I0588401

HONKY TONK COWBOY

THE TEXAS BRAND: GENERATIONS

BOOK TWO

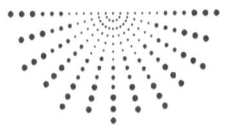

MAGGIE SHAYNE

OLIVER-HEBER BOOKS

Honky Tonk Cowboy Copyright 2025 © Margaret S. Lewis

Cover art by Dar Albert at Wicked Smart Designs

Published by Oliver-Heber Books

0 9 8 7 6 5 4 3 2 1

PRAISE FOR MAGGIE SHAYNE

"Readers will love this novel, which twists Shayne's usual combination of sharp wit and awesome characters with a killer who could have leapt right off of a television screen." ~**RT Book Reviews** on Sleep With the Lights On

WINNER: Paranormal Romantic Suspense of the Year
FINALIST: Book of the Year

"Maggie Shayne's books have a permanent spot on my keeper shelf. She writes wonderful stories combining romance with page-turning thrills, and I highly recommend her to any fan of romantic suspense." ~*New York Times* bestselling author **Karen Robards**

"In this thrilling follow-up to Sleep With the Lights On, Shayne amps up both the creep factor and the suspense." ~**RT Book Reviews** on Wake to Darkness

"Shayne has hit the jackpot with the pairing of self-help author Rachel de Luca and Detective Mason Brown. With chilling suspense and laugh-out-loud one-liners from Rachel, this book will have readers engrossed until the very end." ~**RT Book Reviews** on Deadly Obsession

"This is page-turning, non-stop suspense at its finest. Shayne brings the characters to life for her readers, who will not be disappointed with this fabulously entertaining story." ~**RT Book Reviews** on Innocent Prey

"One of the strongest, most original voices in romance fiction today." ~*New York Times* bestselling author **Anne Stuart**

"Maggie Shayne is a wonderful storyteller. Creepy, chilling, and compelling, her entries into the world of the occult are simply spellbinding!" ~**Heather Graham,** *New York Times* bestselling author

"A moving mix of high suspense and romance, this haunting Halloween thriller will propel readers to bolt their doors at night." ~**Publishers Weekly** on Gingerbread Man.

CHAPTER ONE

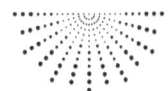

*E*than Brand took a breath of beer-scented air and strummed his guitar on a plank-board stage in a Memphis honky-tonk. He hit the opening notes of the only song the audience wanted to hear, his solitary hit. He'd written plenty of others, had a whole album out, but they didn't care. They wanted to hear the one they knew.

His set tonight was three songs long. His audience was city, not country. They wore shiny, scuff-free cowboy boots and kept their hats on indoors, like they'd been raised in a barn. They danced some, but mostly drank and socialized through his first two numbers. Their applause felt obligatory. But as soon as he started "Country Kind of Love," they cheered and shouted approval, danced and even sang along. That was why he'd saved it for last.

> *She's the perfect one for me,*
> *Loves my crazy family,*
> *Mostly good and sometimes bad,*
> *Dev'lish angel, dang, I'm glad*

Right or wrong, she's by my side
Gonna make that gal my bride.
Lazy Sundays snug at home,
What sane man would ever roam?
Swear she's sent from up above,
She's my country kind of love

He sang about a relationship he'd seen but never experienced. He'd written it based on the kind of love his adopted parents, Uncle Garrett and Aunt Chelsea, had. It was the kind of love his cousin Maria had found with his brand new cuz-in-law Harrison.

That was how he'd met Harrison's sister.

Lily Ellen Hyde had stepped off a small airplane looking like an angel. Her silver-blonde hair floated in the smallest breeze, and she had the big, sparkling eyes of a cartoon princess. Bluer than blue, he'd found, when he'd seen her up close. He'd been dumbstruck for a beat or two and had the oddest sensation of something shattering, way down deep in his chest.

There'd been a spark between them from that day on, for sure. She'd felt something too. Ethan hadn't pursued it, though. She was small and delicate. He was big and lumbering. There was light inside her. He had bad blood.

Besides, she'd fallen in love with Quinn, Texas, and wanted to stay there with her brother and their dad, and enough in-laws to fill a gymnasium, while Ethan had decided that whatever he did, it couldn't be there.

Not in Quinn, among the *real* Brands.

He was not a Brand, not really. He was the son of the man who'd murdered his mother and was serving life without parole at Torres, down in Hondo.

He ended the song, holding the last note a little longer than usual, and the crowd of maybe fifty folks cheered. Then he took his guitar by its neck and left the stage. There was no dressing room in the small honky-tonk. If he ever built a honky-tonk—as unlikely as that was—it would have a couple of dressing rooms, with snacks and water.

But this place had nothing like that for the talent. His options after his set were to walk straight out the back door to his truck, or head for a barstool and a beer.

Several gals were hovering at the polished, curving bar, watching him, their eyes beckoning. One even raised a beer mug his way. She was pretty, and he was flattered, but he touched the brim of his hat with a polite nod and opted for the exit.

"Mr. Brand, just a moment," a male voice called, barely louder than the din of the place.

Ethan ignored it and stepped out into the parking lot behind the bar. Almost all cars, only a handful of trucks, including his own.

Ethan loved his truck.

He headed toward it, breathing in the muggy Tennessee night. He'd been on his own for this gig, one of five featured guests playing with the house band. He'd plugged into their amp, used their mic. So he was free to leave. The owner would mail his check to his home address.

Well, not his *home* address. He didn't have a home. He lived on the road, traveling from gig to gig, motel to motel. Every couple of months, he'd head back to Quinn, Texas, for a week with the family—holidays and special occasions, like Maria and Harry's wedding last month. That was the second time he'd gone home for Maria's wedding. She'd run away from the first one.

He enjoyed the visits home. He'd hang out with his adopted kin, and then he'd take off again. It wasn't much of a life, but he was content with it.

"Mr. Brand."

He'd heard the back door open, just hadn't paid it any mind. Muffled music and voices came from the bar, competing with distant traffic sounds. You couldn't'a heard a cricket if it had a bullhorn. The night was so humid his face felt damp.

"Mr. Brand, please, hold up a sec." The fellow let the door close behind him, dulling the noise again and heading Ethan's way.

Sighing, he turned to look back. The fellow hurrying across the parking lot was wearing a vest over a shirt and tie.

"Can I he'p ya?" he asked the little guy. Maybe he wanted an autograph. That happened from time to time. After all, he did have *one* hit song. It always made Ethan's face hot and his neck itchy when someone asked, but he always obliged them all the same. The only thing this fellow was carrying, though, was a fat file folder with page edges sticking out unevenly.

"I'm Jonathon Harper," he said. "I'm an attorney."

Ethan arched his brows. That was not what he'd been expecting.

"I have news about your father, Vincent de Lorean. Is there somewhere we can—"

"Only news I want to hear about that man is that he's dead. Is he dead?" He glared at the guy, expecting him to say *no*, to which he would reply by getting into his truck and slamming the door. He tapped the key fob to unlock it and took hold of the door handle.

"Yes, I'm afraid he is."

Ethan's hand fell to his side.

"He died peacefully in his sleep."

"That's too good a death for a man like him."

"There um…there was a will. You—"

"Nope." Ethan held his hands between them like a double stop sign. "He was in prison for killin' my mother. You must know that."

The smaller man blinked behind his glasses, backed up a step, and said, "I know."

"Sorry I raised my voice," Ethan said, softening his tone, banking his temper. His size was intimidating enough all by itself. Uncle Garrett had always told him the bigger a man was, the gentler his nature ought to be. "You're just the messenger, after all. Can I refuse it or somethin'?"

"You can disclaim it, yes. But um, there's one item that was transferred into your name before your father died."

"Don't call him that."

The man nodded. He still seemed nervous, and no wonder. Ethan was a foot taller, twice as wide.

"I apologize," the lawyer said. "I'm botching this badly. Look, um, despite its source, you could do something good with this." He said that with a nod at the folder he held. "And even if you want to disclaim, you'll first need to know what it is you're disclaiming. And you'll need your own attorney." He held out the fat folder. "I can send these digitally if you prefer. I'll just need an email—"

"This is fine." Ethan took the folder. He didn't think the guy would have been able to hold it out at arm's length like that much longer anyway. A semi blew past, its wake blasting them with parking-lot grit.

"My advice—if you were my client, Mr. Brand—would be to go home, go through the documents, talk to the people you trust most, and consult with your own attorney."

He heaved a sigh. "You said there was one thing that had already been put into my name. Could he do that without me signin' off on it?"

"I don't know how it was done. I wasn't involved. But yes, there are ways."

He nodded, moving around the truck's nose to the passenger side. The lawyer followed. Ethan opened the passenger door and set the file folder on the seat. When he closed the door, he asked, "So what is it?"

"What is…?"

"What's the one thing that's already been put in my name?"

"It's a taco joint-cantina in a town called Mad Bull's Bend."

Lily Hyde pressed her palms flat to the shiny hardwood bar and leaned over it, trying to see through the porthole windows into the kitchen in back.

Manuel, the short and increasingly round owner, saw her there as he passed, balancing trays full of burritos in both hands. His jet-black hair bore plenty of silver—more than it had when she'd first met him.

The Brand clan frequented Manny's Cantina so much, he was practically family. By virtue of her brother's marriage, Lily was a member of that clan, and she was quite disgustingly hung up on another member.

Manny sent her a big smile, white against his bronze skin. "I'll round him up for you in two shakes, Lil," he called in his thoroughly Texas twang.

It always surprised people who expected him to have a Spanish accent. That would teach them to assume.

"You're busy. Looks like he is, too," she said, noticing the impatience in the air. There were nine filled tables, and only two had food on them. "Where are Rosa and the girls?" Manny's wife and two daughters usually helped run the place. Her dad only helped out part time, in hopes of snagging Rosa's taco recipe. Her precise seasoning blend, he said, was impossible to duplicate. And he'd tried.

Lily went behind the bar, grabbed an apron and tied it on.

Through the porthole windows in the double doors, she

could see her dad's head bobbing around in the kitchen. He wore a white pillbox hat, not a tall puffy one.

"College visits," Manny called. Having delivered the food to one table, he moved to another, pulling out his order pad as he went. "Soon they'll be gone for good, and then what?" He looked around the diner, shaking his head, then attended to the customers.

The kitchen doors split and Lily's father came out with a big tray of food, spotted her, and smiled ear to ear. "Ah, my salvation. Here, table ten. By the jukebox."

She took the tray laughing. "Just like old times, right, Pop?"

"How'd you know I needed you?"

"Didn't. Came in for a taco."

"I'll save you some." Then another group of hungry patrons came in, so Lily got to work.

For the next two hours, she hustled like she hadn't hustled in years, taking and delivering orders, while keeping glasses filled, condiments topped off, and customers happy. Her wad of tips was getting fat by the time the lunch rush flagged.

Only a couple of patrons remained.

One of them was a regular. He must've wandered in during the rush when she hadn't been paying attention. She stole a look at him while wiping down the bar. Nobody seemed to know who he was, and you couldn't really tell what he looked like, with the bushy dirty-blond beard and ever-present sombrero. He kept it down low over his eyes.

He came in most afternoons, always sat at the same table, and usually stayed into the night, sipping tequila, and just... watching.

A handful of times, when there'd been trouble, he'd stepped in to help. But he never said much, just did what was needed and returned to his silent, tequila-fed contemplation. He had a long-nosed, black *pistola* under his blue-and-white woven poncho. Maria said she'd seen him pull it out the day her ex had found her there with Harrison and beaten him bloody.

Lord, what her poor brother hadn't gone through for Maria Michelle Brand. Oh, but at the wedding, while he'd watched that wild redhead walk down the aisle toward him, there'd been tears in Harrison's eyes. Lily'd had a perfect view because she was his "best woman" and stood beside him.

She'd glanced past her brother to where Ethan stood on his other side in the little white church with the red doors and the tall steeple. Cousin and bestie of the bride, he'd served as Maria's "man of honor."

Ethan Brand had caught her looking at him, and they'd locked eyes. His were full of joy for his cousin, but then turned a little nervous when their gazes held a beat too long.

They'd slow-danced at the reception. She'd asked him after a few beers had given her courage. He'd held her close, too, one arm around her waist up high, the other holding her hand outward, like they were going to waltz. She'd wiggled her hand free and hugged him instead. He surrendered with a sigh and wrapped his arms around her.

He was tall and wide, and she was built like her mother had been, small and slight. She was enveloped by him, and she'd liked the feeling. So she pressed as close as she could and sighed out every wisp of breath in her lungs. When she inhaled again, she smelled Ethan. His soap, his clothes, his skin. She'd lifted her head to look up at the cleft in his chin.

They were outdoors, of course, on the front lawn of the sprawling Texas Brand ranch. He was wearing his hat, so his face was in shadows that emphasized the line of his jaw, the slight hollow of his cheek, and the thin layer of dark scruff that covered it. She wanted to run her own cheek across that scruff.

As if he felt her eyes on him, he looked down. She didn't look away. She just held his gaze and let him see what was in her eyes, and she must've done a good job, because his sparked with desire. But then the spark was banked by what looked like worry. Maybe fear. The song ended. He thanked her for the dance and walked away so fast you'd have thought she was a dragon about to flame-roast him.

He'd avoided her for the rest of the night. Not that she'd put up much of a fight, once she realized that was what he was doing. She had some pride, after all.

The next day he'd left without saying goodbye to resume playing in honky-tonks around the south and southwest, ever in search of his second big hit.

Her father's hand came to Lily's shoulder from behind. "You haven't forgotten a thing, have you?"

She blinked out of her memories and back to the moment at hand—the two of them slinging food together again.

"I loved working at the Sunday Café with you, Dad," she said, wiping the memory from her eyes and turning to smile at him. "Those were the happiest times of my life. I don't—"

Then she bit her lip to stop the flow of words. She'd almost blurted, "I don't like being a nurse."

It would've been a stupid thing to say. Her mom had been a nurse, so she was a nurse. There'd never been a question, really. She looked like her mom, she was named after her mom, and she aspired to *be* like her mom.

Everyone had loved the original Lily, Lily Marie. The mourners at her funeral had been out the door and spilled onto the sidewalk outside the funeral home. Angel on earth, the minister had called her. For hours, people had sung her mother's praises.

Lily Ellen, the knock-off Lily, had Lily Marie's angel-blonde hair and her big blue eyes, her slight build and her naturally soft voice. But she didn't have her mother's heart. She wasn't half the woman her mom had been.

Her dad and brother, however, thought otherwise, and they relied on her to fill the hole her mother's death had left in the family. So she was faking her way through life, trying to be this serene, healing angel, failing most of the time, and screaming in frustration on the inside.

"They were your happiest times *so far*," her father said, wagging a finger at her. His smile was bright, and his light-blue eyes were too, but Lily could still see the loneliness behind them. "There are far happier times to come."

"For sure," she replied, though she doubted it. Had it sounded convincing? "Did you save me some tacos, like you said?"

"I did. And before she took Pilar and Pedra on their trip, Rosa finally gave me her precise seasoning blend," he said. "Ever since I started helping out here, I've been asking. I flatter, I flirt—"

"Don't you *dare* flirt! Manny has a baseball bat back here." She nodded at the bat leaning in the corner within easy reach of anyone behind the bar.

"You're right," he replied.

The kitchen doors opened, and Manny came in carrying a large crate of bottles. He must've carried them up from the basement, Lily thought. He was sweating and grimacing a little.

Hyram quickly took the heavy crate from Manny and lowered it to the floor behind the bar. "You should've let me help," he said, as he straightened upright again.

Manny stood rooted to the spot, though, and then he bent forward, and kept going, clasping his chest as he fell to the floor.

"He's having a heart attack!" Hyram cried, grabbing Lily's arm. "Do something!"

"Me?" she blurted.

"You're a nurse!"

"Oh, right." *Shit, shit, shit.* She crouched beside Manny, rolling him onto his back, opening his shirt, and looking around the place for a defibrillator. Several patrons gathered around, trying to see behind the bar.

"Somebody call 911," Lily called. "Is there a defibrillator in here?"

"I got it," said a deep voice. And then the portable defibrillator case was lowered to the floor beside her and she looked up to see the gringo in the sombrero, who gave her a nod and moved to help her father herd the remaining customers out of the building.

"I'll box up your food and bring it outside," her dad was telling them. "Please don't block the way for the ambulance."

"I'll see to it," the gringo said, and he went outside with the rest.

Lily knelt beside Manny, checking for a pulse in his neck and not finding one. Then again, her own heart was pounding so hard her fingertips were throbbing. She attached the leads.

"Okay," she said. "Okay." She'd never done this before, never electrocuted a heart back into beating. She powered the device on. The button marked SHOCK was bright red. She moved her finger over it, clenched her jaw, and started to press.

Manny suddenly sucked in a loud, harsh breath, and she jerked her hand away from the button so fast she fell on her backside on the floor. Then she scrambled forward again, her hands going to his shoulders. "Easy, Manny, you're okay. Help's on the way."

She untaped the leads and pushed the case away from her in horror. She'd nearly pressed the button. She'd nearly…

A siren wailed in the distance.

"My chest hurts," Manny said.

"That's okay, it's okay. You're going to be okay."

She'd almost shocked him. God, she'd almost shocked him. If she'd have pressed that button, she could've killed him. Trying to help him, she could've killed him. And she knew, right then, that she was going to quit her job before she closed her eyes that night.

Her dad and Harrison would be so disappointed in her. She

wondered if all the parts of her phony-baloney identity as her mom's worthy successor would crumble around her feet, now that the avalanche had begun.

Manny clasped her hand. "Rosa can't manage this place with me laid up in a hospital, Lily."

"My dad's here. Your girls will be here. And I'll help out, too." Then more quietly, she added, "I'm gonna have some time on my hands."

CHAPTER TWO

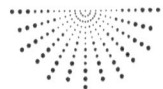

The Saturday barbecue at the Texas Brand was in full swing, with country music playing, grills sizzling, plates heaping, and a whole slew of Brands talking and laughing at once, when a distant dust cloud announced a new arrival.

Lily gazed out past the rolling lawn, over the hard-packed dirt road that ran beneath the tall arch with the words "Texas Brand" carved out of the wood. Sure enough, a vaguely pickup truck-shaped dust cloud moved closer.

Garrett, clan patriarch, was standing near the grill with a two-pronged fork in one hand. He gazed at the approaching vehicle and said, "Don't know who it could be. We're all here."

"Not all," his pretty wife Chelsea said, pointing at the dust cloud. "Whatever's charging this way is big, and I do believe it's also red."

"Bubba!" Maria yelled, jumping up from her plate of food and slamming her hands on the picnic table so hard her glass of sweet tea jumped.

Her new husband, who was also Lily's brother, said something near her ear. Then she shouted, "Ethan!" her cousin's preferred name.

It was, Lily knew, his middle name. Ethan's birth mother had named him after Garrett Brand before leaving him on that wide, welcoming front porch as a baby. The Brands had given her shelter when she'd been in trouble. She'd never forgotten the ways of this family, the closeness, the sheer *goodness*, of the Brands. So when she'd been desperate to hide her child someplace safe, this was the place she'd come. She'd left a note pleading with them to raise her son and to protect him from his criminal father in case she couldn't get back to him herself.

And she never had.

The red truck moved closer, its dusty plume like a comet's tail.

Lily's stomach clenched into a knot so tight she couldn't swallow the potato salad in her mouth. She reached for her water to wash it down. Ethan. Now, of all times? She was already in the midst of an existential crisis; she didn't need him coming around and making it worse.

It didn't matter. She had her first date with Fred, a phlebotomist from El Paso, tonight. Fred was a nice guy. He was smart, informed, could carry on an intelligent conversation. He was well-mannered, treated others kindly, and they liked some of the same TV shows.

Lily had described him just that way to Maria, and her sister-in-law had said, "Sounds downright scintillatin'," ladling more sarcasm onto the words than gravy onto a biscuit.

Trying to look casual, Lily picked up her plate and carried it toward the house, all too aware of Maria and her cousin Willow tipping their heads together as she passed, while Drew, the youngest of the cousins, watched from nearby.

From behind the sleek curtain of her jet-black hair, Willow whispered, "Give her a minute."

The truck's tires crunched over the driveway just as Lily crossed the front porch, and shivers went up and down her spine. She hurried inside. The screen door banged closed behind her, and she stood just inside the cool, dim house.

Ethan had been left as a baby on the very threshold she'd just crossed, she thought. His mother must've known there was no better place on earth for a kid to grow up. Why would anyone ever want to leave?

Why couldn't Ethan bring himself to stay?

She crossed through the big, comfortable home to the kitchen to rinse her plate, and mulled on the Ethan Brand she'd known first, long before she'd ever met him in person. The country music singer. His first hit song had made her long for the "Country Kind of Love" it described. She felt the same longing for it that she heard in his voice, especially when it broke on the chorus. And the ballad "Home" (side 1, track 3) had made her long to be in Quinn, Texas, before she'd even known its name.

> Desert dark and badlands mean,
> alongside fields o' blue and green
> Where horses graze and cattle roam
> and people care, that there's my home

She belonged in that place he described. She'd felt it since she'd first set foot in Quinn. Just like she'd felt Ethan all the way to her soul the first time she'd set eyes on him, a tall, dark cowboy. He had the jawline of a god, the smile of an angel, and the devil's own dimples. And she'd kind of thought she might belong with him, too.

She *didn't* think she belonged in nurse's scrubs though. She was having a full-blown identity crisis. And Ethan was a big, handsome complication.

She could hear the rumble of his deep voice greeting his family outside. His love for them was genuine and deep. She wondered yet again why he stayed away so long between visits.

Her plate was clean and in the rack. The dishwasher was still running, so she couldn't begin to load it with the second batch, but the dishes were rinsed and stacked, awaiting their turn. The cooking was done outside on Saturdays, all the sides having been made the day before, so the kitchen was relatively clean. She had no excuse to stay in there, and if she did so anyway, it would look as if she was hiding from Ethan, and she had no reason to do that either, as far as anyone knew.

So, unless she wanted them to start guessing her feelings for the black sheep of the family, she needed to buck up and get out there.

She dried her hands on a dish towel and went back through the house into the big front room just as the screen door squeaked open and Ethan Brand filled the space, guitar case in one hand, suitcase in the other.

"Oh. Hey, Lily." He dropped his suitcase and took off his hat, ruffling up his dark-brown hair in the process. "How you been?"

"I...I don't know how to answer that, to be honest." He crooked an eyebrow at her. She shrugged and said, "I'm figuring it out. You?"

"Got some figuring out to do myself." He hung his hat on the tall hat rack that stood just inside the door.

"That why you're back so soon after the wedding?"

"Yeah."

He didn't say anything more, and she couldn't think of anything to say either. The silence was getting awkward. "Well. Good luck, I guess," she said to break it. "I, um, gotta get home."

She took a step forward, but he didn't move out of her path. He said, "You're not staying here at the ranch anymore?"

"Oh gosh, no, not since January. I mean, we stayed for the week of the wedding like everyone else, but—"

"Oh. I didn't realize."

"You didn't stick around long enough to find out," she said.

"No big deal." Only it was. "Dad and I sublet a log cabin at the edge of town."

"The Campbell place?" She nodded, and he said, "I always liked that house."

"I like it too. It's perfect for Dad and me. Two bedrooms, full basement with a bar, pool table, and big TV on the wall. Dad's claimed that space as his own."

"And his health? He seemed to be better, at the wedding."

"He is. He walks into town every day, and he's been cooking at the cantina when they need a hand in the kitchen."

"That's great."

"It really is."

Ethan lowered his eyes. "Speaking of, how is Manny doing?"

"He's home," she said. Of course Ethan's kin would've told him about Manny's heart attack. The guy was like family. "He's recovering. But...you should go see him while you're here."

"Yeah, tomorrow," he said, like he already had the visit planned. "It's a good thing you were there, huh?"

She lowered her gaze. "I didn't do anything. But he *is* getting better." She brightened her voice, not wanting to bring him down. "Dad got Rosa's taco recipe, though." Ethan's smile widened as she went on. "He plays poker with two soldiers and the local mailman every week, and sometimes he hosts the game down in his basement bachelor pad."

Ethan's smile became a laugh. "He *is* feelin' better!"

"I haven't seen him this healthy in years," she said. "But I don't think he's really happy. There's still that heartache in his eyes, you know?"

"Yeah."

They were standing in the middle of the living room, between the kitchen and front door, and she didn't know what to do with her hands.

Ethan's smile softened. "And how about you, Lily?"

How about her? He hadn't called her or texted her. He hadn't even said goodbye before he'd left, but now he wanted to know how she was?

"Why do you ask, Ethan?" The question tumbled from her lips without her brain's consent. It even sounded a little snippy.

His face changed. He frowned and seemed puzzled. "Why do I ask?" he repeated.

"I need to go," she said, nodding at the door behind him.

Ethan stepped aside, picking up his suitcase on the way. Lily headed past him and through the screen door without another word. It creaked and banged when she let it go, and she pasted a bright smile onto her face and walked in time with the music.

As soon as he'd arrived, Ethan had hugged his cousins and uncles and aunts, and promised he'd eat as soon as he stashed his gear in his room.

Aunt Chelsea was his only real blood relative here. His mother's sister. She'd come looking for her missing nephew and never left. Chelsea let guests use the other bedrooms, but never Ethan's. He'd asked her once how long she planned to keep it for him, and she'd said until he was married with a home of his own.

No pressure there.

He hadn't seen Lily outside, but he hadn't asked where she was, because the family would've started spinning romance between them if he had. He was surprised they hadn't already, given the sparking chemistry between him and Lily Ellen Hyde.

Forbidden chemistry. She was family. Family was everything.

He'd figured she must be around someplace, because her dad was out there with the fam. So he took his guitar and big suitcase through the familiar screen door with the squeak and creak he intended to sample and put into a song. The door banged and there she was.

She looked like a cool breeze, in a white sun dress with daisies embroidered along the hemline. Her angel's hair was wound up and pinned to the back of her head, but strands had come free and hung long, here and there. Her eyes were wider and bluer than the Texas sky.

He was ridiculously glad to see her. The sight of her sent a heavy weight tumbling from his shoulders. He felt lighter in her presence. He'd long since decided everyone probably did.

They talked. He listened, amused by her story about her dad and his poker crew. Her accent was changing gradually. The hard edges of New York were softening after a year in West Texas, and her eyes seemed to drink him in.

But when he'd asked how she was, her peaches-and-sunshine demeanor had vanished behind a storm cloud. Her jaw and lips had gone tight, and her brows had lowered.

"Why do you ask, Ethan?"

Those were the words she'd spoken, but the tone with which she'd spoken them had sounded more like, "Screw you and the horse you rode in on, Ethan."

And what the heck had he done to deserve *that*?

As she strode out through the screen door, its creak and bang didn't come across as the comforting sounds of home. They sounded angry. She crossed the front porch, and he shook his head in bewilderment and then got stuck following the swing of her hips underneath that dress. The flare of its skirt gave more emphasis to the sway, and he ran a hand across his face and swore under his breath.

Then he headed upstairs. His bed was already made up. He suspected that after each visit home, his aunt Chelsea started changing it up for the next time before his tires had left the driveway. Guilt over his infrequent visits stabbed at his belly, but he pushed it away. He put the suitcase on the bed and stood the guitar case in the corner.

Then footsteps told him someone was behind him.

He turned.

His cousin Willow stood in his doorway with her arms crossed over her chest. She looked furious. "What did you say to her?"

"What did I say to who?" He knew exactly who she meant, but he was buying time. Did the family know?

Know what? he asked himself. There was nothing *to* know. He and Lily had never even kissed!

"Lily," Willow said. "She was fake-smiling way too hard. Didn't reach her eyes. Her stride said she was pissed. So what did you say to her?"

He shrugged. "Hello? How are you?"

"And she said...?"

"Why do you ask, *Ethan*," and he put a mean girl lilt into it, just like Lily had. "Maybe I don't speak the language of women. You care to interpret that for me, cuz? I'm lost."

"Sure. It means, why do you ask, Ethan, when you clearly don't give a hang."

"Well, why would she think that?" he shot back.

"Because she knows you're gonna leave again in a couple'a days. Just like you always do. And if you gave a hang, you wouldn't."

He frowned at his cousin, shoved his suitcase out of the way, and sank onto the edge of his bed. "Well, she's sure fittin' right in around here, ain't she?" he said. "Mad at me for the same reason everybody else is."

"Not *exactly* the same reason," she returned, and when he frowned at her, she rolled her dark-brown eyes. "You're so dense, Cuz."

"You're not the first to say so. However, dense as I am, you're gonna have to be more specific."

She heaved a big sigh. "Come on down and eat."

"She left, did she?" he asked.

"Was fixin' to, but Maria cajoled her into stayin' for dessert." Then she said, "You like her, I know you like her."

"Whole family *likes* her."

She blew like an angry bull and left him, slamming the door on the way out.

Ethan didn't follow right away. Instead, he opened his suitcase, took out the fat folder that was right on top and opened it. There was a list of what he thought were stocks, numbers of shares, value as of close the day before.

And there, right on top, was the full deed to Manny's Cantina, which had his name on it.

CHAPTER THREE

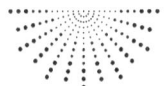

*E*than sat in a rocking chair on the front porch, watching the colors of the sky deepen from blue to purple out past the rolling meadows, stunted woods, and the wooden arch over the long dirt drive.

Uncle Garrett sat in the rocker beside his, doin' the same.

The place had cleared out an hour ago, though Lily and her dad had left early. Ethan had unpacked, and showered up, and then he'd come down, knowing where to find the man who'd raised him. His dad, in every sense of the word.

For a while they just rocked in silence.

Eventually, Garrett said, "You're home without a holiday or party or weddin' to attend. Must be somethin' pretty big goin' on."

Garrett was as big as ever, and not a bit softer. It was only coincidence that Ethan was similarly built. He wore faded jeans, scuffed-up boots, a western shirt over a T-shirt. No sheriff's badge was pinned to his chest, never was on the weekends, unless something happened. His bark-brown hair looked like it had taken a hard frost, and the laugh lines around his eyes were deeper every time Ethan came home.

"Yeah, I…wanted to talk with you."

Garrett looked at him, locked eyes. "I knew somethin' was off. You look troubled, son. Got ghosts in your eyes."

"I was leavin' a gig when a lawyer caught up to me in the parkin' lot. Come to tell me de Lorean's dead."

Garrett's brows rose up high. "An' here I was expectin' you to ask about woman problems."

"Got no woman, so—"

"Could have, if you were…that-a-way inclined."

The phrase was from *Good Ol' Boys*, a western they'd watched together a dozen times. Ethan sent Garrett a questioning look.

Garrett shrugged. "Accordin' to my better half, anyway."

"I still don't—"

"Lily Ellen," Garrett said. "Dang, boy, you're denser'n I was with your aunt Chelsea."

So wait, Aunt Chelsea knew about the…thing between him and Lily? How? He'd never so much as kissed her. "What makes Aunt Chelsea think—"

"She doesn't think, she knows," said Aunt Chelsea, coming out onto the porch with a mug in her hands. "What are we discussing?"

"Lily," Garrett said, at the same moment Ethan said, "Nothin'."

He pressed two fingers to his forehead and said, "It doesn't matter. I came home partly cause I wanted to tell you to your face." He got up from his chair and went to her, put his hands on her shoulders as she gazed up into his eyes. "The man who killed your sister died in prison."

Chelsea dropped her mug. It split on the porch floor and Garrett jumped up and steered her around the broken ceramic and into his arms.

"Michele," she whispered. "Oh, Michele."

"It's okay, babe. It's okay. I got you. I got you." Garrett

repeated nonsense phrases like that and wrapped his arms around Chelsea like he was a big cocoon that could hide her from the world.

Ethan got up to retrieve the pieces of the mug, and Garrett led Chelsea to the porch swing, and settled onto it with her. She leaned into him and drew her legs up, curling into a ball. Her cheeks were wet, and after a moment she took a shuddering breath.

Ethan carried the mug bits inside to dispose of them, and to give them a minute. He grabbed a towel, and filled another mug for his aunt, fixing it the way she liked. Then he returned outside, set the mug on the little glass-topped stand in front of the porch swing, and quickly wiped up the spill.

"Thanks, Ethan," she said. "I'm okay."

They'd had almost a year to get used to calling him Ethan, but in her and Garrett's minds, he'd always be Bubba, and he knew it. Then his aunt frowned and said, "How did you find out?"

"A lawyer notified him," Garrett told her.

She met Garrett's eyes, then sat up straighter, put her feet down, and looked at Ethan. "He left you something, didn't he?"

"Yeah. I can disclaim most of it, and intend to—"

"But Ethan, that could be a fortune," she said.

"The devil's money. It has my mother's blood on it." He lowered his eyes. "I can disclaim it. All of it except one thing he put in my name before he died. And I don't know how or why, but somehow he owned Manny's Cantina. And now I guess I do."

"How could he—?" Chelsea began, but she glanced at her husband and stopped speaking. Garrett was frowning hard, and she said, "Wait, did you know something about this?"

"Manny was havin' money troubles—must've been long about five years back," Garrett said. "I remember he couldn't get a loan from the bank, 'cause he talked about it one night with a few beers in him. A coupl'a months later, he was upgradin' the restrooms. I never did hear where he got the money."

"Well, I gotta go see him," Ethan said. "I got no intention of keepin' it. I'll just sign it over to Manny. At least maybe I can right one of that bastard's wrongs."

"It's a good plan," Garrett said.

"Why don't you tell Manny tonight?" Aunt Chelsea asked. "The stress of being in debt to a loan shark, if that's what this was, must've contributed to his heart attack, so the sooner he knows it's over, the better."

"You think he's up to it?" Ethan asked.

Chelsea nodded. "It was a minor event, as heart attacks go. He's been home a couple of weeks, and I understand he even opened the Cantina tonight."

"How are you so much better informed about what's goin' on in Quinn County than I am?" Garrett asked. "I'm the sheriff."

"And I'm a woman," she said with a loving smile. "I think the sooner you can ease Manny's mind about this, the better, Ethan. This news might be the best medicine he could have right now."

"I think you might be right, about that," Ethan said.

"Lily's been helpin' out at the Cantina, you know," Chelsea went on, trying to act casual about it. "Said she had some vacation time piled up, so she took it right after Manny's heart attack."

"Mighty selfless thing to do," Garrett said. "That's a good woman, right there."

"A *good* woman," Chelsea repeated, nodding.

Ethan closed his eyes, lowered his head, and managed not to cuss aloud. They were onto him. Shoot.

Lily sat across the table from Fred Raspin. He was one of the hospital's vampires—a phlebotomist. He drew blood from patients for testing. She had been a nurse, so they'd interacted many times almost every shift. It had never occurred to her to date him. There was no spark, no attraction. At least not on her part. So she'd been totally unprepared when he'd asked her out for dinner on the day she'd given her two weeks' notice and explained that she'd be taking her two-week vacation during the interim.

She'd blurted "okay" to Fred's invitation without thinking first, then panicked because she wanted to take it back, and then didn't take it back because it felt mean.

"Really?" he'd asked, surprise making the word curve upward at the end.

She'd felt she had to follow through. But she could at least keep things light, casual, and be in a place with backup if she needed to make a graceful exit.

As much as she'd been helping out there, Manny's was becoming her home away from home. Working with her father again, like she had back in Ithaca when she'd been in college, and he'd been a chef trying to manage a diner, when all he wanted to do was cook.

Lily had suggested to Fred that they should go someplace casual and friendly, and asked whether he liked tacos. He'd received the message. Friendly. Okay. She wondered if he'd retract the invitation. He didn't, maybe because he also felt obligated to go through with it.

Why hadn't she just said no?

But she hadn't, and so they were having tacos at a corner table at Manny's Cantina. The Cantina was her sister-in-law Maria's favorite place in the world, and it was rapidly becoming Lily's as well—despite the trauma of having nearly killed the owner.

This was Manny's first night back at work since his heart

attack. He hadn't been out of the hospital long. But it was hard for him to stay away.

Fred was trying to eat a taco without letting any of the filling spill out and having a heck of a time. Lily took a careless bite, letting beans squish out the other end and fall onto the plate, dripping salsa onto her chin. Maybe if she was sloppy it would put him at ease. He seemed so tense he might break.

He was older than she, early thirties, maybe, light-brown hair in a deep side part that might be hiding some thinning. He was taller than her, so she'd never seen the top of his head before, as she did when he bent over his taco.

The kitchen doors swung open, and Manny came through them. "Well, hello there, Miss Lily," he drawled, in a voice meant to carry. "This here angel saved my life," he told everyone within earshot.

Not an angel, and I damn near killed him, she thought.

There was a smattering of applause from a few of the other patrons. Then Manny spoke lower, just for her, not the whole place. "Thanks, Lily, for that and for your help these past two weeks," he said. "I don't know what Rosa and the girls would've done without you and your father. Though I do admit, I was jealous you weren't at the hospital taking care of me."

He was *lucky* she hadn't been at the hospital taking care of him. Aloud, she said, "Well, I still have some more time, so I'll hang out a little longer."

Manny's jet-black waves were streaked with white, and his face had aged years in a couple of weeks. The light in his eyes was still only gleaming at half-power, she thought. He looked... drained.

Fred cleared his throat, reminding her he was still there. "Oh, I'm sorry. Manny, this is my co-worker, Fred."

"Hello, Fred," Manny said, deepening his voice a little, as men did, she'd noticed, when speaking to other men.

Fred nodded hello, and then a big red pickup truck rolled

into the parking lot just the other side of the wide front windows, and Lily almost lowered her head and closed her eyes. Why was Ethan Brand *here,* of all places, at this particular moment?

Ethan got out of his truck, his long legs reaching the ground easily. She had to use the running board to step up, and even then it was a bit high. He met her eyes through the window and touched the brim of his hat. She'd kind of fallen for men in cowboy hats since moving down here. New York men didn't wear them. And those who did, didn't wear them…the same way.

She nodded back and saw Fred look where she was looking. "Seems like you know everyone here," he said.

"I live twenty minutes away," she said, still watching Ethan. He'd shifted his attention to Manny.

Manny said, "Looks like your cuz-in-law wants a word. You give me a yell if you need anything." Then he turned, meeting Ethan at the door, and the two of them went to a table way on the other side. She was curious. Surely Ethan hadn't driven all this way just to have tacos, not the way his aunt fed people under her roof. And he'd had something in his hand, a folder. She'd been so busy watching his eyes and his mouth and wondering what his lips would taste like, that she hadn't noticed it right away.

Could he have known she'd be there? Lily wondered. On a date? With a man? Who wasn't him?

Manny and Ethan sat opposite each other at a little table just the other side of the juke box, left of the bar and double kitchen doors. There were only a handful of patrons at tables in between. Gringo Sombrero sat in his usual spot, all the way over by the right wall, his long legs stretched out, boots crossed at the ankles, drink in front of him. There was a couple she saw there often, and a table full of out-of-towners. There were a few locals she recognized. She was getting to know folks in Quinn.

"This has been fun," Fred said, again making her realize she'd been ignoring his presence. That was rude and not like her. She might want to be rude sometimes, but she almost never gave in to the urge. It's not the way her mother would have acted, so it wasn't the way her only daughter, namesake, and doppelgänger, should act.

"I'm sorry, Fred. I don't mean to be so distracted. I just have a lot on my mind."

"Oh?" Shoot, he was waiting for her to elaborate. "Do you want to talk about it?"

"No," she replied. "It's personal." She couldn't help that her gaze slid toward Manny and Ethan sitting on the other side. Ethan slid his folder across the table to Manny. Manny shook his head and slid it back.

"Okay, good." Fred got up and she faced him again. Oh, shoot, he looked pissed. He took a ten-spot from his wallet and dropped it on the table. "See you at work," he said.

She got to her feet. "Wait, are you...angry with me for some reason?"

"No, I *like* going on dates and being ignored," he said.

"Well, it's gonna take another five to cover your half of the meal and tip there, Prince Charming," she shot back, loud enough to be heard inside. She damn near clapped a hand over her mouth. Who the hell's voice was that?

Fred sent her a furious glare, pulled out his wallet, found a five-dollar bill, and dropped it onto the table, not caring that one end landed in the sour cream. Then he pivoted and strode away, straight out of the Cantina. He slammed his car door to show her how mad he was, and pulled out way too fast. What a jerk.

She looked at the tacos, at the money, decided to leave the cash for a tip, and pay with her card, and got up to take care of the bill—because, honestly, she was dying to know what was going on between Manny and Ethan. She went up to the bar, which brought her within earshot, and slid onto a stool to wait for someone to come and take her payment.

"You don't understand, Manny," Ethan was saying. "I don't *want* it."

"*You* don't understand, Ethan," Manny replied. "*I* don't want it."

"Well, we're at an impasse, then."

"No, we're not," Manny replied. "*You* own it. Says so righ'chere. I, on the other hand, am about to start plannin' my retirement party."

"How can you—what do you mean? A loan shark swindled you out of this place. Why wouldn't you want it back, if only to sell it again?" Ethan spotted Lily just as he completed the question.

She saw him wondering how much she'd heard and tried to cover her intent listening by bringing her phone to her ear and speaking low into it while turning her back to the two men.

Manny said, "Loan shark? Where'd you get that idea?" He picked up the papers. "I sold the place willingly. New owner took care of the operatin' expenses, and I got to keep all the profits for as long as he lived. He even provided me with a bookkeeper. Took all that worry out of Rosa's hands." He shrugged. "I presumed it was a tax write-off or some such. What I don't get it is why he would've signed it over to you. Did you know this fella?"

Lily realized she could see Ethan's face in the big mirror behind the bar. He looked stunned. As she watched him, he nodded, but didn't speak.

"Look," Manny said, "this feller de Lorean and me, we agreed that upon his death I'd retire to make way for the new owner. I been sockin' away money ever since, and we have Rosa's retirement, too. Now, I'll he'p you with the transition any way I can, Ethan, but—I cain't do more'n that. This thing with my heart's made me realize I might not have as much time left as I always thought. I gotta live my life now. Tell ya the truth, the timin' couldn't be better for me."

Again, he shoved the papers across the table to Ethan, then he crossed the room and moved behind the bar, coming over to take Lily's card from her while she pretended not to have heard a thing. As he ran it, Ethan was gathering the papers back into his folder. Lily signed the receipt and headed out before he finished, and since he hadn't locked his truck, she climbed in and waited.

He didn't see Lily at first, but then he felt her there in the passenger seat, or smelled the shampoo she used, or something. He turned his head and met her eyes. They were wide in the darkness.

"Date ditched me," she said. "I rode down with Dad. Wanna give me a ride home?"

The word *date* hit him hard. He was quiet for a moment, and then he nodded. "Lover's quarrel?" he asked.

"First date," she replied. "I don't think he'll ask for a second."

"Then he's an idiot." He started the engine, backed the truck out. When he glanced her way again, her cheeks were pinker than before.

She averted her eyes and said, "So what's all this about you owning Manny's? I mean, I couldn't help but overhear."

"Yeah, you could've."

"Yeah," she said. "I could've. But you changed the subject. What about the cantina?"

He thought for a moment, then said, "Other than my folks, nobody knows about this yet."

"I'll never tell." She locked her lips and tossed the key.

"I don't even know what I'm fixin' to do about it just yet."

"Run it," she said. "What's better than a country singer with his own honky-tonk?"

"I'm not that big a country singer."

"You will be."

"The words one-hit-wonder mean anything to you?"

"So you take that one hit and you milk it for all it's worth. Have CDs and T-shirts on sale behind the bar. Deck the walls with album covers—"

"There's only just the one."

"—and shots of you on stage, and shots of you with other famous people. Use song titles and lyrics in your menu items, maybe even rename the place. Country Kind of Saloon—something like that."

He pushed his hat back on his head. "You're just full of ideas."

"Yeah, I've been getting ideas about this place for a while. Been helping out around here since Manny's heart attack," she explained. "I felt so bad about what happened, I—"

He held up a hand, school room style. "Why would you feel bad? I heard you saved his life."

She bit her lip. "I didn't really do anything. He came to and I held his hand and waited for the ambulance."

There was something more, he could see it in her eyes.

"Anyway, they needed the help, and I know my way around a restaurant, so—"

"Cause your dad's a chef?"

"The owner of the diner where he worked back east made him manager," she said. "He just wanted to cook, but the owner insisted he could do both. And he loved cooking there too much to give it up. It was short-order, but he'd created signature sandwiches and fancy sides the patrons loved. So I started helping him out and taking courses to learn what I didn't know. Next thing I know, I'm the manager. Unpaid."

"How old were you?"

"Mmm, I helped Dad run the diner all through my teens," she

said. "We didn't have entertainment, just food, but—we did all sorts of special events, holiday themes, private parties, and promotions. Gosh, those were great times."

Her eyes were sparkling. He hadn't yet started the truck. He was kind of lost in learning new things about Lily Ellen Hyde. And when she talked about this particular thing, she lit up.

"I was thinking you could knock out the east wall. Build on an addition with a stage and dance floors. Maybe install a second bar out there. And you could plan a huge grand opening and advertise the heck out of it. Bring in every act you've met on the road to perform. Make this little taco bar into a true honky-tonk." She gazed out her side window, then behind them. "You're gonna need a bigger parking lot."

"And I'm gonna do all this...when, between gigs?"

Her face fell. It was like a flame had been doused. "I guess I thought—I mean, is all the touring what you really want out of life? Forever?"

He shrugged. "It's what I do."

"Yeah, but is it getting you anywhere? Is it making you happy, or is it just keeping you busy?" She bit her lip when he looked her way. "I'm sorry, that's none of my business. I'm projecting, anyway."

"Projectin'? What, you're not happy being a nurse?"

She sighed and said, "Nobody knows this yet—"

"I'll never tell," he said, repeating her earlier promise back to her. He even did the lock-the-lips, toss-the-key move.

That made her smile, and her smile made him smile back. Something moved between them, this unseen energy, attraction, something. He hadn't identified it yet, but he always felt it around her.

"The truth is," she said, her smile dying slow, "I almost killed Manny."

He swung his head her way.

"He had a heart attack right in front of me. I froze till Dad reminded me I was the only medical professional on hand. I couldn't feel his pulse, but it was just because my own was pounding so hard. I almost shocked him with the portable defibrillator, but he came around just in time. I could've killed him." She gave a shudder that told him how much this had been bothering her.

"And you haven't told anyone. Not even the She-Brands?"

He knew using that term would bring back her smile. That was why he'd used it. It eased the guilt and shame in her eyes, but only briefly. "I'm just so embarrassed."

"Well, don't be. You've only been a nurse for a year."

"And already almost killed someone. Think of my body count after five. Or ten!"

"Come on, don't be so hard on yourself."

"I just don't…" She lowered her head, closed her eyes. "Your second day back and I'm dumping on you."

"I don't mind. Please, now I'm invested in the story. You just don't…?"

"I just don't *feel* like a nurse. I never have. I thought it would come to me eventually, but it hasn't. Even in school, I felt like an imposter. Like a little girl playing dress-up with her sainted mamma's scrubs." She tried to swallow, then tried again. "It's hard to explain," she said. "I don't expect you to understand."

"Oh, no. I understand completely."

"Do you?" she asked, and he could tell by the way she searched his face that she really wanted to know. "Wait, do you feel like you're not a real country music star because you've only had one hit song?"

"I *know* I'm not a real country music star," he said. "But what I was getting at is…" He'd never said aloud the thing that had been eating at him his entire life. He could hardly believe he was about to say it to her. "I don't feel like a Brand."

He started the truck and backed out, then put it into gear and started toward home before he looked at her, taking his eyes from the road for a second at a time to do so. She was gazing at him in confusion. "Because you're adopted?"

"Because it isn't Brand blood in my veins, Lily. It's not even good blood. It's a killer's blood."

"Ohhhhh." The sound emerged soft and breathy.

She put a hand on his shoulder. So small, her hand. Warm.

"Maria told me the story. How your mother left you on the front porch while she ran from your birth father. How he caught up with her and—" She lowered her eyes.

"Killed her."

She nodded. "But that's who he is, not who you are."

"Was," he said. "He died in prison. Left me some shit, none of which I'll accept, but Manny's place was put into my name before he died."

"And Manny doesn't want it." She shook her head slowly, making sense of the parts of their conversation she'd overheard. "Well, if you don't want it, you could sell it. But it would be a shame if the new owner tore it down or put in a Dollar Mart or something."

"That'd break Maria's heart."

"Mine, too, to be honest." Lily sighed. "I guess you've got some thinking to do."

"Sounds like we both do," he said. By then they were nearing the log cabin at the edge of town, just past Main Street on the right. He pulled in, and she opened her door. "You want to come in?"

Her eyes were so pretty, and big, and blue. He wanted to say yes. "I'd better get back."

"Oh, sure," she said. "Thanks for the ride. And again, your secret's safe with me."

"No secret, really. I'm just waiting until I know what it is I want to tell 'em. You know?"

"Whether you're keeping the place or selling it or what," she interpreted, nodding, standing in her driveway with the truck door open. "You know, maybe you shouldn't wait to tell your cousins. They usually have pretty good insights on things. Talking it out with the gang might help you decide what to do."

He nodded. "How'd you get so smart?"

She shrugged one shoulder. "Well, my brother's a certified genius, so...DNA?" She smiled so brightly he forgot to breathe for a second. "See you around, Ethan."

"See ya," he said.

She closed his truck door, turned, and walked over a footpath with weeds coming up between the stones. She put her key into the lock of a green front door, then turned and waved before disappearing inside.

On the drive home, Ethan kept thinking about the things she'd said, mainly that he ought to run this past the cousins *before* he made any decisions, not after.

He thought about calling Maria, then decided to leave her be. She was a newlywed. And Willow was the newest deputy on the Quinn PD and in a perpetual state of panic about living up to her uncle's legacy.

Hell, now that he thought about it, feelin' unworthy might be a Brand family tradition. Must come from having such exceptional parents.

Ethan told his phone to "call Drew," and she answered on the third ring, saying "Hey, Bubba. What's wrong?"

"Nothin's wrong. I'm callin' a bunkhouse bonfire."

"Hell, yeah!" she said. "When?"

"Tomorrow night, if everyone can make it."

"Well, that's a yes from me. Who's bringin' what? What do you still need?"

"Um...well, I was hopin' you'd help me organize all that. Willow usually does it, but she's busy with the new job and all."

"Huh," she said. "Why does Willow usually do it?"

He frowned. His youngest cousin's tone had taken on an edge. "I don't know, exactly."

"Why doesn't the person who calls the bonfire do it? Oh, wait, is it because he has a penis?"

He almost dropped the phone. Since when did little Drew use that word?

"That isn't what I meant!"

"If it's not what you meant, then why didn't you call Baxter or Orrin or Trevor to organize it? You automatically think of Willow or me, and you'd have asked Maria in between if she hadn't just got married."

He lowered his head. "You're right, Drew," he said, realizing that all four male Brand cousins relied on the females to handle the organizing of their frequent bunkhouse bonfires. "I honestly hadn't thought about it, but you're right."

"Dang straight I'm right."

His hope of help was dwindling. "I don't...It's just that I'm not very good at that sort of thing."

"Neither am I. Neither were Maria or Willow 'til somebody made it their job."

"Well, that's probably true, but—"

"Let me help you get started. We'll need about six pizzas, nobody wants anchovies, multiple bags of chips, various flavors, and a lot of beer. Which of those things would you like *me* to bring?"

She wasn't going to give in, was she? "Um, chips?"

"Very good. Now repeat this phone call to Maria, Willow, Baxter, and Trevor. Better yet, use the dang family text loop you avoid like the plague. Assign each cousin something to bring— divvy up the pizza and beer costs among all of us, so nobody's paying the whole shot."

"What about Orrin?" She'd listed every cousin but her brother.

"I'll tell him. We'll go in together on the snacks and bring enough for everyone."

"Okay." He felt chastened by a child.

"Oh, and don't forget to invite Lily. She's part of the family now. You wouldn't know that, bein' gone most of the time."

Man, she was really letting him have it, wasn't she? "Okay," he said again. She'd managed to make him feel like she was the one pushing thirty and he the barely twenty-three-year-old.

"Good. See you tomorrow night."

She disconnected. He shook his head. The kid was right. She was also growing up and becoming a spitfire too.

He rolled his eyes, then turned on some mellow country music.

CHAPTER FOUR

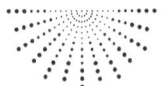

*L*ily couldn't sleep. She wanted to get up and go get herself a snack, but she didn't want to wake her father. He slept so lightly that the least sound or movement would rouse him. He was feeling good, she thought. Better all the time, actually. And his mind was still sharp and clear. He'd made friends, and they played cards and bowled. Cooking at the cantina was healing for him, she thought. So was working with him there, for her.

It had only been two years since they'd lost the real Lily, and none of them had healed, although she thought Harrison had progressed furthest. Finding Maria, marrying into her family, moving down here—he'd found his place.

She still wasn't so sure of her own. And their dad? She didn't know, but she sure wished the sparkle would return to his eyes.

The real reason for her sleeplessness, she knew, was that Ethan was back. She usually knew when he was coming. It had to be an event; a wedding, a funeral, or a major holiday. They always ran into each other when he was in town. She always had a plan to ensure they would, but she'd never had to use one. It always happened on its own.

She'd never been more attracted to a man in her life, from the moment she'd first set eyes on him. No, before that. She'd fallen in love with his voice before she'd ever seen him. She'd heard him on the radio, downloaded his album, followed his fan pages on social.

Seeing him for the first time, face-to-face, had been entirely different from seeing his photos and videos, though. His dark-brown hair had lighter and darker shades in its loose curls that looked as soft as satin. His stunning black-rimmed, light-brown irises seemed to gleam in contrast with his heavy, dark eyebrows.

He was so big, the thought of being with him was a little bit scary. She wasn't big anywhere. But when she thought about being wrapped up in those arms, she didn't feel fear, she felt bliss.

She knew he liked her. More than liked her. Was attracted to her. He was clinging to his lifestyle and now she thought she knew why. It kept him away from his family. He felt unworthy of the Brand name. He hadn't told anyone else about that feeling.

Nor had he told anyone else about his unwanted inheritance, other than Chelsea and Garrett.

In her mind's eye, Lily saw Manny's Cantina from the front. She'd never seen the rear of the place. She wondered what was back there, and how far the property extended. Part of that area could solve the parking issue, and then the front lot could be replaced by a patio, and they could put an entire section of outdoor tables there, rather than the handful tucked up next to the building on the hot pavement.

Her brain wouldn't stop chattering, so she got up, pulled on a light-blue robe, and went to the little desk near her bedroom window. She sat down and flipped open her laptop, opened a blank document and started typing. There would have to be shade, and some kind of sound barrier between the place and the road. She looked around the desk, found a pencil, but nothing to draw on. Not a notepad, not a piece of scrap paper. Ah, the printer! She yanked a few sheets from the feed tray and returned to the desk chair and leaned over to sketch out some ideas. She drew a curving brick boundary wall with a rock garden and pair of cacti. Oh, and off the front, they could add a serving station with warmers and coolers for the most popular dishes.

Her phone chimed and she picked it up and looked at it. And then her heart jumped.

Ethan: You still up?

Smiling so much while all alone in a room was probably a sign of idiocy, she thought. But it felt like there were springs in the corners of her lips. Idiocy.

She keyed back a one-word answer.

Lily: Yes.

Ethan: I took your advice. Called a bunkhouse bonfire with the cousins. Tomorrow night, if you want to come.

Her brain typed out YES!!!! But she forced her fingers to tap the word, "Sure," instead. And then, on autopilot, "What can I bring?"

Ethan: Would love some of that dip you made at Christmas.

She smiled, warm right to her toes.

Lily: Dad's recipe. I'll make a jumbo batch.

Ethan: Thanks.

She held the phone, waiting for more, but he didn't say anything else, and the silence stretched to awkward. She had to reply somehow. *You're welcome? YW? De nada?*

Ethan: What do you think they'll say when I tell them?

She mulled on that for a moment. But it didn't take long.

Lily: They're your family. They'll want you take over the Cantina and stay.

Ethan: Yeah.

Lily: At first. But if you ask them to be objective, they'll try. And good ideas will follow.

He sent back prayer hands. Then...

Ethan: So what's keeping you awake?

Lily looked at her sketches and notes.

Lily: Something that's none of my business.

Ethan: Mysterious.

Lily: Ideas for the cantina. They wouldn't let me sleep till I got them down.

Ethan: Bring them tomorrow night?

Lily: And dip, right?

Ethan: And dip, yes. See you around eight?

Lily: See you then. Good night.

Ethan: Good night, Lily.

She exited the app and pressed the phone to her chest, closing her eyes. Then she popped them open again, and said, "No. You are not doing this to yourself again, Lily."

It happened every time. Whenever Ethan was home, he made her feel as if he must adore her. And every single time, he left again without so much as a kiss.

And yet, here she was, convinced he felt the same thrill in her presence that she felt in his. You couldn't fake something like that, and why would he even want to?

A little voice crept into her head. *How can he feel anything for me when he doesn't even know me? And how can he know me when I don't even know me?*

She looked at the photo of her mom. It hung in a black frame on the wall opposite the window. It was like looking into a mirror that reflected the future. Her mother's face, her palest blond hair, her big blue eyes, her tender smile, they were all older versions of Lily's own. Even their names were the same.

Her mother was a *saint.* And a nurse.

All her life, Lily had tried to model herself after her beautiful, kind, perfect mother. And when the first Lily had died, those efforts had tripled.

Now she felt as if she was buckling under the weight of trying to fill the empty space in her family that her mother had left behind.

The following night, Lily tried three different outfits, and each time, got halfway to the front door, where her father was waiting, then changed her mind and went back to her room.

The third time she came out in jeans and boots and a navy-blue tank with a long, lighter blue cardigan over it. The only special part of the outfit was that the blue tank was made of a sleek satiny fabric that shimmered if the light hit it just right.

Her dad, who'd been waiting near the front door the last two times she'd come down, had taken a seat in a kitchen chair and had a novel open in front of him, but he looked up. "Ready?"

"Yes."

He nodded, set his book aside, got up, and put on the Stetson hat Harry and Maria had given him for Christmas. He never left home without the thing. She noticed he'd dressed up, too. Wore a pair of spanking new Levis and a light-blue dress shirt, all tucked in and buttoned up. Garrett and Chelsea had invited him to have dinner at the ranch with them. Said they were having a friend over anyway and could use a fourth.

She sniffed. He was wearing cologne. Who was this friend, having dinner at the Brands' tonight? Mom had only been gone for…two years. Two years.

She sighed.

He said, "I'm driving. I'll drop you at the bunkhouse and head down to the ranch house," he said. "That way I can head home after dinner. You're staying over, right?"

"That's generally what happens at the bunkhouse bonfires," she said. "Hence the bunkhouse part."

"Slumber party for grown-ups."

"Who you callin' grown up?" She elbowed him and handed over the keys. She'd objected to the pickup truck, but her dad couldn't be talked out of it. She was still driving her little cross-over. She'd flown home to pack up all their things and close down their lives in New York. She'd hired movers for what she'd kept. She'd cried her heart out at everything she'd let go. But she'd felt lighter after. Once everything was donated, sold, or packed into moving trucks and on its way, and the house stood empty, Lily had cleaned it, wall to wall and floor to ceiling.

There had been a few things she hadn't trusted to the movers. Her mom's good china, her teapot collection, and all the family photos, along with her own clothes and belongings. She left the bucket and cleaning supplies on the curb and wrote FREE on the pavement in chalk. Then she'd dropped the chalk into the trash can.

Lily blinked out of the past when her father said, "We're here. You sleeping, sweetheart?"

"Daydreaming," she said. "Thanks for the ride, Dad. Have a good time tonight."

"You too, sweetheart." He eyed her and said, "You look great. You looked great all three times."

"You're biased." She leaned across the seat to kiss his cheek. He was truly thriving in Texas. But only physically. She wondered if he was depressed. She grabbed the huge container of dip in a one-armed bear hug and got out of the truck. As her dad drove away, Lily sent a rapid fire, one-handed text to Ethan's adopted mom, Chelsea, who was a psychologist.

Lily: Dad on way. Seems depressed.

Chelsea: I'll keep an eye on him.

Chelsea always texted in complete sentences, she'd noticed. Most of the elder Brands did that. Her father didn't text at all, unless absolutely necessary.

She said *thanks*, then closed out and returned the phone to her sweater's deep pocket. When she looked up, Ethan's chest was right there in front of her face. She tipped her head up further, and he tipped his down. "Hey," he said.

"Hey." She got stuck looking into his eyes. Damned if there wasn't something there. How could he keep leaving her and not even exploring this thing that simmered between them?

She almost closed her eyes and tipped her head a little more to invite a kiss and see what he'd do. But she caught herself, shocked that she'd nearly done it. And he looked like he was thinking along the same lines.

She thrust the bowl outward, pushing him back a step. Well, more like startling him back a step. Pushing him would be like pushing a tree. "Dip!" she said. Scintillating conversation starter, that.

He took the bowl and smiled. "Thanks. I've been thinkin' about this dip since Christmas."

The dip. He'd been thinking about the dip since Christmas. Not their almost-kiss under the mistletoe.

They'd bumped into each other right under the leaf and berry bundle. She'd looked up at him, then past him, and he'd tipped his head up, too. Glimpsed the mistletoe hanging over his head. It only cleared him by a few inches.

He lowered his head again, real slow, and his eyes locked with hers. She moistened her lips with her tongue, lifted her chin a little.

He put his hands on her shoulders, moved even closer.

And then somebody dropped a glass, and it shattered the moment. He'd been about to kiss her, she was sure of it!

She was so frustrated she wanted to pour the bowl of dip right over his head.

"The dip need the fridge? he asked, distracting her.

"Not right away. But it should be divvied up into smaller bowls."

"I think there are some in the bunkhouse." He'd taken the bowl from her, so now she didn't know what to do with her hands. She shoved them into her pockets and they turned and walked along the path toward the bunkhouse. The bonfire was behind it, far enough out to be safe. She could see the golden glow, smell the burning wood and hear the crackling flames.

They went inside, though, into the kitchen. Ethan opened cabinets, took down four small ceramic bowls just the right size for dip. He set them on the counter, then opened a drawer and took out a spoon.

Lily took the lid off the dip, and Ethan scooped some into each of the bowls, replaced the lid, and put the big bowl into the fridge. He picked up two of the little dishes, offered them to her. She took them, running her hands over his as she did. Dammit, there was a devil inside making her do things she wouldn't normally do.

She thought his breath hitched when she touched him. She had the bowls in her hands then, palms up. Ethan cupped his hands around hers from below, then pulled them slowly way in a matching caress. Then he turned to pick up the other two bowls, and headed outside once more, moving around behind the bunkhouse with her following him.

Everyone yelled greetings, but she was lost in the whirlwind inside her mind. *He did that, caressed my hands like that. On purpose, he did that. Okay. He likes me back. I've been right all along. Ha! I'm not crazy. He likes me back.* She couldn't keep the smile from her face for a moment until the next logical thought jumped in.

So now what?

When Ethan asked himself why he had done that, rubbed his hands across the smooth backs of hers, he already knew the reason. It had been either that or kiss her, something he'd been avoiding since the day he'd first met her. It wasn't a fling he saw when he looked into Lily Ellen's eyes. It was the whole shebang, and the thought of it scared the daylights out of him. The thought of being with someone so good, so light, when his blood was stained dark.

Besides, he couldn't give her what she wanted. His life was

on the road. So he'd determined early on he'd best leave his cousin-in-law's younger sister alone. The problem was, it was getting harder to do that every time he saw her.

And now he'd kindled the spark in her angel-blue eyes into a burgeoning flame with no more than a touch of his hands across hers. And no wonder. He'd felt it clear to his toes when she'd run her petal-soft palms over the backs of his hands, soft on his knuckles, and slow all the way along his fingers to their very tips, leaving a trail of electric sparks in their wake.

There were makeshift tables between their lawn chairs, a tall spool that had held a cable, a tree stump sawed off flat, an upturned five-gallon bucket. Each "table" held a bowl of chips, and he added dip to two of them and looked around for a place to sit.

There were two empty folding chairs, side by side. He headed over to the big table, where the pizza boxes were, helped himself to a slice, and stood there to eat it. Lily placed the remaining two dips, putting one of them on a short, wide, upright log between the two chairs, where a bowl of chips already waited. Then she helped herself to a beer and took a seat. Ethan ate his pizza standing up, then wiped his mouth with a napkin and got a beer. He still hadn't sat down, though. He cleared his throat and said, "So the reason I called you guys here is—well, it's about my birth father. He um…he's dead. Burnin' in hell, I hope."

The cousins exchanged looks, and it was clear they didn't know how to react.

"I'm glad he's dead," Ethan went on. "I wish he'd gone out harder than he did, though. They said it was peaceful."

"Still," Baxter said, running a hand through his shaggy blond hair. "It's a lot. It's your father, man." He wore khaki trousers instead of jeans, loafers instead of boots, and a short sleeved, button-down shirt without snaps. There was an olive drab jacket over the back of his chair. He was the eldest of the cousins at thirty-one.

"A technicality," Ethan replied. "I have no problem with his death, other than that I wasn't the one who brought it about. But there's a will."

"Oh, shit," Maria said, her head coming up off her new husband's shoulder. Harrison watched Ethan, his eyes concerned. His sharp mind was probably already ten steps ahead. His sister was just as brilliant, he thought, sliding a look Lily's way.

Her eyes were on him. She smiled, gave an encouraging nod.

So he went on. "He left me a lot of stuff. And most of it I can just disclaim. I have an appointment with a lawyer tomorrow on that."

"Well, that's dumb," Drew said. "Why not cash out and donate it to the local school or somethin'?"

"He killed my mother. I don't want to touch it."

She rolled her eyes, but Willow said, "I totally get it. I think you're doin' the right thing. Let the state figure out what to do with it."

"Me, too," Maria said. "I mean, you could do somethin' in your mom's name, but...either way. You sound like your mind's made up."

"It is."

"Then why'd you call the bonfire?" Trevor asked. Then he took another sip of his beer and stretched out his legs. "Not that I mind a bonfire."

Beside him, Orrin sat quiet, observing them all. He never missed a thing, Drew's brother. But he said very little.

"Because he saddled me with one item I can't refuse. Manny's Cantina," he said.

Everyone exclaimed at once, and he pumped his hands for quiet. "I assumed it was some kind of loan shark deal, but turns out Manny sold him the place knowingly. He's been able to keep all the profits all this time on the condition that he'd clear out and retire upon de Lorean's death."

"Well, what if Manny doesn't *want* to retire?" Maria Michele blurted, rising from her chair with emotion.

Ethan said, "I tried to give it back to him, no strings. He said absolutely not. Especially after his heart attack. He's ready to let it go, and his deal with my—with de Lorean left him with quite a retirement fund."

Maria crooked one eyebrow. "Really?"

"The only other condition on Manny was that he use de Lorean's bookkeeper. Which makes me wonder if there was money launderin' going on. But we'll be startin' fresh, so it might not matter. I don't want to stir up trouble for Manny if I don't have to. Whatever was done, it's over. Still, I have to look into it, make sure nothin's going to come back on me later."

There were several deep "ohs" and some heads nodding.

Maria sank back into her chair as if her legs had melted. "Well, shoot." She looked heartbroken.

"I don't know what I want to do about it," Ethan said. "On the one hand, I don't want anything from him, and I've had a feller name of Angus Silver, pesterin' me about buyin' it already. Must've stumbled onto the transfer of deed or something in the public records, I don't know. He's eager. I could flip it easy." He shook his head slowly.

"Angus Silver's a small-time criminal, cuz," Willow said. And when Ethan sent her a surprised look, she went on. "It's a familiar name to law enforcement. He's tangled up with his older brother's fentanyl smuggling enterprise, but is mostly a screw-up. Always causing problems big brother has to fix. Often caught, never convicted. You can't sell it to him."

"I didn't know. I'd have checked though. I'd never sell it to anybody like that." "It's Manny's place," Maria said. "That makes it all but family-owned already."

Her eyes held a plea for Ethan.

He sighed. "Manny said knowin' it was goin' to me would let him retire in peace."

"It's part of the fabric down here," Willow said softly. And the others all nodded. "What the heck is Mad Bull's Bend without Manny's Cantina?"

Lily's big brother Harrison looked around at all the faces, and said, "I don't see the problem, then. Keep it. Run it."

Maria put her hand over his. "That would mean givin' up his career as a country singer," she said.

Ethan nodded, too. "So, I don't know. I thought you'd all have input. But Lily said I should ask you to be objective about it, you know, rather than emotional. I know you'd all prefer me to stay, but—"

"We get it," Orrin said, looking around with one eyebrow raised. "But that's easier said than done, Cuz. We freakin' *miss* you."

Everyone murmured agreement, and they all got out of their chairs and surrounded Ethan. Everybody had a hand on him. He wondered whether Lily was among them. He couldn't see her, the way the cousins had closed in.

Then she cleared her throat, from the direction of where she'd been sitting and apparently still was. "I don't see why you think you have to choose," she said.

The sea of cousins parted to reveal her sitting there, sipping beer from a long-neck brown bottle. She'd worn her hair down. It hung like a silvery cloud around her shoulders. The firelight caught and reflected in her blouse, somehow.

"You said you had some ideas," he said.

"Yeah, later on those," she said. "But why not take a short time off from the road, and focus on the cantina? Make it into whatever you want it to be. Use your name and celebrity status to have an amazing launch. Then hire somebody else to run it for you and go back on the road, if that's what you still want."

Baxter got up, paced to the table for another slice, and took a thoughtful bite, nodding while he chewed. "She's right. Lots of country stars own bars and restaurants. It's probably a great tax shield, not to mention a backup in case things go wrong in the singing career."

"Or never go right," Ethan said.

"See that, right there?" Lily pointed at him. "That attitude, that belief that you've failed? That's what's keeping your career from taking off again."

Everyone gasped, and she bit her lip. Ethan could see how uncomfortable she was that she'd blurted what she had. It hadn't seemed intentional.

"That's what my mom would've said, anyway," she finished softly, then rolled her eyes.

"That's exactly what she would've said." Her brother Harrison got up. "She'd say to spend some time doing something you could feel great about. Get your focus off what's not going right. Give it..." he paused, and then he and Lily finished the sentence together. "...room to breathe."

"You're smothering it with your doubt," Lily went on, grinning as she quoted her mother again. Maybe she *could* fill in for her a little bit, here and there.

"Yeah," her brother added, throwing in another old chestnut. "Stop arguing for your limitations." Then he leaned over to high-five her and said, "That was good."

"Like she was right here," Lily agreed.

Trevor leaned forward, reaching for a fresh beer as his chair was near the cooler. "Might be somethin' to be said for lettin' the fans miss you for a little while. Folks want somethin' more when they can't have it."

Orrin nodded his agreement.

Ethan went to his chair, right next to Lilly's, and sat down. "I didn't think about doin' both. Hirin' someone to run it seems like it could work."

"And findin' somebody who can make tacos like Manny's," Maria Michele said. "You have to save the tacos, Ethan."

"My dad's on that," Lily said. "He's been getting hands-on lessons from Rosa. He even sweet-talked her out of her secret seasoning blend."

Ethan looked over at her and wondered where the hell she'd come from. It was like Harrison Hyde, the man who'd come to Texas to sweep his cousin off her feet, had brought an angel along with him. He'd dropped her right into the middle of their lives, and she'd been glowing and gleaming there ever since.

Everybody felt better when Lily was around.

He tapped his beer bottle to hers. There was a satisfied look in her eyes. Then he said, "I really want to hear your ideas, Lily. The ones that kept you up all night."

"Shoot, she could run the place for you, if you wanted," Harrison said. "By the time Dad retired, she was managing the diner more than he was."

Lily raised her chin a little at Harrison's praise and said, "I was managing it entirely. Dad was just cooking. But then he retired, and I went to nursing school."

But her brother's words burrowed into her heart, and into her mind, too. And they settled in there, like they were planning to stay a while. They felt good. And then they felt like a spark, and the spark said, *I really* could *run it for him.*

She looked at Ethan. He was looking back at her, but she couldn't read his expression. "I do have some ideas," she said. "About making the place into a proper honky-tonk."

"Knockin' out a wall to expand, puttin' in a dance floor," Ethan said. He'd been turning her suggestions over in his mind ever since she'd expressed them.

"And maybe put the parking lot in back. It could be way bigger if you did, and the front could be repurposed for—"

"More outdoor tables?" Ethan said. Then he snapped his fingers. "We could host private parties, wedding receptions."

He said we. Okay, okay, stay cool.

"I have some sketches." She opened her phone's photo app and handed it to him.

He expanded the images of her drawings. She'd made several versions of a decorative, sound-buffering barrier between the road and the area in front of Manny's. She'd also drawn ideas for providing shade, from colorful shade sails to transplanting 20-year-old live trees native to the area. Her ideas for an outdoor serving station, placed in various locations, were there too. She watched him looking, nodding, and then he looked up from the phone and met her eyes, smiling,

"These are great. No wonder you didn't sleep last night."

"I got inspired."

Their eyes held until Drew cleared her throat. They both looked up, and Lily realized they'd kind of forgotten anyone else was there. Everyone was looking at them, expressions ranging from speculation to full-on amusement.

Trevor said, "You gotta put in a mechanical bull, Bubba. No matter what."

"The tacos are what's important!" Maria said. "You have to get them right! And we all have to be there for Manny's final night in business, too."

"I like where this is going," Baxter said. "Ethan, you probably know enough country singers to keep big acts circulating. And you could use local bands in between, even perform yourself."

"Say more about moving the parking lot to the back," Willow said. "I think it might be brilliant."

"Say more about the dance floor!" Drew added.

Everyone was smiling, throwing ideas around, talking over each other. But not Ethan. Lily watched him looking from one cousin to the next. His expression was kind of vacant. Yeah, they were doing just what Lilly had predicted they would.

She leaned closer. "They're acting like it's a done deal, aren't they? Maybe this wasn't such a great idea after all."

Then Orrin, who'd been silent throughout, spoke into a lull in the noise. "Place has a basement, you know."

That silenced everyone. The gift of being the silent type was that when you did speak, people listened. "I didn't know," Ethan said. "How do *you*?"

"Was getting quesadillas with friends when that twister came through, my senior year. Manny hustled us into his *sótano*. It was so quiet down there you wouldn't've known there was a storm." He shrugged his shoulders. "Might make a good recording studio."

Lily shifted her gaze in time to see the change in Ethan's face. Behind his eyes, she thought she detected the same kinds of sparks and tiny fires that were hopscotching across her own brain. There was definitely a light that hadn't been there before.

And then Willow said, "Or, you could sell it to strangers who'll do whatever they want to it, and go back on the road like before."

Baxter tipped back his beer, lowered it, thumped his chest with a fist and burped simultaneously. Drew rolled her eyes and Willow laughed at him. "If you want to change the output, you have to change the input," he said. "You keep doin' things the same way, you can't get anything other than the same result."

"Basic science," Harrison agreed.

Maria's husband tended to be way more vocal when he agreed with his in-laws than when he didn't, but that was okay. He was a good guy, for a Yankee. Fit with Maria like he was made for her. Though Ethan wouldn't have believed it on paper, seeing them together left no room for doubt.

Everyone was still discussing. Drew was reciting a wish-list of restroom features, that had Maria and Willow shouting back affirmations like hallelujahs in church. Trevor was wondering aloud about how much land came with the place, and whether there was enough for a rodeo ring. Baxter argued that a rodeo ring beside a bar would be a recipe for disaster.

Orrin was quiet, like always, and Ethan was just taking it all in.

Lily leaned closer to him. "I don't know, Ethan. I'm not hearing too many arguments against keeping the place. At least for now. Do you actually have any yourself?"

"Yeah," he said, tipping his head, so it came nearer, speaking to her alone. His mouth was so close to her ear she felt his warm breath with his words. She shivered, and it was delicious, and she imagined him saying something sexy or at least flirty to her, and shivered even harder.

But what he said wasn't sexy or flirty at all. It was a plea. "One big argument against it," he said softly. "What if I fail?"

CHAPTER FIVE

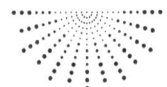

*E*than had several beers, but no buzz. He was a big guy; he metabolized it faster than he drank it, so he rarely got tipsy unless he was specifically trying. Like when his manager Ang had told him if he didn't have an album for them by year's end, his label intended to cancel his contract.

Five beers in, he was uninspired and stone cold sober. He cracked another can.

Lily, on the other hand, was feeling no pain, dancing fireside with the She-Brands, Willow, Maria, and Drew to music spilling from a pickup's open doors.

Eventually, though, the pizza was gone and the beer was warm. One by one, the cousins peeled off. Maria and Harrison went home. Obviously, the newlyweds wouldn't want to bunk down with the whole gang. Harrison drove, since he'd stopped drinking early on.

The others headed into the bunkhouse one at a time, until it was only him and Lily.

She stood near the dying fire with her back toward him. The warm yellow glow lit her bright angel's hair, and outlined her body in that clingy sleeveless, shiny blouse, and butt-hugging jeans.

She rubbed her arms. He spotted her sweater on her chair, got up slow, and slid it over her shoulders.

"Ooh, thanks." She put her arms into the sleeves and hugged the cardigan around her. "I was too warm a minute ago."

"Fire's dyin' down. Probably oughtta douse it and head inside."

"Oh." It was sad, that syllable. Disappointed. She heaved a sigh, then she turned around and put one hand on his chest. She looked up at him and said, "I'm not who everybody thinks I am, you know." She hiccupped, and looking surprised, pressed her fingers over her lips.

"No?"

"Not at *all*."

"Who does everybody think you are?" he asked. He shouldn't have. It wasn't fair to urge her to spill things she might not spill sober. But his desire to hear whatever she wanted to tell him was irresistible.

She turned away, but leaned back against his chest, looking up at the Texas sky—stars from horizon to horizon. Sparks from the fire floated upward now and then, fading as they went. It seemed like they were joining the stars up on the big stage.

He thought about the cantina, about Lily's ideas, about putting in an addition with a stage and dance floor. With the friends he'd made in the business, there were nine or ten acts he could book with a phone call.

Then he looked down from the stars to their reflections in her eyes. Her gaze shifted, so she met his upside down, leaning back against his chest. His arms had locked around her waist and he didn't remember moving them.

"They think I'm my mother, a weaker reflection of her, anyway."

"Because you're named after her. And you look like her."

He'd seen photos. When they'd re-interred Lily Marie Hyde, they'd held a graveside service at the pretty little cemetery on the highest point of the Texas Brand. His birth mother had been moved there, too, long ago. He understood Lily's guilt, wondering if she'd disturbed her mother's rest and whether she would have wanted to be there. For his part, he didn't have any doubts his mother would be pleased. Her sister Chelsea was at the Texas Brand, and so was Ethan, as often as he was anywhere.

But he didn't know whether Lily had come to the same peace of mind about having her mother exhumed, flown across the country, and re-interred on Brand land.

After the graveside service, there'd been a reception at the ranch house. There were photos of Lily Ellen's mamma everywhere. She was a true beauty, and Lily did bear a strong resemblance.

But he could see the differences. His Lily's face was softer, rounded where her mother's was more angular. Her eyebrows arched more gently, and her eyes...

Were staring into his.

"Everyone called her an angel. And she seemed like one to Harrison and me. Perfect in every way. She always knew what to say. She always knew what to do. She was a great nurse, too. In the ER people would ask for her by name. She saved a lot of lives. She'd have saved Manny."

"Manny's fine," he said.

"I know." She closed her eyes. "I'm not an angel of mercy like she was."

"I don't think it's a job requirement for nurses," he said.

"I don't think I'm a nurse." She pressed her lips tight, then shook her head. "It's been tearing me up, every shift I work. So I...gave notice. Two weeks ago, so..."

She stopped looking into his eyes, resumed staring at the stars, but she was still pressed against him. The top of her head was under his chin, her back and shoulders against his chest. He wished he hadn't brought her the sweater.

"I'm really not any kind of angel," she said softly, and then she turned around, stood on tiptoe, and pressed her mouth to his.

Ethan crumbled like a week-old cookie. He closed his arms around her and then some, gathering her close, and he kissed her back. She ran her hands through his hair and arched against his thigh. *Oh, hell no.*

"Hey, hey, here now. Let's take a breath." He held her by the shoulders and peeled his body from hers. The air between them was icy. "We can't uh—you ain't sober."

"I don't care."

"Well, I do. My uncle didn't raise me like that, Lily. Besides, you'd care tomorrow."

"I've been thinking about kissing you way longer than I've been drinking beer tonight. Like, a whole year longer."

He pushed a stray curl off her forehead. "I know," he said. And as she started to scowl, he added, "Me, too."

"Well then why haven't we—"

"This is not a conversation we're fixin' to have tonight, Lil. Not like this."

She hiccupped again, then pouted and lowered her head. "You're prolly right."

"I'm for sure right. Come on, let's get you inside. I'll come back out to douse the fire."

"Okay." He turned her in the circle of his arm and started toward the bunkhouse. She was walking fine, not drunk, just silly and loose.

But suddenly she planted her feet only a few steps from the door and turned and said, "No."

"No?"

"Nope. I'm not going inside unless you kiss me again. I've been very patient, Ethan. I've waited a long time and I think I desherve this. 'Specially after you left me hanging under the mistletoe at Christmas. So I'm not leaving this spot until you—"

He kissed her. Oh man, did he ever kiss her. She tasted like pizza and beer, and all he wanted was more. He didn't want to stop. He knew he had to stop. Dang, he didn't want to stop.

He stopped, straightened, shook his head. "Dang, woman."

"Yeah. Fire, huh?"

He nodded, reached for the doorknob. "You ready?"

She smoothed her hair, pressed her lips, gave a nod. He opened the door, and she went inside under her own steam, heeling off her shoes as she walked straight to the far end and crawled into a vacant lower bunk without looking back. She lay face down with one leg still on the floor and didn't move again.

Shaking his head, Ethan went the rest of the way inside, passing Willow, who was in the kitchen, putting leftover pizza into the fridge. She caught his eyes as he passed, raising her eyebrows in question. He ignored her and continued to the bunk all the way back. Someone was in one of the two showers, everyone else was in the other bunks. Trevor snored softly. Drew muttered in her sleep. Baxter's mouth was slightly open. He didn't think anyone was awake besides him and Willow, and whoever was in the shower. Must've been Orrin.

He knelt low and tugged the blankets out from under Lily. She shifted and muttered, and then her hands were at the fly of her jeans, and before he could do much of anything, she was shoving them off, down her hips, down her curvy thighs and slender calves to her ankles.

"Uh, Willow?" he whispered, and he turned, but she'd gone outside. He could see her moving around out there, picking things up.

Lily was kicking her feet in slow motion in a failed attempt to remove her jeans. She had light-blue panties underneath. He peeled the jeans over her feet, and draped them across the foot of the bed, while she continued writhing around under the covers. When she emerged, she still wore the satiny dark-blue tank top, but her bra dangled from one finger. She started to throw it, but he grabbed it first and laid it atop the jeans.

She flung back the covers then, and smiling sleepily, patted the mattress beside her. The blouse clung to her breasts like paint, leaving nothing to his imagination. He reached down and pulled the covers over her, then he turned to head back outside, moving fast, like the very devil was nipping at his heels.

The brisk night air smacked his face, and he welcomed it as he closed the bunkhouse door behind him.

Willow was out there, gathering beer bottles and cans into their respective boxes. He went to the hose, already attached to an outdoor spigot, turned it on and aimed it at the fire pit. As she moved around in the darkness, Willow said, "Saw that kiss." And when he looked her way sharply, she added, "Kitchen window."

He shrugged.

She moved past him, gathering more bottles.

He set the hose aside, took up a fire-rake and stirred the coals around. Then he turned the hose on again. He didn't reply to Willow's observation because he didn't know how. He'd kissed Lily. He'd devoured her. Twice. What was there to say?

"She's a tender thing, you know that, don't you?"

"Aren't we all?"

"Well, yeah, but if you're just gonna leave again—"

"I know."

She nodded, carried a 24-pack of empties over to the front door. He shut off the water and wound up the hose, satisfied the fire was thoroughly doused.

"It's not just you and Lily involved," Willow said. "You break her heart, it's gonna mess with Maria and Harrison, too."

"I...hadn't thought of that." He started gathering up the chairs, folding them and sliding them into their respective carrying bags.

But Willow wasn't finished. "It could drive a wedge right through the family, Bubba. And family's all we got, when it comes down to it."

He lowered his head. Willow did her best to call him Ethan most of the time, but when she was angry, she reverted to using his childhood nickname to make sure he knew it. "I hear you."

"You'd better." Then she sighed, looking around the site. "I think we got everything. I'm hittin' the rack." She reached for the door, but when he didn't move, she turned back. "You comin'?"

"I'm uh—I'm fixin' to sleep in my truck," he said. "I think it's for the best."

"You'll freeze your hindquarters off. Go on back to the house, sleep in your room."

"I'm good. G'night Will."

"'Night, Ethan."

He went to his truck, got in the passenger side, and pushed the seat back as far as it would go. Then he reclined it as far as possible, and wished he'd thought to bring a blanket. He heeled off his boots and turned onto his side, drawing his knees up, because there wasn't room to stretch out.

There was a tap on the window. He turned the key on and put the window down.

Willow stood there with a bedroll. There were always stacks of clean bedding all bundled together in the bunkhouse closet.

"Thanks."

"You really oughtta go back to the house for the night. Or just come inside. Lily won't know if you're there or on the moon. She's sawin' timber in there."

But *he* would know. "I'm fine. G'night."

"'Night."

He rolled the window up as she walked away. He thought that going to the ranch house for the night would be hurtful to Lily. It would come off like a rejection. Nope, he was gonna be in the kitchen brewing coffee when she opened her eyes in the morning.

And then, he supposed, if his female cousins were anything to go by, Lily would want to talk about all that kissing. It floated into his mind that maybe she wouldn't remember, but he'd been in a lot of barrooms, and the blackout drunks were easy to spot. She'd only had a few beers. Got herself into a state of silly and put her inhibitions to sleep. But she wasn't likely to forget.

Besides, if those kisses had felt to her the way they'd felt to him, they were well and truly burned into her memory. He'd never forget them, that was for sure.

Son of a gun. Staying in Quinn was a bad idea. He'd break that little gal's heart if he stayed, and Willow was right. That could drive a wedge into the closest family in Texas.

He'd best sell Manny's Cantina just as quick as he could and get back to his career. Lily would be hurt, no doubt about it, but if she was gonna be hurt by his leaving now, how much worse would it be later?

If he stayed, they'd be together. He couldn't keep saying no to her forever. He was a flawed human male, and he wanted her more than was reasonable. But his life couldn't be in Quinn, as an upright and noble Brand. The farther he went from home, the less his surname meant to anyone. There was no reputation to uphold—or fail to uphold. Being a one-hit wonder was okay out there. Here in Quinn, it was probably the talk of the town.

There he is, Garrett Ethan Brand the Second, a wanna-be country star.

We expected so much more of him.

Certainly not livin' up to his name, is he?

Could be worse, he thought. At least the locals didn't know his real father had been a criminal, a murderer.

Yep. He had to sell. He'd make sure the cantina went to someone decent, someone local. He'd make it a private contract between him and the buyer, no bank loan necessary—give someone from the community a leg-up.

That was it, his mind was made up. He rolled onto his side, sure he'd be able to go to sleep now that he knew what he had to do. But the minute he started to drift off, a voice—Lily's voice, inside his head—whispered, *That stage could have built-in amps, top of the line. It would save visiting bands setup time and provide quality sound even if the band is just starting out.*

The suggestion was accompanied by an angelic look in Lily's big blue eyes. Now he knew this wasn't Lily's idea, but his own. His subconscious was just choosing to give it to him in Lily's voice.

"Irrelevant," he told the thought, "since I'm sellin' it. I'm fixin' to call Cat Shaw first thing tomorrow mornin'."

Before or after you make me coffee and we talk about all that kissin'? Mental Lily asked in a Texas twang she'd never used.

"One problem at a time." He rolled onto his opposite side, tried to straighten his legs and his knee hit the console. "Dang." He rubbed the pain away, wishing it was enough to distract his mind. He tried the method his aunt Chelsea had taught him when he'd still been a pup, counting backwards from seven, seeing each number as a color. Seven, red, he thought. Six, orange. Five, yellow. Four, green.

You could get the best equipment there is for the recording studio. Can you imagine, recording whenever you feel like it instead of on someone else's schedule?

"Yeah," he muttered. "Midnight inspirations, I could lay a quick track down." Then he popped his eyes wider. "Except that I'm sellin' the place in the mornin'."

Lily woke up reliving those moments alone with Ethan out by the campfire. At first, she was relishing the memory, and then as she came more fully awake, she was mortified. "Oh, no," she whispered, and she sat up fast. Too fast. Her head spun, and her stomach knotted up. "Ah, hell." She sat there in the bunk, upright, legs still under the covers, in her shiny dark-blue tank top and underpants. She'd brought an overnight bag and hadn't even opened it. And she'd kissed Ethan full on last night. Twice!

And he'd kissed her back.

Raising her head slowly brought another wave of pain, but she peered around the bunkhouse through squinty eyes. She saw him about the same time she detected the smell of fresh coffee. He was in the kitchen. He'd already showered up. His hair was still wet. Then she looked at the other bunks. They were empty.

Ethan held up a mug. She swung her legs out of bed, but they were bare, and she was suddenly self-conscious. Her jeans lay across the foot of the bed, so she grabbed them and pulled them on before she crossed the bunkhouse to the kitchen and took the mug from his hand. It was warm, and she sipped, and it didn't make her stomach revolt.

"Drew and Orrin left early," he said. "Willow, just now. Trevor's in the shower."

"I need one, too."

"There's a second bathroom. It's all yours. I just wanted to see you before I headed out."

"Oh? You were waiting for me?"

He nodded. "I wanted to tell you before anyone else."

His tone wasn't all excited like, *I couldn't wait to tell you*. It was, more like, *I thought you oughtta know*.

He took a breath, gave himself what looked like a nod of encouragement, and blurted, "I've decided to sell the cantina soon as I can find the right buyer."

"Oh." She took another sip of the coffee. She didn't say

anything else, but her mind was reeling. This was his reaction to those kisses. In spite of a thousand reasons to stay here, he'd decided to leave.

She took a deep breath, looked him right in the eyes, and said, "Well, fuck you, then."

"*What?*" His face was completely lax, and then his phone went off. He reached down to silence it, but it went off two more times before he could, and he looked down at it then.

Lily set her coffee mug down hard, went to where she'd left her backpack on the floor, and yanked it over her shoulders like she was mad at it.

"Lily, come on, you knew this was my plan." But his eyes kept darting to his phone screen again as it buzzed two more times.

"Sure did," she said. "I'll get that shower at home. You have a nice life, Ethan." And then she went right out the door.

He didn't pay any attention. He didn't shout at her to wait or to stay. He didn't apologize or try to explain. He didn't come running out the door behind her. Nothing. He'd fallen fully into his phone. Like she didn't even matter.

She picked up the pace, hiking the trail back toward the ranch house. Her angry strides ate up the distance, but the whole time she was sure he would come bouncing along in his big red truck and pick her up and say something. Anything.

He didn't. God, she was so humiliated. His reaction to her kissing him was to cut and run. She broke the crest of a rise and saw her dad's pickup parked alongside the house, not in front. Chelsea hated people parking in front.

She crossed the driveway and headed up the porch steps to the door. Breakfast smells came from inside, and her stomach growled. She pushed open the creaky screen door—family didn't knock here—and went inside, following voices into the kitchen where her father was laughing, and as he scooped a perfect western omelet onto a plate, pivoted, and with a flourish, placed it in front of Miz Cat Shaw, the local realtor. She'd found them the little cabin where they lived and had helped Maria and Harrison buy their adorable house on Bluebonnet Lane.

Cat Shaw had a mass of minky-brown hair with silver near the roots and just in front of her ears. Her brows were perfectly arched, and her makeup flawless at seven a.m. on a Tuesday, even though she still wore a fluffy robe and slippers.

So, she noticed, did her father.

Cat saw her first, and said, "Oh, don't look like that, Lily Ellen. I had my *own* guest room."

Her father turned, "Lily! You look...you look a little wobbly, honey. You want an omelet?"

"I do and I don't. Too many beers." She held her stomach.

"Go upstairs, take a shower," he said. "Use mine, I'm in the blue room. While you're gone, I'll make you an omelet. I know just how you like 'em"

"Okay, I'll go, but no omelet. I couldn't do it justice." She frowned, still not seeing anyone else in the house. "Where are Chelsea and Garrett?"

"Went for an early morning trail-ride," Cat Shaw said. "Conveniently," and then she winked. "They're pretty obviously tryin' to play matchmaker with your dad and me."

"Very transparent, aren't they?" Hyram said. "To be honest, I'm flattered anyone would think a pretty lady like you would be interested in a washed-up old chef like me."

"Huh. And here I was, flattered they'd think an accomplished, talented, handsome man like you would be interested in a busy-body small-town real-estate lady like me," she replied.

And the two of them smiled at each other as if nobody else was in the room.

"Welp, that shower awaits," Lily said, and headed up the stairs at the same pace she'd walked over from the bunkhouse.

Once she'd closed the bathroom door behind her, she called her brother.

Harrison picked up with a sleepy, "Hello?"

"I think something's going on between Dad and that realtor lady, Cat Shaw!"

"Good morning to you, too," Harrison replied. "She's the one who helped Maria and me buy our house, right?"

"Yes," Lily said in a stage-whisper. "They're downstairs in their *bathrobes* making eyes at each other over breakfast."

"Aww." He sounded like he'd spotted a puppy.

"What do I do, Harrison? He made her an *omelet!*"

Her brother took a deep breath. "I think it's sweet, Lil. I do. You said you were worried about him, that he seemed depressed, that you think he's lonely. Maybe Cat Shaw's good for him. Maybe…it's time."

"Oh, God," she said. It was a cross between a whine and a moan. She leaned back against the wall and slid slowly to the floor until she was sitting on a fluffy shower rug. "It can't be time."

"Mom would want him to be happy."

"Mom was a saint. *I* don't want him to be happy. *I* want him to keep grieving her forever."

"No, you don't," Harrison said. "I know you better than that."

"No, I don't," she admitted. She took a deep breath and lowered her chin to her chest. Then from somewhere beyond her brother, she heard Maria shout, "Oh no, this is *awful!*"

"What's wrong?" Lily asked. "Is Maria okay?"

"Hang on, she's showing me something…oh, hell. This is bad. I'm forwarding a link. Where's Ethan right now?"

"Out at the bunkhouse, last I saw him," she said. "Why?" Her phone signaled, and she clicked the link her brother had sent. Her eyes rounded, and her jaw dropped. "Holy fu–dgesicles."

And like a bolt from the blue, she understood where her sainted mother's favorite exclamation had come from. She'd used it to keep herself from dropping f-bombs.

That was almost as big a revelation as the gossip site's sensationalistic hit piece about Ethan Brand's drug-lord father having murdered his birth mother.

When Ethan had looked at his phone, he hadn't been able to believe his eyes. There was an image of him on stage, head back, guitar high, wailing, with backlighting that cast everything in red. Underneath the image there was a caption: "Ethan Brand's Wholesome Image Hides a Violent Past."

And then he saw the little inset with de Lorean's face-front mugshot, and the caption, "Brand's father—drug dealer and cold-blooded killer."

He swore softly and tapped the link. It took him to an article in one of the celebrity gossip sheets, claiming he'd just inherited a fortune from the same man who'd killed his own mother, a crime lord worth millions. It made him sound like a greedy, grasping fraud.

"While his music praises his small-town home and family values, it appears Ethan Brand is actually sole heir to the fortune of a murderous organized-crime boss, earned by smuggling cocaine and fentanyl into the country."

The article made it sound as if the idyllic upbringing he'd talked about in every interview and written about in most of his songs had been made up out of whole cloth.

"Hell and damnation." He pushed a hand through his hair.

That was the point where he'd looked up to find Lily on her way out the door.

His phone stopped buzzing and started ringing. Angelo Barrone was on the screen. His manager. He had to answer. He had no choice but to let Lily run off angry. He could make things right later. Or…not. He was leaving. What difference did it make? It might even be easier to let her stay mad.

He answered the phone. "Hey, Angelo."

"For fuck's sake, Ethan!"

He sighed and said, "Look, I was adopted as a baby by the Brands of Quinn, Texas. Everything I've ever said or sung about my childhood is the truth. It's verifiable. My birth father's behavior isn't my fault."

"No shit. It's all true then?"

"Yeah."

"He killed your mother?"

Ethan sighed heavily. "Yeah."

"Jeeze, kid, that's rough. I'm sorry, man."

"Thanks."

"So, what about this inheritance they're talking about?"

"I'm disclaimin' it. Meetin' with a lawyer today."

"But…? It sounds like there's a but."

"There's a but," Ethan admitted. "He put a local cantina in my name before he died. And the previous owner had a heart attack and wants me to take it over. He's countin' on it, in fact. And it's in my hometown, well, hometown adjacent. They count on the place, too."

"Ah-huh." Angelo said. "Lemme think, lemme think."

Ethan could picture him, pacing his cheesy little office in Dallas, rubbing his bald head, and pressing his lips. He'd emigrated from Brooklyn and never lost the accent. Still had an office there, and one in Nashville, too, but he spent most of his time in Dallas, his adopted home. He made good money, lived in a house out of a lifestyle magazine, but you wouldn't know it by his shabby workspace.

The guy was a genius for most of his clients. Kept saying he hadn't quite found the key with Ethan yet, but that he knew he would. Talent will tell, he liked to say.

"I'm fixin' to sell the place as quick as I can," Ethan told him. "I'm hopin' to find somebody local. It's part of the community, you know? I can't sell to some corporation who'd doze it to make a parkin' lot."

"Yeah," Angelo said. "Yeah, a little cantina. Part of the fabric of that small town of yours. Quale—"

"Quinn."

"Quinn, yeah."

"Only it's in Mad Bull's Bend, next town over."

"You're kidding. You're making it up."

"No, why would I—"

"This cantina shown up in any of your songs, Ethan?"

He thought about it for a second, then snapped his fingers. "*Gringo in a Sombrero*," he said. It's a silly song about the bearded, sombrero-wearing Caucasian who hangs out at Manny's place, causing all the locals to speculate about him."

"Yeah? How's it go?"

He sang into the phone:

> "In a small cantina-taco-stand, with the best tacos in all
>   the land, at a table near the soda stand
> Gringo-sombrero man.
> Brim down low to hide his eyes, bushy beard like a
>   disguise. Doesn't care to socialize
> Gringo-sombrero man.
> Watching diners every day, still as if he's made of clay,
>   prob'ly with the CIA,
> Gringo-sombrero man.

*Or maybe casing up the joint, to rob it at some future
    point
Or maybe in the distant past, here's where he saw his
    lover last
And now he waits for her return, And until then, his
    heart will yearn—"*

"I'm not so sure you should sell it," his manager broke into Ethan's number just when he was getting to the big finish. "You got another option besides sell it?"

"Well, I mean…my family wants me to stay here and turn it into a honky-tonk, but—"

"Turn it into a honky-tonk?" Angelo said. "Huh. A honky-tonk."

"Yeah, but—"

"Is it big enough to bring in decent acts?"

"It could be," he said. "If we knocked out a wall, and…But that's not what I—"

"This sounds like the perfect thing, Ethan. You realize that? The solution to your problem is right in your hands."

"No, Ang. It's not."

"First things first," Ang said, brushing off Ethan's denial like a pesky gnat. "You need to make a statement for the press to respond to this hit piece. Make a video, okay? Disown your old man, disclaim the inheritance, and talk about your adopted family being the only one you've ever known, yada, yada, blah, blah. You got me? Then say you need to take some down time to process what's happened. Can you do that for me? On video?"

"I…yeah, I can do that, sure."

"Good. That's first. You make that video on your phone or whatever, and you send it to me. I'll do the rest. And then you go focus on that honky-tonk of yours. You want to sell it later, fine. But listen to me, Ethan. You shouldn't be on the road for a while, especially not with an album due. Besides, a person in anguish wouldn't be out playing gigs, and you gotta show some anguish to overcome the stories already out there."

"But they're lies."

"First lie to go viral wins. How many times have you heard me say that?"

Ethan sighed and didn't answer.

"We can overwhelm the bad press with your genuine, down-home wholesomeness. You ain't faking that. I know fakes, and you're no fake. I know what I'm talking about. Home is the best place for you right now. And saving that fabric-of-Quale cantina—"

"Quinn, not Quale, and it's in Mad Bull's Bend, not Quinn."

"—that small-town cantina you've written songs about and somehow, through a twist of fate, wound up owning, is the best thing you could be working on. I couldn't make up a better project for you. Saving a beloved small-town business. Helping out an owner who has to retire after a heart attack. Expanding to employ more locals, boosting the Quale economy."

Ethan closed his eyes, lowered his head. "I don't know."

"Yeah, well, you can't be expected to know everything, son. That's my job. Besides, you just found out the man who killed your mother died in prison. And he happened to be your father. You most likely *do* need some down time, whether you even know it or not. It'd be harder to believe you didn't. So take it. Meanwhile, I'll work on turning this whole situation to our advantage."

"How in tarnation are you fixin' to do that?"

"It's my job to figure that out. You make me that video. Other than that, you don't talk to anybody. No interviews. Stay off social media until I tell you otherwise. Focus on that cantina. Bask in that wholesome hometown of yours for a while. Consider it a vacation."

"How long a vacation?"

"Eight, ten, twelve weeks. You trust me, right?"

He closed his eyes. "I do trust you, Angelo." With good reason. Ang was an important, successful entertainment manager, and Ethan was lucky to have him.

"Good. Then do what I tell you. It's for the best. And shoot me that video. Sooner the better but do a good job. And remember, you need private time to process all this. Okay?"

"Yeah. Okay."

His manager disconnected without a goodbye, and Ethan figured he was probably already placing another call. He put his phone down. Great. Now he *had to* stick around home.

And Lily.

He glanced up toward the still open bunkhouse door and realized he'd pissed her off for nothing. Hell.

The shower shut off, and he wasn't in the mood to talk, so he headed out. If he was fixin' to have a meltdown, he'd prefer it be in private.

CHAPTER SIX

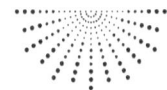

*S*he didn't run into Ethan after her shower, even though she expected to. He wasn't in the kitchen, which was empty. The whole house was empty, except for her dad. He was standing near the front door waiting for her, pickup keys in one hand, travel-mug in the other. He offered the mug to her when she reached him. She slung her bag over her shoulder and took it, and they headed out to his truck together.

"Where is everybody?" she asked.

"Lookin' for Ethan, I imagine. He wasn't in the bunkhouse. Trevor said he was gone when he got out of the shower this morning. His truck's gone, and they're all worried. Did you see—?"

"I saw."

Her father started the engine, then slammed a fist onto the steering wheel, "It isn't right, what they put in that rag."

She put a hand on her dad's shoulder. He'd fully assimilated into the Brand family, was as protective of Ethan and his cousins as he was of her and Harrison.

"Ethan's a good man," he said. "He doesn't deserve this."

"I know, Dad. I know."

"You know where he might be?" he asked.

"I have an idea."

"Well, I don't think he should be alone just now. Do you? It's a lot, what's been laid on him. And I know, he's been giving you a helluva time, but—"

"What's that supposed to mean? Giving me a helluva time?"

"I…" His face puckered like he was trying to squeeze out an answer. "Nothing."

"No, I want to know. Come on, Dad. Out with it."

He shrugged and focused on driving. After a mile he said, "It's clear you two…like each other. Equally clear he's…how did Garrett put it? Saddle shy."

"You've discussed this with Garrett?"

"Not like you mean. Simmer down, Daughter."

That was a Texas turn of phrase if she'd ever heard one. She closed her eyes, shook her head, blew a sigh.

"Besides," Hyram said, "The whole family's rooting for you two."

She swung wide eyes his way.

"You're thinking the burial ground, aren't you?" her father asked, his eyes innocent.

She nodded, still mortified.

"I'll take North Brand Lane, then," he said. "Let's just see if his truck's out there."

Ethan sat on the little stone bench in the family burial ground. His mamma's headstone was on his left in a row of others. On his right there was a small pond, thriving with little fish and frogs and salamanders, and covered in lily pads. Blooms of white and lemon yellow seemed to float just above the water.

He sat there and listened to the slow croak of a bullfrog, closed his eyes and smelled wild roses blooming nearby. Something splashed. Something rustled. And still a whirlwind of questions gusted through his mind about what to do and how to do it and when, and what to say on the video and where to record it, and a million others.

The rustling took on a pattern of pairs. Footsteps. He opened his eyes and for some reason, wasn't surprised to see Lily coming along the same path he'd taken. He rose from the bench. She kept coming, winding through the cemetery, blowing a kiss in the direction of the most recent grave, her mother's. Then she came to him and looked at his face, *really* looked. "You okay?"

He stared back at her, opened his mouth, closed it again.

"Of course you're not okay. That was a dumb question."

"I'm livin' out my worst nightmare," he said. He hadn't intended to say it. The words had just tumbled out. He sank onto the bench. "How'd you find me?"

"Had a feelin' this is where you'd be. Had Dad drop me off on the road where you left your truck. Whole family's looking for you."

"Then they've seen it too?"

"Yeah." She took a deep breath, and then she glanced over toward her mother's headstone, asking in silence, he imagined, what the elder Lily might've said to someone in this sort of a state.

Then she took a long, deep breath and it was almost like she exhaled the words. "So if this is your worst nightmare, then it's happened. It's done, it's out there. And you're still here, still upright and functioning. Aren't you?"

He looked at her, narrowing his eyes. "Mostly. So far."

"Well, what is there to be afraid of now, then? The worst is over."

"It could ruin my career," he said.

"Scandal? Ruin a country music star's career? What planet do *you* live on?"

His dread shifted slightly, letting a little of her light beam in through a crack in the door. He became thoughtful, interested. "Angelo, that's my manager, he said he'd figure out how to make this work in our favor. Damned if I know how." He lowered his head.

"Sounds like that's his job. What's his advice in the meantime?"

"I'm under orders not to sell the cantina right away. He thinks I should stay here, under the radar, and work on the place 'til further notice.

She lifted her eyebrows at him. "So you're staying, then?"

He nodded.

"For the um…good of your career?" she asked.

"Yeah."

"Huh." She rose from the bench and walked a few steps nearer the pond, gazing into the water but not at him. Sunlight gleamed down, reflected, and danced across her cheek.

He was trying to figure out what she was thinking and failed. He stayed where he was, overwhelmed with options and questions and uncertainty. After a long moment, without turning around, she said, "So what are you gonna do about the cantina?"

"What Ang said, I guess. Hang out here, work on the place."

"I got all that. I meant, work on it how?"

"Expand it like we talked about, I guess. Add that stage and dance floor. I liked your ideas about the parkin' lot too, the outdoor tables. Heck, I agreed with most everything you said."

"Uh-huh." She didn't sound flattered by the compliment, and he was reminded sharply that her parting words to him at the end of their most recent conversation had been, "Well, fuck you, then."

"You think you'll be here long enough to do all that?" she asked.

He swallowed hard. "A coupl'a months, anyway," he said. "I could get most of it done, assumin' I can book local contractors on short notice."

"And then what?"

He frowned at her, but she was still gazing into the pond with her back to him. A slash of sunlight on the crystal-clear water gleamed almost the same white blond as her hair. His brain didn't work right when she was around. "I don't under—?"

"When all this blows over and your manager says you can hit the road again, what then?"

"Oh." He could tell by the rigidness in her back and shoulders, and how still she held her head that his answer was important, and he knew it would make her mad all over again. "Then I'll probably sell it—with the stipulation that the new owner keeps it open—and hit the road again."

"That's what I figured," she said.

"I'm sorry," he said. "I'm an even bigger stain on my family's name now that this is out. You gotta be able to see that. I can't stay here. I can't live in Quinn."

She turned to stare at him as if he were an idiot. She didn't say anything or contradict him. Not with words, anyway. But the look in her eyes said it for her.

Eventually, though, she took a deep breath and returned to the bench but stood in front of it instead of sitting. She looked him right in the eyes. "Don't apologize for being honest," she said. "I asked the question because I wanted to know the answer, and you gave it to me."

"It's not you, Lily, believe me, it's—"

She held up a hand, flat palm. "Don't even."

He lowered his head, heard her sigh. Then she said, "Last night, you were also thinking about hiring a manager to run the place for you, freeing you up to go back on the road without having to sell the place."

"Having my cake and eating it too?" he asked. "That's

unlikely. First off, where would I find a person I can trust while I'm on the road, on such short notice?" He looked up as he asked the question.

Lily squared her shoulders, and her chin rose a notch higher. "You're looking at her."

It took him a beat, then he said. "You mean, *you'd* want the job?"

"For now, hire me to help you get the place ready to open. You're already using my ideas, right? I have experience managing a restaurant. Give me a shot. See what I can do, and how well we work together, and we'll take it from there."

"You're that sure about giving up being a nurse?"

She lowered her head, no longer meeting his eyes. "That last day, I had a panic attack right before I went in for my shift. I did the right thing when I gave my notice."

She had his entire attention. He was still sitting, but that put his head lower than hers, so he could look up into her down-turned face. Her eyes had fallen closed. He thought her lashes were wet.

"I didn't realize you were strugglin' so much with this, Lily. Of course you can work with me, of course you can."

She sniffled, twisting her nose, and it made him want to wrap her up and hold her close until she was all healed.

She thrust her hands into the pockets of her jeans and paced the path in front of him, four steps one way, then four steps back. "So we get it up and running and have a knockout grand re-opening. By then you'll know for sure if I'm the manager you want, and I'll know for sure if that's what I'm s'posed to be doing with my life."

He nodded slowly as her words and their meaning marched through his mind. But above everything she'd said, above logistics and her qualifications, and his own plans, all he kept thinking was that he'd be around her all the time. Every day, he'd be around this sunshine-haired, blue-eyed angel. And every cell in his body said yes.

Then he said it aloud, too, and something inside him lifted. "You're on, Lily."

He rose from his bench and went to put his hands on her shoulders, but she ducked to one side, gracefully avoiding contact with a little swoop that surprised him.

"We should keep it strictly business. You're leaving again once we open. Anything between us is doomed anyway, and I'm not looking to break my own heart, so..."

"Oh," he said. "Sure, that makes sense." It should have given him relief. It wouldn't be as hard to keep his hands off her if they agreed that anything else was a bad idea. And apparently they did.

But suddenly the notion of spending every day with her and not touching her felt like it might kill him. And he must be a glutton for punishment, because he asked for more. "Manny's final night is Friday."

"I know."

"Of course you do, you and your dad have been helpin' out there."

"I'm not needed now that Manny's back, but Dad's still helping Rosa in the kitchen like before."

"Manny's saving some tables for the family. You're joinin' us, right?"

She lifted her eyebrows, and he saw something in her eyes, but he was damned if he knew what. Then she heaved a sigh, like maybe he'd exasperated her somehow, and said, "Yeah, sure."

"Good," he said. Then he couldn't think of anything else to add. The birds were singing up a storm, and the sun beamed on the two of them like a spotlight. If he stood up, they'd be so close their bodies would be touching.

He didn't stand up. He slid sideways on the bench first, then rose to his feet, and his whole body howled in disappointment. "Come on," he said. "I'll drive you home."

The line was out the door when Lily and her dad arrived at Manny's. Hyram had been cooking all afternoon, and both he and Cat Shaw planned to assist with the serving tonight. Still, he'd taken a break to dress up for the big event. He wore cowboy boots, jeans, and a brown shirt with onyx snaps. Lily had chosen a yellow sundress with a halter neck and a pale blue sweater. There were cars overflowing the parking lot and lined up along the roadside in either direction. There were tables set up in back, and spilling around the sides of the building to boot.

She clasped her dad's hand.

"This place is going to do great," Hyram said. "Look how many people love it."

Lily nodded. She'd told her father her plan, but not all of it. Now was as good a time as any. "Ethan's hired me to help him get it up and running, and if all goes well, to manage it for him when he goes back on the road."

He clapped his hands and said, "Yes!" And then he frowned. "Wait, he's going back on the road?"

"Right after the opening," she said, averting her eyes and changing the subject. "Think you can handle cooking full-time again?"

"With a small staff," he said without missing a beat. Then he rubbed his hands together. "I want in as much as the two of you will let me."

"Really?" She tilted her head to one side, watching her father's face.

His eyes were sparkling. "It's been like old times, Lily. Cooking, running a kitchen again while Manny's been down, I didn't realize how much I've missed it."

Someone grabbed her forearm, and she turned her head sharply. Ethan, tall and broad in a black shirt with pearl snaps and a matching Stetson. Looking at him, especially up close like this, always made it a little hard for Lily to catch her breath.

"Here, this way," Ethan said. "Manny set us up at a couple'a big tables in the back. We saved you both a spot."

He moved his hand from her forearm to her upper arm, just resting it there, as if to guide her through the crowd. The line was uneven, splitting into multiple lines and uniting again as people milled, edging ever forward. They were going inside, where family members greeted them and pointed them toward the nearest table, some of which were out the rear door in the grassy area between the cantina and the spot where the river ran through.

As they moved away from the door, someone shouted, "Hyram! Hey, Hy!"

They all turned to see Cat Shaw moving their way. She wore a rhinestone-trimmed top, and her wild brown-and-silver curls were all caught up on top of her head.

Hyram watched her approach and elbowed Ethan. "Can we squeeze in one more?" He asked from the side of his mouth, eyes on the woman hurrying toward them. Her tall black boots clicked fast under a broomstick skirt of green and gold.

Ethan said, "Sure we can. Cat, come join us at our table."

"Thank you, Ethan!" She linked her arm right through Hyram's.

Lily pressed her lips into a smile that felt thin and tight, and cursed her inner pettiness.

Ethan said, "You remember Cat, don't you Lily?"

"Hello again, Lily," Cat said, smiling like she hadn't detected Lily's flash of annoyance. If she'd been an *actual* cat, her back would have been arched and her claws would've extended. Lily wanted to hiss at her but that was unreasonable and childish.

Instead she said, "Hi, Cat," and tried for a genuine-looking smile.

"This way," Ethan said, hand still on Lily's arm, moving to the top of her shoulder as they left the line behind. "There's a side door I never knew about, all the years I've been comin' here. Right in that wall we want to knock out."

He pointed at the door as they neared it. On the right side of the clapboard-sided building, there was a double door for deliveries. There were also two huge trash bins, a stack of crates, and a lot of scrubby brush. About fifty feet from the building there was a small garden shed, red with white trim.

"It's just wasted space now," Lily said. "Aside from the shed."

"It's already mostly level, too. No trees in the way," Ethan added, looking around as he reached for the door. "Perfect for the addition." He opened the side door, and the noise of human voices, laughter, clattering dishes, and a mariachi band gusted out. Ethan led the way, waving her in behind him with the hand that had been on her shoulder. She missed his touch but knew she should have shrugged it off sooner.

"It's a packed house," he said. "Best take my hand." He reached back and clasped her hand in his big, warm one, and she got a chill right up her spine. She liked it too much to remind him of their hands-off policy. Her spine was like jelly where he was concerned.

He pulled her through the crowd, and just before they were swallowed up, she reached behind her to take her father's hand, and grudgingly hoped he had hold of Cat Shaw's. Locals called out greetings as they made their way. Mariachis were working their way through the crowd while playing their instruments and singing. She didn't know how they managed it.

Eventually, she spotted her brother at a long table in the back, four chairs on each side, one on each end. Harrison was beside Maria and had two empty seats to his left for her and Dad, she figured, but it would have to be Dad and Cat. They'd want to sit together. She spotted Orrin and Drew sitting together with their backs to them. Baxter was twisted around looking back at them from one end, and Willow was at the other end of the table, waving.

There were two empty seats on the facing side, next to Orrin and Drew. Lily headed toward one of them, not surprised when Ethan slid into the one beside her. He gave her a casual smile and reached for a big cloth napkin. There were two smaller tables filled up with the Elder-Brands, close but not close enough for conversation without shouting.

Trevor came in, late and laughing about it and yelling, "Anybody save me a seat?"

"Take mine," Lily's father said. "I have a *mission* in the *kitchen*." He said it as a rhythmic rhyme with a wink at Lily, then he got up and moved away, heading behind the bar unchallenged, and through twin doors with porthole windows into the kitchen.

Cat looked around the table, maybe feeling a little uncomfortable. She got up, and said, "I'll see if I can help Hyram."

She left, weaving the same path Hyram had. Lily looked at Harrison and they shared one of those brother-sister conversations that didn't require words. They needed to show Cat a better welcome. They acknowledged it and vowed to do better without a word exchanged.

Then Maria leaned over the table a bit to ask, "Has your dad perfected Rosa's taco-makin' process? Tell me he has!"

Lily said, "He's been cookin' all afternoon, so you're about to find out."

"Hot damn and hallelujah!" Maria rarely cussed, but this was apparently a special occasion.

Hyram returned a little while later with a huge platter of tacos, and Cat behind him with all the sauces, salsas, and chips galore. A cheer went up, and Lily sent an extra bright smile Cat's way when she leaned over to put some of them on the table like only a pro could do. "I didn't know you'd been a server. We should compare notes sometime."

Cat beamed. "I'd love that. I tended bar for twenty years, too," she said, then with a wink, "I *know* things." Then she continued placing condiments, before she and Hyram headed back to the kitchen for more.

As usual, all the Brands were talking at once, yet somehow communicating perfectly. She noticed the way Ethan looked around the crowded cantina after taking off his hat.

People were looking at him. Not because he was a small-time celebrity, but because they'd known him for most of his life and had probably never known his true origin story. Maybe the left-on-the-doorstep part, but not the father-murdered-mother part. She'd certainly never heard anyone mention it outside the family.

He was hot gossip, all right. It was obvious, now that she was paying attention. People looked openly and even glanced her way with speculation in their eyes. And then they whispered behind their hands. Not very subtle, were they? She saw one person doing that and stuck her tongue out at them, an act witnessed by most of those staring Ethan's way since she was sitting right beside him.

People turned their attention back to their own business in a hurry.

Lily faced front in her seat again to find Ethan looking at her.

"Thank you," he said. "That was…" And then instead of finding the right word, he just smiled, all the way to his eyes. "That was very cool."

"Screw the gawkers," she said. "You *own* the place. You can throw 'em out on their collective backsides if you want. I'll help. I'd enjoy it!"

There was a bite in her voice. She heard it herself and it surprised her as much as it seemed to surprise him.

"Huh," he said.

"What?"

"You're really *not* all sweetness and light after all, are you, Lily?"

She looked across the table at her brother, talking and laughing with his new bride. "Don't blow my cover with Dad and Harrison, okay?"

"That's a promise." Then he said, "Do you feel like you can't be real around them?"

The taco platter was passed their way, saving her from having to answer right away. Ethan took the tongs and set three of them on her plate. He was going for a fourth but she held up a hand, so he started filling his own. And man, did he fill it.

She asked for the mango salsa, her favorite, and slathered it over her tacos. "It's more that I don't want to disappoint them."

"I don't think that can happen."

"Oh, it can," she said. "Mom left a big hole in our family."

"And you've been tryin' to fill it."

She nodded. "Trying, and failing, mostly."

"But you're so—"

"Don't tell me it's not a valid way to feel. You don't feel worthy of your family, either. Ridiculous as that seems to me." She dug into her tacos. And she didn't talk again until her plate was clean, and she was chugging sweet tea to wash it down.

She wasn't too busy eating to notice when Maria took her first bite and looked as if she'd tasted heaven.

The family was noisy, all talking over each other and laughing. The Brands really enjoyed being together. You couldn't fake that kind of affection. And she enjoyed it, too. So did her brother. They'd melded seamlessly into the clan. The Brand brothers, Garrett, Ben, Wes, Adam, and Elliot, and their baby sis Jessie, treated Hyram like a long-lost seventh sibling.

A fresh tray of tacos came, and she took one more as it made the rounds.

They took their time, eating until they were full. She knew when the bellies were topped off because the conversation got louder again. And that's when Ethan said, "So on the advice of my manager, I'm gonna be stayin' home for a while."

His announcement got the attention of everyone at the table.

"Two months, anyway. Durin' that time, I plan to keep the cantina closed while we get it ready for a grand reopenin'. And after that, I'll decide how to proceed."

He looked down at Lily, and she saw the question in his eyes. Did she want to tell them her news, too? She bit her lip, cleared her throat. "Ethan's hired me to help him get the place ready and manage the grand reopening."

"What about your day-job, Sis?" Harrison asked.

"It's...it's been...I've recently decided it's just not what I'm meant to do." She couldn't look at her brother when she said it. "And the time I was happiest with my work was when I was helping Dad at the diner."

"So this is..." Harrison looked from her to Ethan and back, over and over. "It's a long-term arrangement?"

"It's a two-month arrangement," Lily said, before Ethan could try to answer. "After that, we'll recalculate."

"But Lil, where's the job security in that? You need to think about your future, and—"

Maria interrupted with, "Because there's fixin' to be a shortage of nursin' jobs in the next quarter?" She put her hand on her husband's shoulder. "An RN can *always* find work, hon. She's okay."

Harrison shifted his gaze to Ethan's, and Lily saw how unhappy her brother was about all this. Didn't he realize that if she could've forced herself to keep working as a nurse, she would have? She'd have spent the rest of her life tied up in knots at work, terrified of making a mistake that would kill someone, just to make her dad and brother happy. Just to make them miss Mom a little less.

She'd been trying for a year to do just that. But it was no good. She couldn't force it, and it would be wrong to try. Wrong for the patients, and wrong for her.

Ethan cleared his throat and pulled everyone's attention back to him. "My manager says I have to make a video." He said it loudly enough for most of the table to hear. "You know, to address that article. What it said, what the truth is and like that. I was supposed to have done it two days ago, but…" He ended with a palms-up gesture.

Baxter looked around the crowded place, and said, "Why don't you do it right here?"

"Right here," Ethan repeated, as if trying to interpret the words.

"Yeah, go on up front and talk to the locals. Tell 'em your side of it."

"Baxter's right," Willow said. "That would stop the gossip in its tracks. Just be the guy they know."

Maria was nodding. "We could livestream it," she said. "We can, right, Orrin?"

Orrin nodded. "Already gettin' out my phone."

For some reason, Ethan looked at Lily, as if wanting her opinion more than anyone else's.

She said, "It would shift the focus from the dark stuff about your parentage to the brighter news about converting the cantina into a honky-tonk. If it works, mission accomplished."

He looked around the packed cantina. Even as he did, Manny was climbing up onto an overturned whiskey crate in the front of the room. He had a microphone and held up his other hand for quiet.

The mariachis stopped playing and the diners stopped chattering.

"Too late," Ethan said. "Manny's already underway, I can't—"

"He'll call you up there in a minute," Lily said.

"Why would he do that?" Ethan asked.

"Cause you're the new owner."

His eyes widened at her.

"Well, it seems obvious that's what he's about to tell them, doesn't it?"

CHAPTER SEVEN

anny started talking, and Orrin aimed his phone to record. Lily turned in her chair to pay attention. She thought Manny looked ten years older since his heart attack. There was a lot more white in his hair, and his face seemed thin and tired. But he was smiling, thanking the communities of Mad Bull's Bend, nearby Quinn, and all Quinn County for their years of friendship and fun in his molasses-thick Texas drawl.

"And y'all know how much I love this place, folks, and all y'all, too. I couldn't retire and heal from what happened to me, to heal my heart, if I didn't trust the new owner completely," he said, looking across the room at Ethan.

Lily got a little choked up. God, she was glad she hadn't killed him.

"But I know this place'll be aw'right," he said. "'cause I'm giving the keys to one of our own. Ethan Bubba Brand." Then he shoved the mic into his back pocket and started a slow clap.

Everyone joined in the applause, albeit half-hearted, and Ethan looked Lily in the eyes.

"You've got this," she said. "Face that nightmare head-on.

Look around the room. These people want to be behind you. Now go tell 'em what they need to hear. That you're exactly who they always thought you were. Orrin'll get the video for your manager. Two birds, right?"

"How do you always know what to say?"

"Trust me, I don't." It was an automatic reply, straight from her gut. She wanted Ethan, of all people, to know who she really was. She didn't know the right thing to say. Her mom had, though. She'd just said what she thought the first Lily would have said.

He gave her a nervous nod, got up, and made his way to where Manny was standing. He did not need to climb up on the box as he stood a head above most people in the room.

He said, "Hey, folks," and he waved awkwardly. A few people waved back, but most just watched him, waiting. "Y'all know my story. As a baby, I was left on the doorstep at the Texas Brand and adopted by Garrett, who married my aunt Chelsea. That's the happy part of the tale and the part I don't mind sharin'. But there's a dark side to my hist'ry. The gossip rags got that part right. The man who sired me was a full-on criminal."

A murmur rolled like a wave through the crowd. Lily got out of her seat without forethought and wove carefully and slowly through the patrons toward where Ethan and Manny were standing.

"And it's true what you've read—that he...he killed my mother."

This time the murmur was louder. Lily pushed a little more aggressively. No one was seated, everyone had risen on their feet to see and hear. She navigated between bodies and tables and chairs, trying to keep an eye on Ethan as she went. He looked shaky.

"'Course, I never knew him. I was knee-high to a grasshopper, I didn't know much of anything. But now, well, he died in prison. And he named me in his will, but I've already declaimed it or disclaimed it or however you say it in legal terms. I don't want his blood money."

People muttered, and Lily heard snippets.

"Sure, he can *afford* to turn it down…"

"…could've done some good with that kinda money."

"I knew he'd never take it. He's a Brand, through and through."

She stopped moving, because she'd broken through the crowd to the three feet of open space between her and Ethan. She turned, though, to see who'd spoken last. A reed-thin man with a handlebar mustache and a face like a baseball mitt sent her a wink and she knew it was him. He worked at the feed store, she thought. Arthur…something. Bryce, that was it. Arthur Bryce. He had Ethan's back.

Lily moved closer to Ethan, out into the open space between them. He saw her and relaxed visibly. He wiggled his fingers at her, so she went up to stand beside him.

"What happened with this place is a little bit different," Ethan began.

"Yeah, it's different aw'right." Manny reached up to pluck the mic right out of Ethan's hand. "I sold it, an' now it's yours. What the people want to know, Bub—Ethan, is what you're fixin' to do with it."

Manny and Ethan locked gazes for a long moment and Lily held her breath. Then Ethan's chin lowered so slightly it was barely a movement at all. And yet, it spoke volumes. He was taking Manny's unspoken advice to leave out the details of how the cantina came into his hands. It was nobody's business, anyway.

Manny handed the microphone back to Ethan and said, "Tell 'em, son."

Ethan took it. Lily squeezed his hand.

"What I have in mind is to grow this place into a top-notch, full-fledged honky-tonk."

Silence. Lily cupped Ethan's hand with her own, pulled the mic down low where she could reach it, and said, "And he's keeping the tacos."

Applause burst out, swelling until she thought it should lift the rafters. Lily took the microphone from Ethan's hand, found the button and turned it off, then handed it to Manny to put away.

"I was fixing' to introduce you and tell 'em how long it'll be closed and whatnot," Ethan said.

"Why not end on a high note?" she asked. "We can put the details out tomorrow." She took Ethan's hand and pulled him back toward the table.

He turned his hand around to clasp hers, though. She glanced back at him, surprised. Their eyes met, and his were full of something. He was probably grateful for the moral support.

They arrived back at the table to a smattering of applause from the family. Orrin said. "I sent the video to your phone. Decided not to live-stream, just in case. I suggest you cut it after you say, 'I don't want his blood money.'"

"Killer line," Drew muttered. "You nailed it."

"I don't know. It feels like I should tell 'em how I came to own the cantina."

"Since when does everyone in town need to know the details of your business?" Baxter asked.

"Anybody goes digging, it'll come out," he countered.

Maria said, "Oh, come on, you're not all *that* famous, Cousin. Nobody cares."

Willow nodded hard. "People will forget all about it in a few weeks. Especially if you put out another hit song."

Lily had a mouthful of taco, so she couldn't chime in. It turned out she had room for one more after all, and a fresh platter had been delivered in her absence.

"Chances of that are slim," Ethan said. "I'll be too busy with this place for the next few weeks to record. And I haven't written a word anyway." Then he took a big bite himself.

Lily swallowed, drank some sweet tea to clear her mouth, and then said, "You don't need a new song. You have a whole album full of songs. Just release one as a single. That's a thing, right?"

"Sort of. I mean, I don't release it, the producer does, but—"

"'Home,'" she said. "That's your next hit."

"What makes you think—"

"Because it's my favorite song on the whole album."

For a moment it felt as if they were alone in the room, eyes locked, hers, she imagined, brimming with excitement. His were alight with hope. "You think?"

"It is a dang good song," Trevor said, from somewhere outside the spell between the two of them. "You know, I think it might be my favorite, too."

"You have my album?" Ethan asked, as he shifted his gaze to his cousin.

"Of course he has your album," Willow said. "We all have your album."

Maria said, "I have it in vinyl *and* MP3."

Drew added, "I give it to friends for birthdays."

Baxter, the eldest, leaned forward in his seat. "Wait, Ethan did you think we *didn't* have your album?"

"I didn't know, I guess." He was genuinely touched, and there was red creeping up his neck and into his face.

It crossed Lily's mind for the dozenth time that he was the best-looking man she'd ever seen, even when he was blushing hot.

"Thanks," he said. "That means a lot. I guess I'll call my manager."

"We can do some pushin' on social," Drew said, "Maybe get a little momentum goin'."

"Yeah," Orrin added. "I can set up social media accounts for the honky-tonk, too, if you want. All the usual places. It's the perfect time, you bein' in the press right now."

"And once what you just said goes viral," his sister put in, "you will be even more."

"We can help with that, too," Orrin said.

Lily saw the way Ethan's brows furrowed. In the year since she'd met this family, she'd never heard anyone offer an opinion or advice to Ethan on his musical career until now. And it was *good* advice, at least to her novice mind.

She finished the last taco she could possibly hold, knew for sure there was sauce on her face, and put her hand on Ethan's shoulder, whispering, "You need a media budget to pay those two."

Ethan looked gobsmacked. "Honestly, I didn't think you were payin' any attention at all," he said. "Much less full of ideas."

Willow heaved a sigh, met Maria's eyes, then rolled hers. "We always got the feelin' you didn't want our input," she said.

"What gave you that feelin'?" he asked.

She shrugged. Trevor said, "Mainly because you don't talk that much about it when you're home."

Ethan shook his head in self-deprecation. "I didn't want to come off like I was braggin' all the time, you know?" he said.

"Braggin'," Willow said, shaking her head. "Well, now that we've got that out in the open, I have a few ideas about your next album cover."

Amazing what a little communication could do, Lily thought

The cantina looked entirely different the next morning. It was empty and spotless, the chairs were flipped over, atop the tables. The 'Closed' sign hung crooked in the front window. Ethan stood in the middle of the open floor looking around. What the hell was he doing? What did he know about running a business? He should be writing and touring to test out songs for the next album.

He was supposed to have been doing those things ever since the first album had dropped. "At least now I'll have an excuse for my failed career."

"You're twenty-nine years old, Ethan," Lily said.

He'd felt her come in just the instant before she'd spoken. A chill of sheer pleasure danced up his spine any time she was nearby. He cursed his luck yet again for being this attracted to a woman who was off-limits for a one-night-stand or a casual fling. She was family. His cousin-in-law's sister. That might not be considered close in most families, but it was in his.

He didn't turn, since she was moving up to stand beside him. "We have our work cut out for us, huh?"

He looked down at her then. She wore a denim shirt, unsnapped over a black tank-top, and jeans over heavy-duty work boots. A tool belt was buckled around her waist, he noticed, and he couldn't hide his smile.

"Oh, you like that?" she asked, hooking her thumbs behind twin screwdrivers. A hammer hung at her hip like a six-shooter.

"You borrowed it from your dad," he said.

"How do you know it's not my own?"

"I can read you like a book."

Lily fell silent, her eyes widening slowly.

Then he added, "And his initials are on the nail-apron."

She looked down at her own front, where HH was the same upside down. "I should've remembered. I'm the one who got it for him. Father's Day, five years ago, I think."

"It's worn well," he said.

"Mainly, I wore it for the tape measure, and to carry my tablet around." She pulled her iPad out of the apron's nail pocket.

"And in case we decide to knock down a wall?" he asked, with a nod at the hammer.

"Well, yeah. Obviously." She smiled brightly, then pointed to the table directly inside the door where she'd deposited a cardboard tray with a pair of extra-large coffees and a bag he hoped held donuts. "From the donut shop up the road," she said.

He made growly sounds and headed for the table, taking the coffee with the E on the lid, and then peering into the bag. "Yes, raspberry jam, my favorite."

"I know. I'll take that glazed one, if you don't mind."

He plucked the donut and brought it to her along with both coffees.

"Thanks," she said. She was surveying the room. "While the rest of us pigged out, last night, Dad jotted a few notes for the kitchen."

"He did?"

"He's not trying to butt in, just wants to be helpful. Says it's just stuff he'd want if he were in charge of it."

He crooked an eyebrow. "Does he want to be?"

"Want to be what?"

"In charge of it. Head chef."

She caught her lower lip in her teeth. He'd noticed she did that when she was holding something back. "He does, yes. I'm not sure he can handle it on his own, though. If this place goes as big as I think it will...but that's another conversation. Let's start in the basement and work our way up, all right?"

Without waiting for a reply, she headed behind the bar and through the red doors into the kitchen. He caught up with her and asked, "What changes did Hyram ask for?"

"A second cook surface, to keep the meats separate from non-meat items. Reduces cross-contamination risk. He'd put a produce prep station over in this wasted space near the basement door." She opened said door as she spoke, felt around for a light switch and found one. The steps were finished, not open, not rickety as he followed her down.

"Wow." Lily was standing in the middle of the finished basement turning in a slow circle. One end held a furnace and large water heater. The rest was empty, aside from crates of booze, in stacks. The concrete block walls were painted white. "This is a lot of space."

"Not good for much besides storage," he said. "Too far from the rest. Good to have in case of a twister, though."

"It's a shame not to use it for something." She set her coffee on the water tank, held her remaining half-donut in her teeth like a fat cigar, and tapped on her iPad with one finger, which she'd wiped on her jeans, making a note. "What about that recording studio idea?"

"I mean, it could work, sure, but...it's a distraction. We should focus on the honky-tonk."

She muttered something. The words "God forbid" and "time at home" in the mix, and maybe a cuss word, which was unlike her.

Or not.

Having looked his fill, Ethan made an "after you" gesture toward the stairs, and Lily started up.

"Second floor next, huh?" she asked. "I've never seen that part. Have you?"

"Never had call to be up there, no." He followed her out of the kitchen, around the bar and just past it, and up the stairs. It was impossible not to notice how those jeans hugged her backside, since it was level with his face as she trotted ahead of him.

The entire second story was a big open space. It had windows on all four sides, and a support beam in the center. Aside from a few boxes stacked along two walls, and a whole lot of dust, it was empty.

"Office space," Ethan said.

"For you or me?" she asked, moving to the back, where a

picture window took up almost the entire rear wall. Wiping the dust way with her hand, she looked out.

"It's big enough for both," he said.

"Wall down the middle? Who gets the window with the view?"

"I'm okay without a wall if you are," he said. "Keep it open."

She grinned. "I like it. Okay, desks should be on that side, so we're facing this *amazing* view. No curtains, but maybe blinds, so we can block the sun when it's too much." She pulled her tape measure off her tool belt and stretched it across the room. He held the end for her as she made notes on the tablet. "A private restroom would be nice, too," she said. "There's plenty of room for one, and it would be better than sharing with the gen pop downstairs."

"If there's room in the budget, I'm all for it."

"There's a budget?"

"Not yet, but it seems like there ought to be, doesn't it?" He looked at her with one brow raised, half-kidding, but not really.

She nodded, biting her bottom lip.

"What?"

"Nothing."

"There's something. Go ahead, ask. You want to know if I can afford it."

She shrugged, lowered her eyes. "Yeah, I do. I mean it *is* just the one hit song."

"Thanks for reminding me."

"*De nada,*" she said. "We can get by up here with a fresh coat of paint. The floor is…" She bent to pull up the corner of old indoor-outdoor carpet. "Plank, probably original too. Look at that. Just needs to be sanded down and refinished. We can DIY this space, save us a bundle."

"You really want that bathroom."

She took a few more measurements, then ran back down the

stairs, into the main room. "Down here, though, I think we need to consult with an expert," she called.

He headed down to the ground floor too, and wondered how he'd keep up with her energy. "I agree. That could be a load-bearin' wall, for all I know."

She went to the wall in question, with the double glass doors in its center, nodding her head and examining it as if she knew more about construction than he did. Maybe she did. She sure as hell knew more about running a business than he did. "This doorway should be arched, out to the addition, don't you think?"

"More room if its squared-off."

"More memorable arched. More beautiful."

"More expensive?"

"Seriously, you have to tell me," she said. "I feel like your family's pretty wealthy, even though they don't seem like rich people. You all get a cut from the ranch or something, don't you?"

"It's an ever-dwindling cut, but we've invested the profits in the past, and that part of it's doing pretty well."

"So between that and the hit song...?" She left the question hanging in the air.

"I'm going to take out a loan."

She smiled at him, moving close enough to poke his chest with a forefinger. "Including enough for my salary," she said. "I'm on the clock as we speak."

So if he pulled her in for a kiss, it would officially be sexual harassment, Ethan thought.

He blinked the impulse away, kind of stunned by it. Then his phone went off and hers did, too. "It's Orrin," he said. Then he read the text on his screen aloud. "'Video's gone viral, just not the way we expected.' There's a link." He held the phone low so she could see, too, and tapped the link.

The video of him talking last night was flirting with a million views. "That's good, right?"

"Seems good, to me," Lily said. "Look at the comments and see how it's going over."

He scrolled with his thumb, and there were several comments like, "love his music" and "good for him" and a few folks claiming their dads had murdered their moms, too, which just made him sad, and a handful of trolls calling him a washed-up wanna-be, which made him wonder if it was possible to be both.

But then came the most popular comment of all, the one that asked, "Who's the girl?"

That comment had 1,207 replies, including, "He's really got a death grip on her hand, doesn't he?" and "check out the way he looks down at her at 3:47." And "You can practically see the hearts in his eyes." And "I feel a love song coming on."

He couldn't bring himself to look at Lily, so he had no idea what she was making of it all.

Just then another text came through with another link. He tapped that one, and it went to a truncated version of the original video that zoomed in on his and Lily's clasped hands and then cut to him gazing down at her like he'd just crossed a desert and she was a popsicle.

They'd slowed that part down, into ultra slow-motion, and they'd put pulsing heart graphics over his head. His volume was up, so the swelling romantic music they'd inserted behind the clip played full blast.

He tapped and tapped to silence the dang thing, then glanced at Lily's face. Expressionless. Too shocked to react?

Orrin was still texting screenshots of headlines. "Who's the mystery woman healing Ethan Brand's heart?" And "Ethan Brand's Heartache Honey?"

That was downright insulting. Aloud, he said, "Lily, I'm so

sorry. I never meant to drag you into my mess. Hell and damnation."

She took his phone from his hand and clicked again on the doctored video. "I mean, they're exaggerating the moment." Then she tapped the looped arrow and played it again.

"I was shaky," he said. "And when you came up, I was relieved."

"Right. You were just glad to see me. That's all that look is. And you know, they slowed it way down, and then they put that Bugs Bunny music behind it, and—"

"Tchaikovsky," he said. "The Romeo and Juliet Overture."

"I knew that." She blinked and lowered her head. "Not really. But I'm impressed you did."

"I'm a musician. I take it seriously."

"I know you do."

He smiled, then realized he was probably looking at her again exactly the way the camera had caught him looking at her in the video. Yeah, they'd slowed it down and added one of the most romantic songs ever written. But they couldn't fake the look in his eyes when she'd come to stand beside him. And it wasn't a one-night-stand or casual fling kind of look, either.

This wasn't good. There was too much to lose if things between them went sideways.

She glanced up, caught him looking, and even though he quickly tried to change his expression, she'd seen it and her eyebrows bent in an analytical frown. He cleared his throat and looked away, toward the front where a pickup truck full of cousins had just pulled up. Thank the Lord.

"Well, at least it looks like everybody's forgotten about your scandalous DNA," Lily said.

"Yeah, but now you're a target."

"I'm a target of whom?"

"The press. The media. The fans. The—"

"Honey," she said, and not as a term of endearment, "As your cousin Maria reminded you recently, you're not all that famous." Then she winked at him. "Not yet, anyway."

Lily wasn't mortified by the rash of videos featuring her. She probably should've been, but she wasn't. She was flattered, and frankly it was gratifying that the small part of country music fandom who followed Ethan Brand were as confused by him as she was. He looked at her like he adored her but refused to do anything about it.

And now his ever-present family was spilling in through the front entrance. And while she loved them, had adopted them as her own over the past year, it was awfully difficult to get any alone time with Ethan. They were always around.

She sighed too loudly. He heard it and glanced her way. "You all right, Lily Ellen?"

God, she loved when he called her that. Nobody else called her that, only Ethan, and it made her belly clench up every time.

"I just…we should talk about this, you know? Privately."

He held her eyes, nodded. "Before the day's out, okay?"

"Okay." She pasted a big, fake smile onto her face, and welcomed the gang, who'd come to help in any way needed.

By lunch, the dining room had been cleared entirely, all the tables and chairs had been loaded on the back of the pickups in which the cousins had arrived. Orrin, Drew, and Trevor had taken the loaded trucks back to the ranch, where they'd found room to store everything in one of the outbuildings.

Lily had been making notes and even a few sketches on her iPad to keep herself distracted. Ethan kept an arm's length between them all day, to the point that she felt it had to be obvious to everyone. No one said anything, though, so maybe she was being hypersensitive.

None of the cousins had mentioned the *Ethan Brand's mystery gal* memes making the rounds on the internet. She'd checked social media multiple times, unable to stop herself. Nobody seemed to be talking about his father, the recently deceased criminal kingpin, having murdered his mother anymore. Everyone was speculating that his announcement of a two-month hiatus in his hometown had more to do with the mystery gal than with transforming a cantina into a honky-tonk.

She'd bookmarked the pieced-together video with the closeup of him gazing down at her. Someone had made a version where hearts were popping out of his eyes rather than pulsing over his head, but she didn't like that, because they hid the real thing. She liked looking at him, looking at her. There was something there. He could deny it all he wanted, but it was plain as day. And that made her start hoping again, and that was the most self-destructive thing she could probably do.

Willow and Baxter left to get pizzas, Willow sending her a nod, like she knew there were things her cousin and cousin-in-law needed to discuss in private. The two of them got into Baxter's Jeep Wrangler and bounded away.

Lily turned to face Ethan.

He looked down at her and smiled. "Okay," he said. "It'll be at least a half hour. You wanted to talk about the video."

"No," she said. "I wanted to talk about...you're so dang tall, you know that?"

"I'm...sorry?"

"Could you sit down, please, so I can look you in the eye."

His eyes widened, maybe in alarm, but he reached behind him for the three-rung stepladder and backed his butt onto the second rung. Then he said, "Better?"

She moved right up in front of him and said, "Much." Then she slid her fingers into his hair, right past his ears, until they met at the back of his head, and then she kissed him. He jerked in surprise, but then his mouth softened, and his breath kind of whispered out of him. He tilted his head a little, moved his lips against hers. He moaned all soft and raspy. He closed his arms around her waist, pulling her between his legs until her chest was up against his, and so was everything else.

He was cupping her head with one hand, and the other was moving down her back, lower, toward her butt, and then he clasped one cheek and pressed her closer.

She was so surprised she broke the kiss, opened her eyes, had to back away to bring him into focus. And then she said, "I knew it! I knew you felt something for me."

"No. Nonononono, this ain't right. It can't happen." He rose, pushed a hand through his hair, and paced away from her. "You're Harrison's baby sister, Lily. You're family."

"What does that have to do with anything?"

"I can't...you know...start somethin' up with you. It'd be disrespectful. Harrison would hate me, probably try to kick my ass, and I'd have to let him. And Maria! She'd never forgive me."

"For what, exactly?"

"For breakin' your heart, obviously."

She said, "Oh," and raised her eyebrows. He turned to look at her, so she went on. "So you're pretty sure that's how it would go, then? You, breaking my heart?"

"Well, yeah. I'm not gonna stay here long term, you know. I have to get back on the road. My career—"

"Yes, of course, your career."

"So nothin' can come of it."

"Right."

"It would just be a fling. And I can't have a fling with Maria's husband's sister."

"Because it would be disrespectful," she said.

"Yes."

"And you don't find it at all disrespectful that what I want hasn't even entered into your thinking?"

He opened his mouth, closed it again.

"My body, my choice."

He shook his head like a dog shaking off water. "Well, no, that never occurred to me. I guess I just assumed you'd want... more."

"Maybe I will. Or maybe I'll want less. Hell, maybe *I'm* the one who'll break *your* heart." She picked up her tool belt from where she'd left it on a wall hook. "I'm done for the day. I'll send you my notes. Do whatever you want with 'em."

She went right out the door into the bright, midday Texas sunshine, got into her car, and left without looking back.

As she went, she passed a big brown car that had to have been from the seventies, parked on the side of the road. It was an odd place to just sit, so she tried to see inside as she passed. The guy behind the wheel was vaguely familiar, but she couldn't quite place him. He had a shaggy blondish beard, sunglasses covering his eyes, and his hair was apparently pulled back.

Then she was rounding a bend and he was out of sight behind her.

On the way home, she relived every moment of that kiss. The way Ethan had wrapped her up tight in his arms, the way he'd held her pressed against him from collar bone to hip bone and everywhere in between.

Her stomach knotted up all over again with the memory.

Okay, okay, this was not a bad thing, she thought. Even though she had broken her own rule, and that wasn't really fair, she'd learned the truth. He obviously wanted her as much as she wanted him. That was progress, she supposed. Toward what, remained the question.

The thing was, they had to work together, for a little while at least. And her bold move, while proving the attraction between them was real and reciprocal, had also ensured things would be awkward. She was going to have to come up with a solution for that.

CHAPTER EIGHT

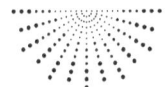

*E*than didn't know quite where he'd gone wrong, so he was clueless about how to make it right. Anyway, it was no fun working on the place without Lily. He didn't even want to buy paint or order office furniture without her input, since she'd be working there as much as he would. More, really. Because he was only going to be around long enough to get the place open. She'd be the one running it for him while he chased his country music dream as far as it would go—providing he didn't alienate her entirely before then.

Oh, sure, she thought he'd decide after the opening, but he'd already made up his mind. If Lily still wanted the job after working with him for two months, it was hers.

A big black Cadillac complete with a set of steer horns on the grill pulled into the parking lot beside his truck. And for some reason a chill of foreboding crept up the back of his neck. He stepped outside.

A man got out of the SUV's rear door. There was somebody else behind the wheel, but he couldn't see too much of the driver because the windows were tinted so dark. The passenger who'd got out wore dark sunglasses so you couldn't see his eyes.

He had male-pattern baldness and a shiny blue suit that said "money."

"Ethan Brand?" he asked. His voice had an irritating scratchiness to it. Not the kind you got from a cold, the kind that was permanent.

Ethan nodded once. "That's right. Who are you?"

"I'm the man whose messages you've been ignoring."

"Only messages I been ignorin' were the ones that sounded like scams. You the feller offerin' to list the place on Google, or the one offerin' free accountin' services?"

"Angus Silver." He offered a hand. Ethan didn't take it. "I'm the one offering to buy it for twice what it's worth," he said.

"Oh, *that* Angus Silver." He'd done a little checking after Willow had mentioned that the guy so eager to purchase Manny's from him was a small-time criminal. Apparently he aspired to be big-time like his older brother, but he just wasn't very good at criming. "I didn't ignore your messages. I replied that I wasn't interested in selling."

"I e-mailed you three more times."

"'No' is a complete answer. Or so the womenfolk tell me."

"You have a lot of those around, don't you? *Womenfolk?*"

The way he said the word was mocking. Ethan didn't reply, but he did take a step closer, spine straight, shoulders square, eyes mean.

The smaller man averted his eyes. "So you're making changes to the place?" he asked.

"Yeah, so it's closed to the public. You understand."

"There's a second part to my offer," he said.

"There's nothing you can do—"

"There's something I could...not do. I could *not* inform the FBI about the previous owner's money laundering deal with your late father."

"I've already talked to 'em," Ethan said. It was a bold-faced lie.

Angus Silver pushed his sunglasses up on top of his head, and looked Ethan right in the eyes, as if he could tell whether or not he was lying. Ethan gazed right at the feller's blue and bloodshot eyes, unblinking.

He lowered the sunglasses again. "Well, that was only off the top of my head. There're other things I could *not* do.

"That sounds like a threat."

"People don't say no to me."

"We both know that's a lie, as I've said no to you multiple times now." Ethan leaned sideways to get a look at the guy's license plate. Silver-1. Of course it was. He straightened again. "Look, lemme save you some trouble. My father is Garrett Brand—"

"Your father was Vince de Lorean."

"*Sheriff* Garrett Brand. And my uncle's his chief deputy—"

"And your pretty cousin Willow's his rookie. One of your *womenfolk.* I know 'em all. Make it a point to know about the families of the men I deal with. Especially their women."

Just then Ethan saw motion at the far corner of the cantina. He didn't want to look and give anyone away, but he had a strong feeling someone, maybe one of his cousins, had been watching all this go down.

"That redheaded veterinarian, Maria," the criminal droned on. "And sexy as sin and barely legal Drew. That hot little nurse-turned-bartender, Lily—"

Ethan had the guy by the front of his shirt before he could finish the sentence. The car door opened, and the driver stepped out, put his hand inside his coat and said, "Let him go."

He was a big guy, not as big as Ethan, but young, with a thick neck, and a blond crew cut, extra high.

"You ought not be tangled up with this kind of filth," Ethan told the driver. "There's no future for you. A man like this one will get you killed or tossed behind bars. I've seen his kind before. Trash." Then he let Silver go with a shove that sent him staggering backward. He slammed into the driver, who braced him up to keep him from falling on his backside, only to have Silver wrench away from the guy like it was his fault he'd stumbled.

He grabbed the driver and shoved him aside to take the wheel himself.

"Get the hell off my property, Silver," Ethan said. "Don't ever come back."

The driver barely had time to get into the back seat before Silver was laying rubber in reverse, skidding to a stop in the road. The window lowered and he shouted at Ethan from a safe distance, inside his Caddy. "You're gonna regret this, you son of a bitch!" Then he threw something like crumpled paper. It fell to the pavement and moved with the breeze as the Cadillac lurched away.

Ethan walked out to the road, keeping an eye on the Caddy. It passed a brown car that was sitting on the roadside in the distance, and then it sped around a bend, out of sight.

Ethan crouched to retrieve what Angus Silver had dropped. Looked like a crumpled photograph, and as he smoothed it out, his blood chilled. It was a snapshot of Lily, unlocking the front door of the cabin she and her dad rented at the edge of Quinn.

A clear threat.

An engine started, and he looked up fast, thinking the Caddy had returned, but no. This engine was loud and old, and belonged to that ancient brown Buick that had been parked up the road. As he watched, it executed a three-point turn, then drove away from him, the same way the Caddy had gone, vanishing around a bend.

Ethan ran back inside just long enough to grab his keys off the bar, then locked up on the way out. He dove into his pickup and told its dashboard, "Call Uncle Garrett on speaker."

As he sped toward Quinn, a solid twenty minutes away, he

heard the phone ringing and eventually, his uncle picked up. "Bubba?"

"Lily might be in danger," he said. "Get somebody out there, ASAP. I'm on my way."

"So'm I, son." He rang off, no questions asked.

Ethan pressed harder on the gas and told his phone, "Call Lily."

It rang and rang.

Hyram was out with Cat Shaw. The two had signed up for square-dancing lessons at the volunteer fire department, and tonight was the first class, so Lily had the house to herself. She'd filled the bathtub as deep as possible, drizzled in some sandal-wood essential oil, and was soaking neck deep with cucumber slices over her eyes.

She'd done it up right, deciding she deserved a little self-care, now that she was a b-list internet star. Maybe c-list. Her Bluetooth speaker played Ethan's debut album. She'd turned off the lights and had three scented candles burning. Vanilla-citrus. The flames cast dancing light over her skin as she lay there, soaking in the steamy water. She arched her back until her nipples breached the surface and pebbled at the touch of the cool air. Grinning at the naughtiness of it, she submerged them again, and sighed, closing her eyes.

And then opened them when she thought she heard her name from a great distance.

"Lily!"

There it was again, but muffled. Then the front door banged open, and footsteps came thundering through the cabin. She started to sit up and reach for a towel when the bathroom door opened.

"Lily!"

"Ethan!" She was upright in the clear water, breasts above the surface. His gaze was caught, too, so she let him look for a long moment before slowly sinking beneath the water again, almost all the way. "What's the matter with you?"

"This guy came to the cantina," he blurted, but he was looking everywhere other than at her. His gaze jumped from the medicine cabinet to the sink to the towel rack. "Said he wants to buy it, and when I said no, he threatened you."

She sat up out of the water again, and not for his ego-feeding reaction to the sight of her boobs this time. "He threatened *me?*"

His eyes were glued. He said, "Could you—" as he reached for a towel and held it in her direction.

"Yeah, sure, of course," and then like a dummy, stood right up, and stepped out of the tub. And his eyes were glued again, and not to her breasts this time. He held the towel in midair, having forgotten it was there.

She had to lean closer to snatch it from his hand, and he only blinked again when she'd wrapped it around her. "What did he say, exactly?

"Who?" He blinked twice. "Right. The guy. Angus Silver." He pulled the photo from his jeans pocket and handed it to her.

He'd rolled it, so it was all curled, and bore the marks of having been crumpled earlier. But it was clearly a shot of her standing at her own front door. She frowned. "This was earlier tonight. Those are the clothes I wore today."

"Son of a—"

"I need to get dressed. I don't want to die naked."

"You're not fixin' to die at all. There's already a deputy out front, and Garrett's on his way," Ethan said.

"And you're already here." She smiled but it felt unsteady. "You came running when you thought I might be in danger."

She moved past him out into the hallway, then down it to her

118

bedroom, and logical or not, she was more touched by his protectiveness than she was frightened by the threat. She was constantly surrounded by Brands. It would take an army to do her harm.

Ethan followed, then leaned in her doorway while she opened dresser drawers and took out clothes. She stepped into panties and pulled them up under the towel. Then she grabbed a sports bra and turned her back to him, dropping the towel entirely. She pulled the bra over her head, and then the first blouse she'd found, and when her head popped out, she realized she was facing the mirror, so he'd had the full view the whole time.

She grabbed a pair of socks, then opened another drawer and took out a pair of jeans. As she pulled them on, she said, "Given how far your eyeballs have emerged from their sockets, I don't think my hands-off policy is our solution."

"Why not?" His voice cracked like an adolescent boy's.

She buttoned the jeans and sat on the bed to don the socks, then stood up again. "Because you're not gonna be able to keep your hands off me. Are you, Ethan?"

"Not unless I leave town."

"Oh, I see you've given this some thought already."

"A little, yeah. And you're the one who kissed me, today. After you said hands off at work. To be honest, I don't know if I'm comin' or goin'."

She nodded. "I'd apologize, except I mostly don't either." She crouched to pick up her dropped towel, and when she straightened again, he was right there, close to her. "Are you gonna run from me again, Ethan? Leave in the morning like the stars at sunrise?"

"I feel like the mornin' might be too late." He slid his arms around her waist.

"Hot damn, I was hopin' you'd say that." She put a little Texas twang into the words, then slid her arms around his neck and leaned up close to nibble his lips before kissing them, and then there was a shout from the front door.

"Lily! Bubba! You okay in here?"

She jumped away from Ethan a fraction of a second before Garrett Brand appeared in the doorway, the badge on his chest. "Everybody okay?"

"Yeah, fine," Lily said. "Um, Ethan, why don't you fill him in? I'm gonna um…dry my hair. Yeah." She went into the bathroom and closed the door. Beyond it, she could hear their male voices, tones muffled, concern evident even though she couldn't hear their words.

She stared into the mirror. Ethan wanted her so much it was undeniable, yet he was willing to leave town to get away from her, yet he'd raced to her side, terrified she might be in danger.

What the hell was a woman supposed to do with a guy like him?

Terrence Clay had been Angus Silver's driver for three years. His dad had been Angus's father Devon Silver's driver. Terrence had made it clear from the get-go that driving was all he did. Oh, he could keep his mouth shut all right. Mr. Silver never needed to worry about Terrence running his mouth. He was no rat. His dad had taught him better. To work for the Silvers, all you had to do was follow orders and keep your mouth shut. He'd never been asked to do anything illegal.

But he didn't like that his boss had threatened those women. He'd threatened women in the past, and some of them…well, bad things had happened to some of them. He didn't *know* his boss had anything to do with it…but he suspected it.

Angus Silver drove recklessly as hell, while in the back, Terrence held on for dear life. He hadn't buckled up, and the sharp curves sent him sliding across the seat, smashing against the door, then sliding to the other side.

"Boss, Jeeze, slow down!"

They came to a crossroads in the middle of nowhere, and Angus didn't even let up, just blasted right through the stop sign. A brown car came flying from the left and T-boned them, hitting the driver's side, just ahead of where Silver was sitting. The Caddy's nose snapped right, the car went into a skid, fishtailing wildly as Silver fought the steering wheel.

He brought the car to a stop off the road in a cloud of dust. The other car was off the other side in the road. It had wound up in a weed patch with a steep ravine behind it. The engine had stalled, and the driver was trying to start it.

The big guy's words back at the cantina floated back into his head and he thought they must've been prophetic. He opened his door, started to get out.

"I'll kill that fucker," Silver yelled. He wrenched the wheel, jamming the car into drive.

Terrence pushed off, barely clearing the car door, landing in a tuck-and-roll that hurt like a bitch. He got up on all fours in the road in time to see the Caddy speeding away from him toward the brown car, which had its nose smashed to hell and gone. The driver kept cranking it, over and over again, but it wouldn't start. Silver gunned the Caddy, aiming it right at the guy, and Terrence was sure he was about to witness a murder.

Then the brown car caught and started, and just as Terrence braced reflexively for the crash, the car shot forward. The Caddy blasted right through the spot where it had been, kept right on going, over the drop-off on the other side of the road. It sped to the brink, then vanished from sight.

The brown car sat rumbling in the road. Terrence pushed himself up onto his feet, stunned and shaking. He wanted to see what had happened to the boss and ran closer. The mangled wreckage at the bottom gave all the information he needed.

It occurred to him that he probably ought to run for it. Then the brown car's window lowered, just a crack. And from within a voice said, "He did that to himself. No point you or I gettin' dragged into it, is there?"

"Nope."

"You had a blowout. You lost control and got thrown clear before the Caddy went over. You never saw any other vehicle."

"That's just the way it happened," he said.

The window rolled back up and the brown car rolled away into the road.

Lily took her time getting herself put back together. Ethan was driving her so crazy she felt like her hair must be standing on end. But no, she didn't look as crazy as she felt. She pulled on a flannel over her T-shirt, which was slate blue and bore a pair of stylized aviator sunglasses on the front.

By the time she emerged from the bathroom, Ethan was the only one waiting for her. Garrett had already gone.

"Hey," Ethan said. He was standing in the middle of the living room.

"Hey." She looked around her empty house. "I thought Garrett would want to talk to me."

"They got a hit on that guy's car already. Willow called. It's been in an accident. No wonder, the way he was drivin'."

"Oh." She looked at the sofa, but didn't sit down.

"I'm hoping Garrett can put him on notice that his welcome in this county is revoked. Scare him off."

She realized she should be more interested in the criminal who'd threatened her, but most of her mental capacity was busy with the fact that they'd probably have had sex if Garrett hadn't shown up—a fact that sat between them like a boulder. They both ignored it.

"The guy's license plate didn't exist," Ethan said. "Silver-1. Garrett says it's probably a custom fake."

"But we know his name."

"Yeah. So he's keepin' a deputy watching your house."

"That's good. I guess."

Ethan was not sitting down. It felt as if he intended to leave. So she said, "Dad texted while I was getting dressed. He's spending the night at Cat's."

"That progressed quickly, didn't it? Are you okay with it?"

She took a breath and wandered past him into the kitchen, opened the fridge, and took out a pitcher of sweet tea. "I'm processing it," she said. Then she got two glasses and filled them both without asking if he wanted one. She carried them into the living room, set them on the coffee table, and sank onto her plush brown-teddy-bear of a sofa. "I think my mom would be okay with it. She'd say, 'Life's short, and you ought to be as happy as you can every day of it.'"

With a sigh, he came around the sofa, but instead of sitting beside her, he took her dad's recliner and reached for the tea. After a sip, he said, "He's been lonely without her," he said.

"He's been heartbroken without her. And it's been two years now. I don't think she'd have wanted that. Now, though, since Cat…" She shook her head.

"He's lit right up," Ethan said. "Looks ten years younger and it's only been, what? A week?"

"A week that I know of," she said, in a tone that suggested there might be weeks she hadn't known of. "I think he's been tinting his hair. That stuff that works gradually?"

"I think it's more than that," he said.

"Yeah." She shrugged. "He seems happy, doesn't he?"

Ethan nodded.

"Well, I'm glad he's happy. I think Mom was right, you

should grab happiness wherever you can find it. And on that note—"

"My label's releasin' 'Home' as a single."

His attempt to distract her from talking about the two of them maybe having sex tonight was a complete success. A smile stole control of her face. "That's fantastic!"

"My agent said they couldn't argue with the numbers. I'm all over the internet, thanks to you."

"Yeah," she said. "I've been unmasked already." She grabbed her phone off the end table and tapped one of the saved reels. It was a series of photos of her; receiving her R.N. pin, the shot from her ID badge at the hospital, a shot of her with Ethan outside the Cantina. Under the photos were bullet points.

- Lily Ellen Hyde, R.N. from Ithaca, New York
- Works at a small-town hospital
- Father Hyram Hyde, chef & restaurant manager, retired
- Mother Lily Maria Hyde: R.N. Died of cancer two years ago
- One brother, Harrison Hyde
- Brother is married to Ethan Brand's cousin, Maria Brand
- Lily moved to Texas a year ago with her father and brother

Ethan looked at the post, rolled his eyes. "I'm real sorry, Lily"

She shrugged. "At least they aren't saying anything mean. I've been branded a 'nice girl,' so far at least." She lifted her eyebrows. "Wait until they find out I quit my job to work for you at the Cantina. Bet they change their minds to gold-digger in a hurry."

"When I go back on the road, they'll get over it," he said.

The thought of him dancin' with some honky-tonk honey had her seeing red. "That's not for a while, though."

"We'll see. I can get things pretty well underway here in a couple of weeks."

She set her iced tea down on the table and tried to catch hold of his evasive eyes. "You *are* running away," she said. "Just like I said you would." Then she heaved a huge sigh. "And it isn't right. I can't have you running away because of me. You need to be here for the good of your career, and I think for your own good, too. I don't *need* to work for you. They'd take me back at the hospital, or even at the clinic in Quinn."

"That's not what I—"

"I can call the hospital right now, prove it to you so you don't feel bad about letting me go and—"

"I don't want to let you go."

She stopped speaking. God, she loved how those words had sounded. If only they meant what she wanted them to mean. "Well, I don't want you to leave town, so…"

He closed his eyes. "I think your first idea was probably the best one."

"What first idea?" she asked with bunched-up brows and an irritated tone. Sexual frustration would do that to a girl, she reasoned. Although it had never been a problem until now.

"A hands-off policy while we're working together. You said that, remember?"

"Yeah. Before I kissed you. Twice. Which you liked as much as I did."

"Maybe more," he admitted. "But I've told you why it's a bad idea for us to be together just now. So your hands-off policy makes sense. And I don't have any better ideas, besides hittin' the road."

"Well, I have a better idea."

He looked at her with naked fear in his eyes and did not ask.

So she asked for him in her best Ethan voice, all deep and drawly. "What's your better idea, Lily?"

"Why thanks for asking, Ethan," she replied to herself. "My idea is that you stop worrying so much and make love to me like you want to."

She didn't get up and go over to him, though. She thought about it, but sliding onto his lap on her dad's recliner would feel disrespectful of her dad, and besides, he needed to have a choice. She didn't think his brain would keep functioning if she sat on his lap, and that wouldn't be fair. And if their roles were reversed...damn! She wished their roles were reversed.

So she stayed where she was, on the sofa, gazing at him and he stared back at her, looking deep into her eyes. He swallowed. She could tell by the bulge and retreat of his Adam's apple. And then he said, "Lily Ellen Hyde, you're the prettiest, sexiest, most amazin' female I've ever set eyes on, and I've never wanted to say yes more than I do right now."

He closed his fist around the iced tea, brought it up and guzzled it, rising to his feet as he drained the glass. "I think your first idea was best, though," he said. "A hands-off policy while we work together. And if we can't make that work, then I'll go back on the road." He set the glass on the table and started for the door.

She rose, too. "You're out of your mind. I'm a grown-ass woman."

"Family's too important," he said, his back to her. "This...us, if it went bad, it would drive a wedge through our families. Between me and Harry, between me and Maria, between your dad and the whole clan." He shook his head. "No, I can't. We can't."

He'd said it all without turning to look back at her. But at the very end, he did. And when he saw the tears on her cheeks, he reacted as if the sight pained him. "I'm so sorry, Lil."

She shouldn't have stayed on the sofa. Dammit.

"There'll be a deputy watchin' your place all night. But if Angus Silver's not in the hospital, he'll be in a jail cell, Garrett'll see to that. You'll be safe here the rest of the afternoon and overnight. Might be best if you don't go out the rest of the day."

"Wasn't planning to."

He opened his mouth, closed it again, then said, "I hope you can come to the cantina tomorrow," he said. "I have a contractor comin' at noon to discuss the addition. I need you there to help me flesh out my vision with your ideas."

She rose and moved closer, so she was standing right in front of him, and raised her hand to his cheek, and stood on tiptoe, and kissed him. He shuddered all the way to his toes, and just when his hands touched her waist, she stopped and stood flat-footed again. She was pretty sure that if she kissed him one more time, he'd scoop her up and carry her into the bedroom… and maybe never forgive her. So she sighed, and said, "Okay, fine. We'll do this your way. See you tomorrow, boss." Then she reached past him and opened the door.

He stepped through, looked back, and she closed the door gently in his beloved, bewildered face.

CHAPTER NINE

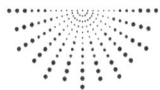

"We had a blowout," the driver told Willow. He was a shaken-up young fellow trying hard to pretend he wasn't. His name was Terrence Clay. "We lost control. I was thrown clear before the car went over. But no, I never saw any other vehicle."

Willow was in her Quinn County Deputy's uniform at the top of a ravine. The car at the bottom of the ravine matched the description of the one they were looking for, but this guy wasn't Angus Silver. A couple of deputies were scrambling down the stony face toward the car.

"Who was your passenger, today?" she asked.

Her uncle the sheriff stood beside and a half-step behind her, a six-foot-four-inch reason to take her seriously.

"My boss, Angus Silver," the driver said. He was a short guy who spent too much time in the gym. "But actually, I was the passenger."

She hadn't seen that coming. "Your boss was driving?" Willow glanced over at Garrett, but his expression never changed, so she kept hers stoic, too, and focused on the witness. "That's weird, isn't it?"

"Not for him. He gets in the mood to drive sometimes." He thinned his lips, shook his head slightly. "Frankly, he's not a very good driver."

He was holding his right arm with his left hand. His suit jacket and matching pants were scuffed at the elbows and knees, and there was a tear in his white shirt right under the collar.

She shot a look at her uncle, and he nodded at her to go on. "We had a report your employer made threats against a local business owner earlier tonight. You know anything about that?"

"No, ma'am," he said, rubbing his elbow. "Mr. Silver keeps his business matters private."

"Why don't you take me through your time in Quinn? You think you can do that?"

"Yes, ma'am, I sure can. I drove him to a cantina that looked to be closed. He talked to somebody there for five minutes or so…big guy, dark hair. Then we left."

"And who was drivin' at that point?"

He nodded. "He wanted to drive, so I hopped in the back before we left the cantina. Then we headed home."

"And where is home, Mister Clay?"

"El Paso," he said. "I have one of Mr. Silver's cards…" He reached around for his wallet, then winced and continued more slowly. Eventually he extracted a business card. It was black with silver foil letters that spelled out the last name. SILVER. It had a cell number on the reverse. A lot of space for a little information.

She heard a shout and looked down over the drop to where her uncle Lash, the chief deputy, was pulling a limp form from the vehicle, which had landed upside down in the creek. He looked up at her, shook his head side to side.

Angus Silver was dead.

An ambulance pulled in and medics scrambled down the ravine, breaking her line of sight.

Garrett was looking at the marks in the dirt, but it was hard-packed, not damp enough to keep good impressions. Still, he was frowning as if something was off. She looked where he was looking.

"Looks like he drove straight off," Garrett said to the driver, "How fast was he goin'?"

"Prob'ly a little too fast, to be honest."

Willow's phone started pinging as the crew below took photos and uploaded them to their secure site. As each notification appeared she clicked through to see the images.

Behind her, a fresh set of medics were trying to get the driver to let them look him over, while he kept saying he was fine.

She scrolled through the photos and saw the shots of the Caddy. It had rolled all the way down the steep drop, but one side had vastly more damage than the other. She spread the photo larger, moving over every inch of it. And then she blinked and tried to zoom further. But it wouldn't get larger, so she pulled out her radio, and keyed the mic.

"Uncle Lash—Deputy Monroe," she corrected quickly. "Is there brown paint on that passenger side, rear door?"

"Stand by," he replied, and she watched as he moved to that side, hunkered low, and looked close. "Good eye," he said. "I'll scrape a little off for you."

She glanced toward the ambulance. They'd argued Terrence Clay inside. The medic reached to close the doors, but she moved in and grabbed on to hold them open, then leaned into the back. "It looks like another vehicle hit that Cadillac, Mr. Clay. There's brown paint on the more heavily damaged side. You want to change your statement that there was no other vehicle involved?"

"Brown?" He blinked. "Paint?" He blinked again. Not the brightest bulb, was he? "Oh, yeah, right, right. That was a minor fender-bender, just the other day. Such a small thing I didn't even report it. Intended to buff out the dings myself. I do a bit of body work on the side, you know. That vehicle was brown, as I recall, so…" He lifted his hands to his sides, then lay back on his gurney.

The medic looked at her. "Okay?"

She let go of the door. "Yeah. Go."

He closed the doors and went around front to get behind the wheel.

As the ambulance trundled away, Willow turned to her uncle Garrett and said, "What do you think?"

He pushed his hat back farther back on his head, crossed his arms over his chest. "I think he was lyin'."

"Yeah, that's what I thought, too," she said. Then she heaved a big sigh. "Looks like Lily's probably safe for the night. But I been textin' the gals. We She-Brands are headin' over there to keep her comp'ny, just in case."

Garrett's smile was half a mile wide. "Sounds like just the ticket to me."

Lily was bored. The afternoon had waned into evening, and Ethan hadn't come back, or even called. Her dad was spending the night over at Cat's, after their square-dancing lesson. The sparkle had returned to his eyes. She had Cat to thank for it.

She was happy for her dad but feeling lonesome and angry with herself for feeling that way. So she'd decided to make the best of the night. She'd already accomplished the relaxing bath part of the plan, even though it had been interrupted by Ethan in a near-panic, thinking she was in danger.

It gave her a warm feeling, remembering that.

She'd got dressed after, but she didn't stay that way long.

She'd since changed into her softest, fluffiest pajamas—light-gray plush with pink. Then she pulled on her thickest socks and put her hair into a ponytail with a thick scrunchy Drew had told her was out of style. To which Lily had replied, "Scrunchies forever!" and they'd laughed together.

She really loved her cousins-in-law. Maybe Ethan had a point about a relationship between them messing with the family.

She settled onto the sofa and reached for the remote, and when she aimed it at the TV, someone knocked on her door as if in response. Frowning, and immediately thinking about the threats against her today—by a dead man, she reminded herself. Garrett had updated her a little while ago. Angus Silver was no threat anymore. He'd left the cantina all pissed off, had a blowout, and wound up at the bottom of a ravine, according to Ethan's uncle the sheriff.

She turned the TV off and went to the door, peeked through the glass pane, then smiled all the way to her toes and pulled the door open.

All three Brand *cousines* yelled, "slumber party!" and Lily burst out laughing.

They came crowding in, her sister-in-law Maria, and Ethan's other two gorgeous female cousins, Willow and Drew, opposites in every way. They were like day and night, Willow with her copper skin and raven hair, Drew with her porcelain and blonde. They all carried canvas grocery bags and wore long sweaters or hoodies in deference to the chilly night.

Lily closed the door as they headed for the kitchen, chattering all the way.

"Heard your dad's at his new girlfriend's for the night," Drew began.

"So we figured the timing was perfect for a get-together," Willow continued.

"And we brought goodies," Maria concluded.

They set their bags down on the counter and shed their coats and sweaters. Underneath, they were all wearing pajamas. Drew's were *Barbie™* -themed, the fashion doll having recently earned her stripes as a feminist icon. Drew had memorized the film's America Ferrera monologue about being a woman. Willow's pajamas were plain and blue, and Maria's were white and looked as if she'd borrowed them from Harrison. In fact, there was an HH embroidered on the pocket.

She saw Lily notice. She said, "What? At this point in my marriage, all my jammies are naughty," and everyone laughed.

"We heard you had a rough day," Maria went on, sending Lily a smile. The grocery bag she'd brought in was insulated and held ice cream and soft drinks. She unpacked them and put them into the fridge and freezer.

"And we're also aware that our cousin's an idiot," Drew put in. She'd brought multiple varieties of junk food, chips, and pre-made dips. There were Oreo cookies and peanut butter cups, God help her. Oh, and chocolate syrup and sprinkles. Okay, she got it. The evening would include making sundaes.

"Don't be speculating about me and Ethan," Lily said. "There's absolutely nothing going on."

Willow's laugh came through her nose because she clapped a hand over her mouth. The others just let it rip. They stopped giggling when she scowled at them, though. Then Willow wiggled her eyebrows and started taking glasses from the cabinet, lining them on the counter, adding ice, and pouring booze.

"We never celebrated your career change," Maria said, then muttered, "or even discussed it."

Lily lowered her head. "I was...embarrassed to admit I couldn't hack it, to be honest," she admitted.

Willow shoved a drink into her hand. "Look up," she said.

She looked up while taking a long drink. The three cousins were surrounding her, looking her in the eye.

"You see these faces?" Willow asked. "These are the faces of your sisters. There's no embarrassment among sisters."

The others nodded, there was a group hug, and then the drinking began in earnest.

"I think he's scared of me, the big goof," Lily said, then she bit a full moon Oreo into a waning crescent.

"Big goof," Drew said, and she snort-laughed which made them all laugh.

"He's nuts 'bout you," Maria said. "He was terrified when that stranger threatened you."

"Aw, yeah," Willow said. "He loo—" *Hiccup* "—looked terr'fied."

And then everyone laughed at the hiccup.

They'd put a movie on. A rom-com nobody was watching. Lily decided to turn it off, and did so, and then Maria set her phone in the speaker dock and got some country music playing.

Drew said, "Does anybody else think it was weird, how that guy threatened Lily, then died before he ever got out of town?"

"Oh, I sure do," Willow said. She looked around as if somebody might be listening, which made Lily giggle a little more. But then she said, "There was brown paint on that Caddy."

"Brown paint?" Lily asked. "What would that mean?"

"You think another car hit him?" Drew asked.

Willow nodded hard. "Driver said it had happened a coupla days ago, but—"

"So the car that hit him was brown?" Lily asked.

Drew was dancing. She grabbed Willow's hand and pulled her up to her feet to join her.

"Mud brown," Willow said, swaying to the music as if she did it every day. "I got a sample, so we might even be able to get make and model."

"Old Buick," Lily said.

Maria, a green-eyed redhead like her mamma, tapped Drew's phone to stop the music. "How do you know that, Lil?"

She frowned, recalling the brown car she'd seen parked near the cantina. But she didn't want to get someone into trouble until she knew more. So she said, "My neighbor back east had an old Buick. Thing was mud brown, that's how I always thought of it. When you said that, it reminded me of it."

"Got you. Yeah. Well, we'll check all the possibilities," Willow said. But she was looking at Lily as if she saw through the lie. Or maybe Lily was imagining things because she was a little bit drunk and a little bit paranoid.

Lily said, "So, Maria. Is the honeymoon phase over yet?" mainly to change the subject.

Maria smiled slowly and said, "Not even slowin' down. It's. Just. Perfect. Oh, ladies, I highly recommend marryin' your soulmate."

"Not me, Drew said. "I intend to live long enough to be an old maid."

"What about you, Willow?" Lily asked.

Willow smiled. "It'll be hard, you know? My parents are kind of sickening over each other."

"Mine, too," Maria and Drew said as one, then laughed because they had.

"So how does anything ever live up to that?" Willow asked. "How's a girl s'posed to settle for good enough when they've been raised up by Romeo and Juliet?"

"Scarlet and Rhett," Maria added.

"Bella and Edward," Drew said.

"Lily and Ethan," Lily said dreamily, then widened her eyes and clapped a hand over her mouth as the others roared with laughter.

Maria turned the music back on, grabbed Lily's hand and pulled her up to dance. "Don't give up, you hear? You're good for him."

"Best thing ever happened to him," Willow said.

"The big goof." Drew giggled, then tugged on Willow's hand and Will let herself be pulled. The four girls silly-danced and laughed, and talked, and took breaks for snacks and drink refills.

The clock read 8:45 a.m.

It was the wrong clock—her dad's mini-grandfather clock, with its swinging pendulum, on the living room wall, not the digital one on Lily's bedroom nightstand.

She seemed to be half on the sofa, half on the floor, and her mouth felt like the ring after a rodeo. Slowly, she sat up, her butt sliding the rest of the way to the floor as she did. The world tilted and she pressed the heel of her hand to her forehead and moaned.

A soft whirring sound came from the kitchen and made her open her eyes, but only a little. Maria was splayed across the chair that matched the sofa, and Willow was sprawled in Dad's recliner.

Where was Drew? Right, kitchen. Lily used the coffee table to push herself up onto her feet just as Drew came in, with a blonde ponytail bouncing high and a glass of something thick and red. She was clean, as if she'd been up and showered already. She was even dressed in regular clothes she must've brought along.

She took one look at Lily and her face turned into a blend of amusement and sympathy. She smiled, and her eyes were soft. "Here."

"That better not have raw eggs," Lily said.

"Fruits, veggies, a few herbs, tomato juice. Chase it with an electrolyte drink, it'll fix you right up."

She sipped it. Tasted like V8. Her stomach accepted it, and a second sip eased the queasiness.

"I don't want to ruin your mornin'," Drew said, "But last night you said you and Ethan were meetin' a contractor at nine."

"Oh shoot! It's a quarter of!" Then she looked down at herself. "I need a shower. Can you text Ethan that I'm running late?" She looked at the clock again. "Tell him I'll be there by 9:15."

"Got it. Go shower. I'll tuck a bottle of Gatorade into your purse."

"I don't have any Gator—"

"I brought some. Go on, I'll take care of all this," she said with a look at the mess they'd made of the house.

"Just leave the cleanup," Lily said. "And let the girls sleep as long as they want. Thanks, Drew." Lily ran up the stairs, sipping the juice on the way, impressed right to her toes with the youngest Brand.

Ethan got a text from Drew just as he was unlocking the cantina to go inside.

Drew: Hey cuz. Lily's runnin' late.

Ethan: She ok?

What the hay did that mean?

Ethan: How late?

Drew: 9:15

Drew: Go easy on her.

Ethan: Thought you said she was ok?

Drew: 📱😅😵

Ethan laughed out loud, shaking his head. Then he texted a thumbs-up, and hesitated before going inside. The donut place was nearby, so he looked up the number and called.

"Dan's Donuts."

"Yeah, This is Ethan Brand. I have a contractor coming over to Manny's place in fifteen minutes. Can you deliver?"

"Hell, yeah, I'll bring it over myself. What do you need?"

He rattled off an order, and by the time the contractors arrived—he'd added an electrician, a plumber, and a floor man to the mix—he had a vat of coffee and several open boxes of pastries and donuts spread out on the bar top.

The food was down to crumbs by the time Lily arrived with her tablet in her dad's tool belt. She wore big, dark sunglasses, a flannel unbuttoned over a blue shirt, and faded jeans. Her hair was in a long, white-gold braid that hung in front of her left shoulder.

Ethan couldn't take his eyes off her, until the general contractor cleared his throat and elbowed him. "Intro please?"

"Samwell Burdick, this is my manager, Lily Hyde."

"Shoot, did we save her any donuts?" he asked. Then grinned. "Good to meet you, Lily."

"Same," she said.

Ethan reached beneath the bar for an insulated travel mug of coffee, fixed the way she liked it, and held it up toward her. She came across the room to take it. There was pure appreciation in the way she hugged the mug between her palms.

"I stashed a couple'a donuts too, if you—"

She held up a stop-sign hand, and he nodded, straightened, left the spare donuts where they were.

"I was just sayin'," Burdick began. "That shed might have to go. Do you think you want it torn down or relocated?"

"Let's take a look at it," Ethan said. Then he headed outside with Sam and Lily. She put the iPad in the apron's nail pocket and brought the coffee with her.

"The shed, right there," said Burdick, pointing.

"We haven't even looked inside that yet, have we, boss?" Lily asked.

Calling him boss was, he guessed, her way of reminding him of his stupid adoption of her stupid rule. Hands-off while they were working together. He was already regretting having re-invoked it.

Burdick was busy measuring the outside of the wall they wanted to knock out, so Ethan and Lily focused on the shed. It was a large garden shed, the kind you could buy ready-made in the Lowe's parking lot. Red with white trim boards. Two doors in front that opened in the middle. It had a barn-shaped, gray-shingled roof and about enough head room to stand in upright —for most people. Not for him.

The door handle had a keyhole in it. He was surprised when he twisted it, and found it unlocked, then pulled one door open. Its partner was held in place by a bolt at the top and another at the bottom. There was no power, no light switch. He peered into the dark space and spotted a lawn mower, an electric weed trimmer, a bucket full of sponges with a bottle of car-washing soap, a sleeping bag on the floor…

Wait a minute.

Yes, that was a sleeping bag on the floor, unrolled, with a pillow on one end, and a flashlight, water bottle, and paperback book on the other. On the left there was an unopened packet of cheese-like substance and crackers, the kind with the wooden peg to use for spreading.

Lily took off her sunglasses and whisper-shouted, "Whoa, someone's been sleeping out here!"

Behind the two of them, Ethan felt Burdick's interest, but he was several yards away and probably hadn't heard. He met Lily's eyes and found them so wide that it felt like he could fall right into them.

CHAPTER TEN

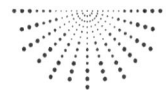

"*W*ho could it be?" Lily asked.

Ethan had to look away from those eyes to process her question, much less come up with an answer. In fact, he had to focus so hard, he remembered that brown car.

"I keep seeing someone around," he said. "Well, twice now. Parked on the side of the road, like a hundred yards north."

"Old brown Buick." Lily replied. Then she looked around as if to be sure no one else was within earshot. "Willow says there was brown paint on Angus Silver's Cadillac. As if it had been hit by another vehicle. A brown one."

He lowered his head. "It was parked there that day." He checked to be sure the contractor was still far enough away and lowered his voice to a whisper. "It was facing this way when the Caddy left here. It turned around to take the same path, like you'd do if you were following it."

"Holy…" Lily breathed.

"Silver's driver denied any other car was involved, though. Said the paint was from a fender-bender a few days ago."

"Yeah, that's what Willow told me, only when she wanted to question the driver again, he'd vanished. Nobody knows where."

"Huh," Ethan said. "So you've seen the brown car too, then?" She nodded.

"Close enough to get a look at the driver?"

"Momentarily, as I passed. I wish I could freeze-frame it, because there was something familiar about his face, even though I could hardly see any of it. It felt like that was the point."

"What parts could you see?" he asked.

"Dirty blond beard, long and untrimmed. Sunglasses. He was wearing a bandana but I got the impression of long hair pulled behind his head. Kind of a chiseled face, what you could see of it."

"Chiseled? You mean as in handsome male model?"

"As in grizzled gunfighter."

"Older?" he asked.

"No, but hard. Like he's been through some things, you know?"

"Like this ain't his first rodeo," he muttered. Then he looked down at her. "Got all that just from a glimpse as he drove by, did'ja?"

"Yeah, I did."

"Huh." He tilted his head. "You think it's the same guy who's been sleepin' in the shed?"

"Unless we have two odd strangers hanging around," Lily said. "I think we need to talk to him. *If* we can catch up with him."

"He takes off as soon as he's seen," Ethan replied. "The two times I've spotted him, anyway. And I could've...nah, it's stupid. I'm reachin'."

"No, go on. Say it. You could've what?"

Ethan sighed. "I could've sworn someone was watchin' that conversation I had with Silver. I assumed it was one of the cousins and then forgot all about it, but it seemed like someone was here."

"Where?"

He turned and nodded toward the cantina. "Right there, front corner."

She was quiet for a moment. Then she said, "Maybe we should watch the shed overnight."

He met her eyes and imagined he could see every single thought running through them. *So, big guy, what do you say we spend the night together, in the dark, all alone, just the two of us? Let's see how this hands-off bull goes then.*

"Okay," he croaked.

"So how is it?" Burdick called.

Ethan had forgotten to look. He turned his attention back to the shed. It was in great shape. The lumber still smelled new. Cedar, he thought. He turned around and said, "We'll move it."

"Let me know where you want it and I can pour you a slab," Burdick said. "Take a couple of hours. You buy the concrete and I'll do it for no extra charge, assuming you hire me for the addition."

"That's a generous offer," Ethan said.

"Well, this would be a notch in my belt, and I don't mind sayin' so. A honky-tonk, owned by a country star, right here in Mad Bull's Bend. You're fixin' to put this town on the map."

"I don't know about that," Ethan began

"I don't see how it can miss. And I'm hopin' you might let me leave a little sign someplace. 'A Samwell Burdick Project.'" He spread his hand apart as he said it.

"Sign? Heck, I'll put up a plaque, you do a good job." Ethan said, "So, like I said, I want the addition to be the dance floor, with a stage, backstage area with a dressin' room."

"With a flagstone patio out front, running the whole length of the place," Lily said, "where the parking lot is now."

Burdick rubbed his chin. He had a yellow legal pad he was scribbling on. He said, "You know you could have that whole front wall all glass. It could slide open. We could continue the floor from inside to outside.

"That would be…" Lily began, then glanced at Ethan.

"Amazin'," he said, finishing her sentence.

Lily flashed him a message with her eyes. He read it as something like, *This guy gets us. He sees our vision.*

"We could do the same in the old section," Burdick said, looking at the wall they were going to demolish. "So dinin' tables too, could continue outside. Maybe…put in a patio bar separatin' the outdoor-dinin' side from the outdoor-dancin' side."

"That's a great idea. Taco bar or beverage bar?" Ethan asked, looking at Lily.

"Why not both?" She crossed the lawn with the men on her heels, until she was facing the parking lot in front of the building. "And there has to be an open-flame aspect to it, I think. Wouldn't that be cool?" she said.

"I know a guy," Burdick said. "Wait, wait, wait." He scrolled his cell phone while Ethan and Lily exchanged a smile. She arched her eyebrows and hitched her chin toward Burdick, as if to say, *This guy, right?* He acknowledged with a slow blink that served as a nod.

Then Burdick said, "Here it is. Check this out. This guy's local, Julio Gomez, a real artist, but doesn't charge like one. He's a plumber, and this is his side gig." He turned his phone around.

Ethan bent lower to look at a video of a water-bubbling fountain surrounded by fire.

"Of course, that's a freestandin' feature," Burdick said. "He does tabletop versions, though. Just fire, just water, or both. Every one's unique. He can size it for the space. And you have plenty of room."

Ethan could tell Lily wanted him to say yes. He said, "Let's get some numbers from the guy first," because it seemed like what a reasonable entrepreneur would say. What he wanted to say was, "Anything that makes Lily's eyes light up like that is a go." But he couldn't really say that out loud.

She looked disappointed while nodding in agreement. "Yeah, I suppose we should see how big a dent it would put in our budget."

They didn't actually *have* a budget yet. He had a round figure in mind and intended to borrow it from the bank. But he thought it might be a good idea to get some of the biggest numbers in hand before he applied for the loan. If the honky-tonk did well, it would pay the loan back itself. But if it failed, he'd still have to pay it back. And that was no small deal, even for a Brand with a hit song.

They gave the plumbers and electricians the specs and sent them on their way to crunch numbers and write estimates. But they spent the rest of the morning with Samwell Burdick, because they both knew he was the man for the job. They discussed the addition, the dance floor, the stage, the parking lot in back, the improvements Hyram had mentioned for the kitchen, and the bathroom for the second floor.

Several hours later, Burdick left with a paperback's worth of notes and promised to have an estimate and a timeline for them within a day.

Then Ethan was alone with Lily.

"We worked right through lunch," she said. "And the kitchen's empty. And there's not a decent taco for at least…?"

"A mile," he said.

"No, I said a *decent* taco."

"Fifteen miles," he corrected.

"See what I'm saying?" Lily smiled and went to the bar top, where she'd left her keys. "I'd keep the barstools. They're perfect as they are, if a little worn. We can have them re-covered to match the new look. Save us a bundle."

She took her keys and headed to the entrance, and he followed, wondering what she was up to. Outside, it was warm and dusty—the kind of day when breathing through your mouth would leave dust on your tongue. His boots tapped the concrete parking lot, and he watched as she thumbed a button and opened the trunk.

"Would you put that savings toward the private bathroom upstairs, or the fire-and-water feature? If we had to choose," he asked.

She pulled a white picnic cooler from inside and then slammed the trunk. "If it were up to me? Fire-and-water feature first. It's gonna be one of the things we're known for. That and you." She was staring at his chest, not his face, when she got stuck. Then she met his eyes, her cheeks went pink and she lowered them again. "You and the acts you bring in, I mean."

"I hope those are all we're known for. But this whole thing with Silver's threats, and then his death and this brown car squatter, whoever he is—"

"I know. It's like, will this be the end of it, or is there a bigger bad guy behind this one?"

"There's always a bigger bad guy." He took the cooler from her as she passed him, because he hadn't been raised in a cave, then followed her back inside. The coolness hit him. "Must be the adobe, keeps it so cool in here," he said. "I'll tell Burdick we want to keep that."

"He's something, isn't he?" she said, as Ethan put the cooler on the bar and opened the lid. He took partially melted ice bags off the top and pulled out a gigantic bowl with a plastic lid, two smaller bowls, and a plethora of silverware.

"I can't believe you left food in your trunk."

"I parked in the shade, and it was very well-iced. Feel. Still cold."

She held out the bowl, and he touched it, then pried off the lid. The bowl had compartments. One was full of small, round, cooked potatoes. Another, what looked like Spanish rice, and another had a mix of broccoli, cauliflower, and carrots, drizzled in something dark brown. The fourth compartment had fat slices of bread.

"Have you ever had salt potatoes?"

"Never," he said.

She nodded. "It's a New York thing." She slid a bowl in his direction.

He helped himself to a fork and put some of everything onto his plate, then relaxed onto a barstool. The first thing he tried was a tiny potato, and found her watching him, waiting. He popped the whole thing into his mouth.

"Well?"

"Salty," he said.

"Yes! That's the point. Most people dip them in melted butter, but I didn't know how to manage that in a cooler."

"They're good just like they are. Like pre-sliced, pre-fried potato chips."

"Dad made everything. I think that's aged balsamic on the veggies. It's thick and sweet."

He tried everything. The Spanish rice had a twist of something that made it even better. Was it lime? "He's a top-notch cook," he said.

"You're changing the subject. We were going to talk about Cadillac guy. What did Manny say? You did call him, didn't you?"

"Right after I paid for the fire & flood insurance." He had called Manny that morning, as he'd told her he would. "He doesn't know this Silver character. But I also asked about how the finances had worked before. He said de Lorean's guy took care of everything. The bills got paid, and profits piled up."

"No shit."

He shrugged. "I asked the bank to give me access to the account associated with the cantina. Sent them proof I bought the business. They're reviewing my request and will get back to me."

"And then what?" Lily asked.

"Then we hire an accountant to go through the transactions with a bullshit meter. Find out what, if anything, is goin' on."

"*Was* going on," she corrected. She'd eaten every bite of her food and dipped back in with her fork for another potato. "An accountant would be obligated to report anything that looked… fishy."

"What are a few more crimes on my sperm-donor's long list?" he asked. "Too bad he's dead. He'll never pay."

She put her hand on his upper arm in a way that told him to listen up, to pay attention. "Manny's an immigrant, Ethan."

"I know, but he's legal, and he didn't know what de Lorean was up to. He's got nothin' to worry ab—"

The look on her face, eyebrows up, chin down, made him break off mid-word and replay what he'd said. Then he said, "You're right. It could be bad for him."

"It could get him deported," she said, blunt as always. "Or worse."

"I'll talk to Garrett," he said. It occurred to him how often that phrase was his solution to a problem. Uncle Garrett always knew the right thing to do. "Until then, I wonder if you and Hy would consider stayin' at the ranch?"

"But the guy who threatened me is dead."

He nodded. "We've just established there's always a bigger bad guy. And I don't want to scare you, but Garrett says Angus Silver has an older brother. Nathan Silver."

"And?"

"He's as big a criminal as my old man was. And I was the last person to see his brother alive. It would be a lot easier to keep you safe at the Texas Brand. There's always family around, and you can see anyone comin' for a mile in every direction. We've got fences, gates, and guns."

She closed her eyes and he wondered what she was thinking.

But she said, "Yeah, sure, I'll talk to Dad after we finish up here tonight."

"So what did you have in mind for the afternoon? It's too early to start surveilling the shed." He finished his last bite, then gathered up all the dishes and headed around the bar and into the kitchen.

Lily followed. "Why? You have something in mind?"

"I thought we might pick paint colors for upstairs, then start prepping the room. Spackle the cracks and tape the trim," he said as he put the dishes into the sink and turned on hot water. He'd left some basics around, so there was dish soap to squirt in.

Lily seemed to think about it, then said, "If I'm moving to the ranch tonight, I'm gonna need to pack a bag. And you can handle paint prep without me," she said. Then she dove into her tool belt and pulled out a handful of paint-sample cards, each one striped in shades of color. "I marked my favorites, but you're the owner."

Lily spent the afternoon with her dad, packing up for a few days at the Texas Brand. She was sure it wouldn't be longer than that.

It wasn't yet dark when she headed back to Mad Bull's Bend and pulled her car around onto the grass behind the cantina. She headed in through the rear door, which led to the kitchen. "Ethan?"

"Upstairs," he called.

She headed upstairs, surprised to find blue painter's tape bordering every bit of window trim and crown molding.

Ethan was on a ladder, carefully smoothing spackle over nail holes in the wall. He wore jeans and boots and a tight-fitting black T-shirt. She got stuck watching the flexing and relaxing of his biceps as he worked.

Her own T-shirt was tight, too. A lot of good it did, with her flannel over top. She took it off right then and there, dropped it over a tall bucket and said, "It's warm up here. You've been busy."

"Couldn't help myself. This room has a perfect view of the shed, so I figured two birds, one stone."

She looked around noting he'd taped her paint sample strips to the walls in several locations.

"Now that I'm up here, I'm liking that pale lavender," she said. She untaped it from where it was and re-taped it to the spot where the light still hit. "Even prettier in the light."

"That was my favorite, too," he said.

"Maybe with a creamy trim?"

Ethan snatched a paint strip off the wall, moved it to the spot beside the lavender sample, and awaited her opinion.

"It's a good look," she said. "Peaceful, but feminine. You sure it's not too girly for you?"

"I'm secure in my manhood."

"Glad you're secure about *something*," she muttered.

"What?"

"I said, you should be. Secure in your manhood, I mean. And in your decency, and in your talent."

He ignored the direction she was trying to steer the conversation and changed the subject. "Besides, after the opening, I won't be here much anyhow. This is really *your* space. But like I said, I like it, too." He pointed to a right angle he'd drawn on the floor, like he hadn't just twisted the knife in her heart a little bit. "That's the bathroom. There's already plumbing run to the spot, as if that was the plan to begin with, so that'll save some money."

"Very cool." She turned again toward the window, gazing down at the shed. "Have you seen any movement out there?"

"Not a bit," he said.

"I wonder if you should move your truck around back."

He shrugged. "He's been sleeping out there with us in and out every day. I don't think my truck's fixin' to deter him."

She shrugged and turned away from the window to face him. "I brought a bedroll and an inflatable mattress. You?"

"I brought paint, rollers, and brushes," he said. "And an extra pair of overalls. In case you came lookin' pretty. You do look pretty, by the way." He tossed her a pair of lightweight overalls, like a mechanic would pull on over his clothes.

"Thanks. Just make sure one of us is always watching the shed." She unfolded the overalls, unzipped them, and stepped into them, sighing because her jeans and top were particularly cute and had been painstakingly chosen.

According to some article Maria had read and then conveyed at some laughing-til-their-bellies-hurt part of last night, she was supposed to douse something in her *signature scent* and then leave it somewhere to waft, so he'd be thinking about her even when she wasn't there. Since she didn't have a signature scent, but always used the same shampoo and conditioner, she'd dabbed a little bit of them on a piece of gauze. It was in a plastic bag in her tool apron where they'd stashed it last night, so she wouldn't forget, and it would probably stay there, because it was a dumb idea.

It only took a couple of hours to get a coat of primer on the entire room, since Ethan had already done most of the prep. It was gray and dull, but also fresh and new. She stood in the center, turning in a circle, imagining furniture placement. "One desk near each of the east-facing windows, you think?" As she spoke, she pointed, and then somehow lost her balance.

Ethan grabbed her quick. "Paint fumes," he said. "You good?"

"Yeah. Yeah. I'm good."

He took his arms away and she immediately wished she'd said no. Then he went to open the windows. She went over to the one just to the right of the top of the stairs, braced her hands on the sill and leaned her face into the warm night air.

"The addition might block the view, if you go two stories with it."

"I only want to go one-story, but with a tall ceiling," he said. "We'll keep the view in mind, though. Be a shame to ruin it." He was at the other window, a few feet to her left, leaning on the sill just as she was. Every time she glanced his way, she found him looking at her, not the view.

"Could go two stories, though," she said. "What couldn't you do with all that extra space?"

He nodded slow. "Could put a handful of rooms in there."

"Your theme is honky-tonk, not hotel. Your business model is a country bar and dance club, not an inn. Let's not lose focus."

He smiled at her. "You sound like my manager."

"I *am* your manager."

"I meant the music one. Angelo Barrone. Why are you so good at this?"

She shrugged. "I took a few electives in college, but I don't think it's that. It's almost intuitive."

"Your brother told me you were brilliant running that place where your dad cooked."

She shrugged, turning back toward the view just as a shadow moved past the small paned window in the shed.

"Did you see that?" she whisper-barked.

"See what?" Ethan looked outside again, too.

"Someone's in the shed. Come on." She pivoted from the window, peeled off the overalls and paper shoe covers, and dropped them onto the floor of the freshly primed room. Then she ran down the stairs with Ethan right behind her, around behind the bar and through the kitchen to the back door.

"Wait!" Ethan called. "Jeeze, let me grab a weapon."

She sent an over-the-shoulder scowl. "Sure we'll shoot him for squatting in a vacant—" But she stopped when she saw the weapon he'd grabbed was a rolling pin. She almost grinned, but there were more important things to do. She grabbed a tenderizing hammer as she passed the utensil rack, just in case.

Ethan opened the back door. They tiptoed to the right side of the building from behind, toward the shed, then froze in their tracks when the motion-sensing spotlight came on from somewhere up high on the side of the cantina. She hadn't even realized it was there. It blazed directly onto the little garden shed, illuminating a surprised face in the shed window. Then the shed door burst open, and a tall, bearded fellow exploded from it and ran full bore toward the road and right into the path of a pickup truck.

CHAPTER ELEVEN

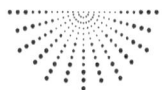

*E*than flinched when the truck hit the guy. His body bounced off the hood onto the far side of the road and rolled into the deep ditch as the truck's tires skidded and squealed. Everything went still and the scent of hot rubber filled the air.

Ethan ran into the street, crossing in front of the pickup, which was Willow's, he realized. She got out and came to the front, shouting, "I didn't see him! Jeeze, he ran right out in front of me! Where is he?"

"Went in the ditch," Lily said, pointing.

The three of them went to the edge of the road. Ethan had his phone out, flashlight app on, aiming it into the deep gulley alongside the road, but there was nothing moving down there.

"Come on, there's water in the bottom," he said, sliding down. It was only six feet or so to the bottom of the ditch, but as soon as his boots splashed down, he realized the water was shallow. Not deep enough to hide a whole human. He aimed the light up one way, and down the other. "Well, where the hay did he go?"

He was looking up at the women when he heard a vehicle

starting up from the distance. He scrambled up the bank and joined them in time to watch a set of taillights about a hundred yards farther up the road, and fading fast.

"Son of a—" Willow opened her truck door.

Lily put a hand on her arm. "Maybe let him go," she said. "He's hurt." And she nodded at the pavement, where there were dark smears. "I think that's blood."

"He moved too fast to be hurt very bad," Willow said. "Besides, I can't do that. I'm a deputy. I can't hit a pedestrian and not report it. If he's hurt, that's even worse. Who the hell is he, anyway?"

Ethan said, "We don't know who he is. It looked like somebody'd been sleepin' in the shed, so we waited up to catch 'em and find out who."

"And do what? Add him to the menu?" Willow nodded at the weapons they were still carrying, a rolling pin and a meat hammer, then lowered her head, shaking it. "Let me get the truck out of the road, and we'll check the shed. If I can get some prints and he has a record, it might be just that easy to ID him."

She got into her truck to move it into the parking lot. As they walked back across the street, Ethan noticed Lily shiver and automatically slid an arm around her shoulders. She looked up at him, and he thought her expression was grateful. Then she pressed a little closer to his side, and he squeezed a little more.

The shed door still stood wide open. Willow shut her truck off and came to join them, then flicked on her Mag Light and aimed it around the inside of the shed.

There was still a sleeping bag and pillow, a bottle of water, and a granola bar. All the same things as before. Except for two new additions, hanging from a nail on the wall. A large Mexican style hat and a woven poncho.

"Holy crap," Lily said. "It's Gringo Sombrero."

Willow moved closer, examining the articles and nodding slow. "I'm pretty sure you're right. At least I can get a description out with the APB. Six-two, maybe six-three, long hair, full beard, both dirty blond. Electric blue eyes. Missin' his hat."

"*Electric* blue eyes?" Lily asked.

"Sure, you've seen him. Keeps that hat low, but not low enough to hide those eyes. They're kind of…intense."

"I heard him described as chiseled," Ethan said, and Lily elbowed him for teasing her.

"Did either of you see what he was driving?" Willow asked.

Just as Ethan was opening his mouth to describe the old brown Buick, Lily said, "Nope," and clasped his hand *hard*. He figured she had a reason, so he kept the car to himself.

"All right," Willow said. "So what happened, tonight, exactly? Before he ran in front of me?"

"We saw him movin' around in the shed from the upstairs windows," Ethan said. "We sneaked outside to confront him," Ethan began.

"But we triggered the motion-sensing floodlight," Lily put in.

Ethan nodded and completed the tale. "He panicked, and ran—"

"—and *bam*," Lily said.

Ethan noted the curious look in Willow's eyes as her gaze shifted from him to Lily and back again, following the conversation.

"Huh," Willow said.

Ethan heard more than the three letters of the word.

"Well," she went on, "he ran fifty yards in the time it took us to check the ditch for him. He can't be hurtin' too bad. I'll get that APB out and file a report. Maybe you should give Manny a call, see if he knows anything about the guy."

"Will do."

"You think this was connected to that shakedown attempt?" Willow asked.

Ethan pushed out his lower lip and shook his head. "Don't see how it could be. That guy's dead. This feels like a fellow without a place to sleep. I wonder if Manny's been lettin' him use the shed the whole time? How long have you been noticing him at the Cantina?" he asked, addressing both women. He wasn't home often enough to know for sure himself. He felt kind of ashamed when he thought on that.

"As long as Dad and I have lived here," Lily said, "So at least a year."

Willow nodded. "Yeah, I'd say right around the time Lily and her dad moved down here. Maybe a month or two longer. Maria will know for sure. She gets tacos at least once a week."

"She'll be going through withdrawal while we remodel," Lily said, shaking her head sadly.

They left the shed without disturbing any of the stranger's belongings. Willow used her jacket sleeve to pull the door closed. "I'll call this in. Get the guys out here with a kit so we can check for prints and—"

"I really wish we didn't need to do all that. Make it all official and everything," Ethan said. And he didn't know what made him say it. There was something about the guy that got to him. Hell, he'd written a song about him. "Seems like he's havin' hard times. I don't want to make them worse."

Willow looked from him to Lily, as if she might be able to explain.

Lily said, "I kind of agree. Could we keep this off the books, Willow, just until we find out more about what's going on?"

Willow sighed, then said, "I have to put in a report, but it can wait a day or two. I'm still gonna get his prints. I need to go get a kit from the office and hope he doesn't come back for his stuff in the meantime."

Ethan said, "We can watch the shed until—"

"No. You two get the hell out of here until I come back, so I know you're safe. Go...go over to the Waterin' Hole." She nodded in the direction of the local dive bar, three quarters of a mile away, in the middle of the Mad Bull's Bend business district. "Get a beer and some pretzels. I'll text you when I'm back. Stay outta trouble, okay?"

"Sure," Ethan said. "We can do that. Can't we, Lily?"

She shrugged and tried to stop worrying so much about the stranger, and the brown paint, and the dead crime lord who'd been trying to make Ethan sell the place to him. And it wasn't hard, not when Ethan Brand was holding out a hand and had a mischievous glint in his eyes.

"Sure we can," she said. "Long as you're buying."

Ethan figured his cousin the deputy was right. He had no business risking Lily's safety by trying to ambush a squatter, and he was a little embarrassed that he'd tried. The notion of spending the night on surveillance with her had probably kept him from thinking about much else. He'd been equal parts excited and terrified at the notion.

Besides, Willow wasn't leaving until they did. So he shrugged and extended an elbow. "Shall we?"

"Yeah, but first I have an idea." She ran toward the cantina. From the driver's seat of her truck, Willow rolled her eyes.

Ethan followed Lily inside, expecting her to grab their jackets and her handbag off the bar, but no, she ran past those things, all the way upstairs. He saw lights glowing before she came back down.

"Turn on all the lights!" she said, as she moved back through the place into the kitchen to do just that.

He would have obeyed, had she not lit the place up like Christmas already. She came out of the kitchen and ran to the vintage juke box, patting herself down for quarters.

"Behind the bar. I put a jarful back there."

"Smart." She ducked behind the bar, and he heard the jar of

coins rattle. Then she dropped a lot of them into the coin slot and poked buttons to select songs. Hank Williams came on first. "Long Gone Lonesome Blues."

She came back to him at the front door. "Okay, great," she said, full volume, because the music was pretty loud. "With any luck, the lights and noise will fool him for a while and his stuff will be here when we get back. Front door's locked. We'll lock the back one behind us on the way out. Oh!" She moved past him and flipped on the outdoor lights, flooding the front parking lot before heading through the kitchen and stepping out the back door.

"We can take my car," she said. "Leave your truck out front, so he thinks we're still here."

"Why not leave 'em both and walk? It's not even a mile." Ethan closed and locked the back door. It muffled Hank, though.

They walked around the building on the side where the shed was. It was empty, dark, its door wide open. He glanced up at the motion sensing light. They were too close to the cantina to set it off.

"I got this," Lily said. She walked toward the only plant on the lawn, an overgrown thorn bush. As soon as she got near it, the light came on. "Perfect." She untied the scarf she'd used to cover her hair while painting and tied it to a thorn-covered branch. The breeze made it dance, which kept the motion detecting light on. "There."

"So he thinks we're still here, and doesn't dare take his stuff before Will gets a chance to look it over," Ethan said. "Meanwhile, just in case he sees through the ruse, we're safe over at the Waterin' Hole."

"More or less," she said,

"Maybe your brother isn't the only genius in the family," he said.

They went around front to Willow, who was waiting impatiently in her SUV. "Tonight would be nice," she called.

"We're fixin' to walk," Ethan said. "Such a nice night."

"Get in, I'll drive you."

Ethan put a hand over his heart. "You don't trust us?"

"Not as far as I can throw you," Willow replied.

"Here, then." He pulled out his phone and tapped, causing a whoosh sound. Then a Ping came from inside the SUV.

Willow glanced at her phone, which was in its holder on her dash. "Why're you sharin' your location with me?"

"So you can track us. Now, go get your Sherlock Holmes kit and git back here, will you? I want to know who this guy is."

"I'll do the best I can. You sure you don't want me to call this in? Make it official tonight?" Willow asked.

He glanced Lily's way, met her eyes. They shared a smile. "I'm sure."

"I hope he's okay," Lily said. "Maybe you should check the hospitals and clinics, Willow."

"Already on it," she said. Then she looked at the stretch of pavement they'd be walking.

It was the entirety of downtown Mad Bull's Bend. Just the other side of a one-lane bridge, lay the grocery store, drug store, all the fooderies, a bar, three used car lots, a pair of gas stations, a donut and coffee shop, and a library. It was lit up like a carnival, despite that most businesses were closed for the night. This was the one thing Ethan would change, if he could. He'd like to pick the cantina up and move it somewhere quieter. Like Quinn, and maybe not even in town. Probably wouldn't get much business, though.

Lily didn't clasp his hand, so he dropped it to his side and they started walking. He put himself between her and the traffic. Willow backed out of the driveway after they'd gone a ways, heading back in the other direction.

"She really *doesn't* trust us," Lily said.

"Me, not you, I'm sure."

She looked behind them, then up into his face. "Okay, she's out of sight. Let's head back."

He lowered his head, shaking it slowly. "Actually, I agree with our resident law woman on this. If I'd been thinkin' straight, I wouldn't've risked it to begin with."

"Oh?"

They were passing a gas station-convenience store, which was open 24/7, but looked quiet as a tomb. You could see a young man inside with thick, dark hair. He sat behind the counter with his head tipped downward, scrolling his phone.

"So why weren't you thinking straight, do you think?" Lily asked.

He glanced at her, frowning. "Sorry?"

"You said, if you'd been thinking straight, you wouldn't've risked confronting our squatter. So why weren't you in your right mind?"

"Oh." He shrugged. "I don't...I was uh..." He'd been excited about spending the night with her. But he couldn't very well say *that*. "Hey, did I tell you? My manager called. The single's droppin' tomorrow."

"Wow, that was fast."

"Ang said they've been trackin' searches on me and whatnot. I don't know how all that works. They liked the timin', with all the press. Decided jumpin' on the wave was more important than pre-release publicity."

They walked in silence for a while, crossing the narrow bridge over the river. There was barely space for a vehicle and a pedestrian to cross together, and if the vehicle was a truck, forget about it. No traffic just then, though. It was a quiet night, not too warm, not too muggy, with crickets singing up a storm and the shallow river rushing below.

She said, "I was thinking Fourth of July weekend for the grand opening," she said after a while.

"That's only eight weeks, though."

"Biggest holiday in the window," she said.

A car passed so close he could feel the engine's heat and the rush of displaced air. "You think we can be ready?" he asked.

"Hell, yes, I think we can be ready. If you can get us some acts."

"It's short notice. People will be booked."

"Then get some local bands and perform yourself."

Music came spilling from a slab-sided building that didn't look like much more than a lean-to. Neon beer signs hung in the two front windows. Parking was in back.

They headed up to the entrance, through a set of batwing doors, and into the din. The place smelled like beer and sounded like a good band with bad amps. Ethan caught cigarette smoke and a whiff of something stronger. He put his arm around Lily's shoulders, because he had an excuse, as they wound through the barroom. It wasn't packed, but there was a decent crowd.

When they reached the bar, he held up a hand and the barkeep saw it easily. One of the benefits of being as big as he was. He held up two fingers and pointed to the taps.

The barkeep nodded, reached for beer mugs, filled them up, and slid them along the hardwood. Ethan handed one to Lily, then replaced his arm around her, and guided her back away from the bar and through the crowd of locals.

"Table!" Lily said, pointing to where two people were rising, pulling on their jackets, and picking up their possessions. She grabbed his hand and pulled him toward it, stopping short to give the occupants room to exit. Then she pounced, putting her beer on the table and sliding into the chair.

"You're good at that."

"I've got some experience," she said.

That made him look at her quickly. "Have you, now?"

"Yep."

"Date a lot, do you?"

"Every chance I get," she said. "I know what I want, and I'm not gettin' any younger."

He was supposed to ask her what she wanted, but he wasn't walking into *that* minefield. Time to change the topic. "I assume you had a good reason for stopping me from mentioning our squatter's car? Or what we *think* is our squatter's car?"

"I did," she said. "There was brown paint on the dead crook's fancy Caddy."

He frowned. "Brown paint," he repeated.

"The driver said it was from a fender bender earlier in the week, but it would be a heckuva coincidence. And nobody's seen him since."

"So you think our squatter...what, committed vehicular homicide?"

"Well, that would be a leap." She shrugged. "But I do think we oughtta find out before we give up that piece of information."

"Even to Willow? She's family."

"But it's Gringo Sombrero! He's never caused anybody any trouble. He just sits there and minds his own business. He helped my brother when Maria's ex beat him bloody. He helped me, when Manny had his heart attack. And we don't know the guy even *did* anything. Shouldn't we at least make sure before we go pointing the police his way?"

"That's what the sheriff's department is for, Lil."

"I know," she said. "Still...I just have this feeling about him." She took a long drink.

"Yeah. Me, too," he admitted.

The band started a new song, a cover of Patsy Cline's "Crazy."

Lily popped up and grabbed Ethan's hand. "I love this song." She tugged him a few steps away from the table, hooked her hands behind his neck, and started to move to the music.

He put his hands on her waist, when what he wanted to do was wrap his arms all the way around her and pull her right up close. He couldn't do that, but she kept inching closer, and he wasn't doing a very good job stopping her. She turned her face up to his, and her breath smelled like that beer, and her eyes sparkled.

His arms tightened around her waist all by themselves. A sigh escaped, or maybe he'd squeezed it from her. God, she was beautiful.

Oh, he was in so much trouble, here. The place was dim and smoky, the music was good and yearning, and she was warm and sexy in his arms.

He wanted to kiss her, and he thought she knew it. She pressed a little closer, and their hips moved together from side to side in time with the singer's deep, dulcet heartache. Around them, a handful of couples hugged close, heads rested on shoulders and cheeks against cheeks. Somebody was smoking at the bar. Nobody cared. His arms closed around her a little more.

She took one of his hands in hers and put it right on her butt, and he squeezed without even meaning to. His hand just acted on its own. She laid her head on his chest. "This is nice."

"What, uh—" His voice came out all raspy. He cleared his throat. "What happened to hands-off at work?"

"This look like work to you?" She didn't lift her head as she spoke. "Try pretending there's nothing else in the world right now except the two of us and that song. There's only one more verse anyway."

Ethan heard her and felt the suggestion straight to his bones, which surprised him because he was feeling so much else at the same time. Arousal, mainly, but with a healthy dose of fear and trepidation.

"It's just a dance, Ethan," she whispered.

He sighed, releasing all his resistance with his breath and

deciding to take her suggestion. Pretend there was nothing else. Stop being afraid of this, just for one dance.

He wanted his fingers in her hair, so he moved his hand from her waist to the back of her head and threaded them there. Her hair's herbal scent wafted up, and he closed his eyes and breathed her in.

"Nice, right?" she asked softly.

"Nice," he said. "But we—"

Her finger was across his lips faster than a quickdraw. So he shut up and relaxed into the dance. The song ended, and she smiled up into his eyes. "That was amazing." Then she returned to her chair and drank deeply of her beer.

Ethan didn't order a second beer. He got a sweet tea. He didn't trust himself to drink around her even though he rarely got a buzz from beer.

He looked at his phone again. Watching for that text from Willow, telling him it was safe to head back to the cantina. Hell.

"I was probably out of line on the dance floor," Lily said.

"You were wonderful on the dance floor."

She lowered her chin. "If a guy acted like that..." She didn't finish, just shook her head. "I'm sorry if I made you uncomfortable."

"The only discomfort you gave me was the kind a cold shower'll fix," he said.

Her cheeks got even redder. "I'm not usually so...I mean..."

"You were fine," he said. "You *are* fine."

A waitress came by to plunk two bowls on their table. One held pretzels, the other, Cajun mixed nuts. She leaned low to put the bowls down, as if her arms wouldn't reach unless her chest was at Ethan's eye level. She took her time about it, too, moving the bowls, turning them, as if their positioning had to be perfect before she straightened again. She had lovely round breasts, elevated by a red pushup bra, the lace edges of which were visible in the scooped neckline of her tight, tight blouse.

"You're Ethan Brand, aren't you?" she asked.

"That's Fred Brand, Ethan's brother," Lily said. "A *true* fan would know the difference."

"Oh." She shrugged and walked away.

Ethan was rapt, watching Lily in action, thinking how quick she was, how clever, how freaking funny. How irresistible.

She caught him looking and arched her brows. "That was a fan. I should've let you handle it. I just keep messing up tonight."

"She wasn't a fan. Not like you mean, anyway. She just wanted to add me to her body count."

"Well, to be fair, so do I." She clapped a hand over her mouth and her eyes widened. She looked around as if for something to blame, and her blue gaze fell on her two empty beer mugs.

"When did you get so sassy, Lil?" Ethan was flattered right to his boots.

She lowered her hand from her mouth. "It's the beer," she said. "Why don't we start back? I think the fresh air would do me good."

"Okay. I'll take care of our tab." He got up, plunked some cash on the table for the waitress, and walked back to the bar to settle up.

CHAPTER TWELVE

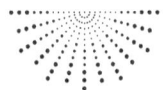

*L*ily gathered her jacket and purse and went to wait for Ethan outside. She stood on the sidewalk, looking up and down the small town's main thoroughfare. It was late, nearly midnight. Most everything was closed. There was a Denny's up a little ways, and the gas stations were mostly open all night. And the bars. That was it. Every other business was closed up tight.

She breathed deep, let the night air clear her head a little. It had been smoky in there. Not all of it tobacco. But she couldn't really blame her bold moves on that. Maybe she was feeling desperate. And that was dumb. Her mom used to say that a girl should never love a man more than he loved her.

Not that she *loved* Ethan Brand. It would be self-destructive to fall in love with him. But she liked him a lot. And she wanted him a lot. And she was convinced they belonged together.

He came out the door with a bottle of water in his hand, which he offered her.

She took it, twisted off the cap and took a long drink. "Thanks. Again, I'm sorry—"

"Stop apologizing, Lily. I...I wanna add you to my body count too. It's just..."

"I'm family," she said. "I know. I don't want to mess up the family dynamic any more than you do, you know. My dad and brother are all I have, and Maria's more than just a sister-in-law."

"She's my best friend," Ethan said. "Has been our whole lives."

They'd started walking back toward the cantina, going slow so they wouldn't arrive too far ahead of Willow and tick her off. When they'd gone far enough that most of the lights were behind them, Lily started hearing the whir of nighttime insects again, a constant, ever-shifting hum that was the backing soundtrack to every West Texas night. Warm night air on her face, big, hot cowboy by her side. She didn't think life could get much better.

As they crossed the bridge, she sighed a dreamy sigh, then felt a rumble beneath her feet and looked up as a semi sped their way, faster than was smart. Just as the truck reached the bridge, Lily said, "He doesn't see us."

"Run!" Ethan grabbed her arm and ran, but they were not fast enough. The grill of the semi was bearing down. Just before contact, Ethan tugged her with him right over the side. They dropped twenty feet and splashed into the cold water, sinking straight to the bottom.

She panicked, but as soon as she started flailing, she felt solid ground under her feet, and pushed herself upright, breaking the surface in the shallow river only to fall down again.

"Lily!"

Ethan reached her and grabbed her under her arms to pull her up, but the current was fast and the water chest-high. As soon as they rose and moved two steps toward shore, it knocked them down again and swept them further downstream.

He got his footing eventually, and helped her get hers, and then they stumbled onto the shore arm-in-arm, soaked and spluttering. They fell together with their feet still in the water, panting, lying on their sides, face-to-face, legs entangled, arms clinging.

So close. His breath on her lips. His warmth penetrating her chill.

"I can't…" he whispered.

Lily closed her eyes in disappointment.

"…resist you, Lily Ellen Hyde." His lips met hers and her heart sprouted wings. Hummingbird wings, it felt like.

She kissed him back, and they wrapped themselves in each other there on the pebbled shore. He rolled over, pulling her on top of him, one hand in her hair, the other on her backside as he fed from her mouth and then her neck, pushing her blouse aside as he went.

Lily pushed his shirt off too, then shucked her jeans and got to work on his.

Ethan lifted his head. "Are you sure this is—"

"Heaven? Yeah, I'm sure. Shut up and kiss me."

So he did. It was not easy peeling off their remaining soaked clothes, but they managed it, and then they were there, on a tree-lined riverbank, skin to skin, every part of them touching, and then closer still. Her breath whispered from her lungs and something caught fire in her soul as she held and kissed and loved him with every cell in her body, right there on the riverbank.

Afterward, she lay atop him. He was stroking her back with his big hands. He hadn't said a word and she didn't know what to say.

And then someone shouted, "Hey!" From the bridge, twenty yards upstream. "Bubba! Lily, are you down there?"

"Willow," Ethan said softly.

Lily rolled off him and re-dressed in her soaked clothes with no small effort. It took her about twenty tug-and-hops to get her wet jeans up far enough to zip them. The top was easier. Ethan was dressed again by the time she was pulling on her shoes.

The beam of Willow's flashlight swept closer from above.

"Right 'chere, Ethan called, and the beam found him.

"What the heck are you doin' down there?"

"Semi thundered through while we were crossin' the bridge," Ethan called. "Had to jump for it." He reached back for Lily, and their eyes locked.

Realization hit her like a freight train.

Oh, no. She loved him.

His hand closed around hers and he pulled her along, angling up the steep bank to the road. It was cold now that she wasn't in his arms. She shivered, and he put an arm around her shoulders as they ascended the steep bank. He kept looking down at her, his eyes full of questions, obviously aware that something momentous had just happened.

They made it to the road and Willow, who'd returned in her Quinn County Sheriff's Department SUV, handed them each a blanket from the back. "You guys hurt? Anything broken?"

"We're fine," Lily said, and she took off her soaked flannel. "The river broke our fall."

"Blouse too," Willow said. "Turn your back, Ethan." She made a circular motion with her finger and Ethan, who'd barely taken his eyes off Lily, turned his back.

She peeled off her blouse and noticed there were some stray leaves and twigs stuck to her belly. Probably more on her back. She wrapped the blanket around her and hugged it close.

"All this for nothin'," Willow said. "I didn't get a clean set of prints off anything in there."

"You checked already?"

"Yeah. Texted you I was back a while ago." She frowned from

one of them to the other, and reaching out, plucked a twig from Ethan's hair. Then she said, "Come on, Lily, take the front seat, you're shiverin'." She opened the SUV's door and reached in to turn on the seat warmer before letting Lily climb inside, then she closed the door.

Lily searched the dashboard, found the heat and turned it on, settling deeper into the seat, huddling in her blanket and still shivering. She was hyper-sensitized, feeling everything, the car's warm air on her legs and face, the brush of the blanket against her skin, the soft seat that cushioned her.

She'd have liked to take off the wet jeans, too. She was probably getting the seat all wet.

What did all this mean? she wondered. Where did things stand between her and Ethan now? Had they started a relationship? Or had they just made a misstep on their platonic path? How was he going to play this?

Motion drew her eye, and she noticed Willow and Ethan had moved further away from the truck, and Willow was speaking to him pretty emphatically. Had she seen them all wrapped up in each other's arms? She couldn't have, not in the dark from so far away.

The memory of their lovemaking washed over her, and she closed her eyes and relished it. This thing between her and Ethan was more than she'd realized.

Maybe it was everything.

Back at the ranch, Lily stood in a hot shower long enough to finally get warm again after her icy plunge...and the absence of Ethan's arms around her, too, she supposed. She closed her eyes, and wished she knew what he was thinking.

She turned off the water, toweled down, and wished she'd brought her thick, fluffy robe into the bathroom with her. Wrapping herself in a towel, she opened the bathroom door just as a soft knock came from outside the bedroom. And then the door opened, and a female hand poked through holding a robe. *Her* robe. And that looked like Chelsea's hand.

"I heated it up in the dryer," Ethan's aunt called.

Lily hurried to take the robe from the hand—oh, it was warm! She pulled it around her and opened the door wider at the same time. "Oooh, that's so nice." She rubbed her hands up and down the sleeves. "What a thoughtful thing to do. Thank you."

Chelsea was always kind, unless someone hurt her family, but this was above and beyond. "And chamomile tea," she said, taking two cups and saucers from the stand in the hallway just outside Lily's door.

Her good china, Lily noticed, with the pink roses and gold rims. That seemed rather...special. She looked at Chelsea more closely, suddenly wondering if Willow had seen her and Ethan after all and had said something.

Chelsea was a beautiful woman. She was letting her hair age naturally, and it was coming in light silver. She had big, brown eyes, a smile that could light up a room, and Lily thought she was one of the smartest people she knew.

She carried the tea to the nightstand, set one cup down, and took the other with her to the rocking chair near the window. "I was thinking," she said, "about when I first came to Texas, and right into this house. How confusing it all was, and how much I wished for my mother, just...to talk to."

"Your mom died young, too?"

"My mom died the same way my sister did."

"Your sister...Ethan's birth mother?"

She nodded. "My father...he beat my mother their whole marriage. One day he went too far."

"Oh my God. I didn't know. I'm so sorry, Chelsea."

Chelsea smiled sadly, then nodded toward the second window seat, a small, overstuffed chair in pale blue. "Sit with me a while?"

Lily took her cup and saucer from the nightstand and went to the little chair, moving aside its lacy white throw pillow before sitting down. She sipped the tea, which had cooled to the perfect temperature and tasted like heaven.

Chelsea said, "I thought you might be longing for a mom to talk to, like I was then. And I thought I'd let you know I'm here to stand in, if you think it would help."

The teacup in Lily's hand was jiggling on its saucer with a soft *ting ting ting ting ting.* She looked at her hand in surprise. And then Chelsea came to take it from her trembling hand and set it on the windowsill. She crouched in front of Lily's chair and opened her arms.

Lily burst into tears and leaned right into them.

Chelsea held her and stroked her hair until she'd cried herself out. She had no idea how long that had taken. Her face burned from the salt of her tears, and her nose was running. Little spasms kept tearing through her chest—aftershocks. She straightened and pressed the heel of one hand to her cheeks in turn, embarrassed to her very toes.

"I don't know what's wrong with me."

"You're in love. You know that, right?" Chelsea tilted her head, searching Lily's eyes as she rose from the floor where they'd wound up. She eased Lily back into her chair, and then she took her own.

"Yeah," Lily said. "I've come to that conclusion." And then she panicked, and blurted, "But you can't tell him!"

"I will never betray your confidence," she said. "Besides, I'm here as your stand-in mom. I asked her if it was okay, and she said go for it, so…"

Lily smiled at the notion of the two of them chatting. It felt completely plausible when Chelsea said it. "I just...I don't know what to do. How do you make someone love you?"

"You can't make someone love you, hon. That's not possible. But the question is, why would you want to try?" She reached across the space between them, took Lily's hands in hers. "You are an amazing, brilliant, ambitious, beautiful, funny, kind, gemstone of a female, Lily Hyde. Your mother must've been so proud, and she'd be even prouder today. And I think she'd ask you the very same thing I'm about to. Do you really want a man you have to work this hard to land? Wouldn't you rather have a man who'd work this hard to land you?"

"Sure, I'd love that. But only if it was Ethan."

"Well, then?"

Lily frowned. Chelsea was looking at her as if she'd just answered her own gnawing questions, but she was no clearer on anything than she'd been before. "I don't understand."

"Know what you're worth, Lily. There's no man you ought to be chasing, not even our thick-headed Bubba. And the sooner you stop, the sooner he's gonna realize it."

Chelsea got up. Her teacup was empty. She was going to leave. But she couldn't leave! She'd given hints but not real answers.

"But...but what if he doesn't?" Lily asked. "What if he just doesn't feel the same?"

Chelsea pressed a warm, soft palm to Lily's cheek. "Then he's not the one for you, and the sooner you know it, the better. Don't you think?"

"Oh." It was, even to Lily's own ears, a heartbroken syllable.

"I don't think that's the way this is will go, though. I know Ethan pretty well. Better than anybody, I think. And I don't think that's anywhere near the way this will go."

"No," Ethan said aloud. "No, no, no. I'm *not* goin' out there to see if she's still up."

He was alone in his room at the Texas Brand with his hand on the doorknob, but he forced himself to let it go and pace back toward the bed.

His room was just the same as it had always been. Chelsea had deemed it off limits to everyone but him, even though he was only home a handful of times a year. That made him comfortable leaving things around. He had clothes in the closet and dresser drawers, and enough belongings for comfort—books, a spare phone-charging cord, shaving gear, shower supplies, and a stack of CDs he refused to get rid of.

Mail was stacked on the dresser, because he'd never changed his address. Once a month Chelsea would bring it to a show if he was playing nearby, always with a sad-sounding comment about how coming home would be so much nicer than a hotel.

He wished he was in a hotel instead of a few doors away from Lily.

No, he wished he was in her room with her, in her bed with her, instead of a few doors away. Being with her had been earth-shaking. Shattering.

He didn't even know who he was anymore. It had rattled him right to his core.

Cold shower, that was the ticket. A nice, cold shower would shock the horny right out of his body and clear his mind. He strode into the attached bathroom, yanking his jeans and shorts down on the way and kicking out of them before he entered the little room. He peeled off his shirt and tossed it behind him, then leaned through the shower curtain to crank on the taps. Mostly cold. Clenching his jaw, he stepped right in. The icy blast made him yelp, but just once, and not very loud. Other than that, he took it like a man.

After the bracing shock did its job, he adjusted the flow warmer, which felt even better after the cold. He was in no hurry to finish up and go to bed, because he wasn't going to sleep anyway. So he took his time and let the pounding heat massage his back a little, let it soothe his head. It didn't ache, exactly. It felt like his brain was firing sparks in all directions. He couldn't seem to quiet it, so he stood in the water for a long time, and when he got out, he shaved, trimmed his nails, combed his hair. Finally, with nothing left to do, he stared into the mirror, thinking about making love to Lily Ellen Hyde right there on the banks of the river, under the bridge.

If they ran into each other again tonight...

"No, no, no," he said again. "I'll stay in my room; she'll stay in hers." And yet he had to keep working with her, and she probably thought now that it had happened once, they were in a relationship. Did she think that? Was that where they were?

He was between a rock and hard place. A persistently hard place, whenever he thought about Lily Ellen Hyde.

He stepped back into the shower for another cold blast.

When he finally re-entered his bedroom, wearing nothing but a scowl, Lily was sitting on his bed. She looked up, her gaze locking on his junk and warming, before sliding up to meet his eyes.

He took two steps backward, grabbed a towel, and wrapped it around his hips. It was very close. He'd nearly taken two steps forward instead.

She rose to her feet. "I was just going to leave it, and—"

"Leave what?" He felt the brush of terrycloth and mentally ordered his lower body to stay the hell down.

She tilted her head, but not her eyes, toward the bed. Her eyes stayed on him. He managed to look where she'd indicated, but the only thing there was her tablet with a pink sticky note on its face.

"It's for you to take to the bank with you in the morning. You're going about the financing first thing, right?"

He nodded and wondered why she was still talking about the cantina.

"So, about earlier," she began, but then she left off there.

It wasn't a statement, Ethan realized. It was a prompt for him to make one. "I don't know what to say about earlier," he managed. "I'm...processin' it."

"Yeah, me, too." She sighed, looked everywhere but into his eyes, then said, "Well, regardless, I'm not here for...you know, more. This isn't the place. Even if we wanted to, I mean."

For the first time in his adult life, Ethan fully understood why he needed a home of his own in Quinn, even if he didn't want to live there. On the road, it was hotels and motels and sometimes a camper. And so far, on the road was the only place he'd...hooked up. Never with anyone he truly knew, much less from his hometown, much less a part of his family.

He couldn't think of anything to say but he didn't want her to go, so he said the first thing he could think of. "Estimates've been comin' in all night. We should go over 'em."

"Pick whoever you want. You're footing the bill."

He nodded and lost his words. All he wanted was to wrap his arms around her and tumble into the bed.She was still standing in front of the door. It was like she didn't dare get any closer to him but couldn't quite leave. She reached behind her for the doorknob. He was still only wearing the towel. He went to her anyway, not close enough to touch, but almost. The air between his body and hers was damn near crackling.

Their eyes locked. She said, "I'm feeling like maybe I have something to say after all, about our...lovemaking."

A few tendrils of icy panic crawled through his veins, both at what she was going to say, and at her chosen terminology. "Oh?"

"I know being with me like that is the very thing you've been trying to avoid. I just...don't want you to think it changes anything."

But it had changed *every*thing. "I don't understand what you mean."

"I'm not gonna chase after you like a lovestruck pup just because we...did it."

"I didn't think you were."

"I don't want a man I have to chase down and rope, like your cousin Trevor with a stray calf. That's not what it was about to me." She was opening the door. She was backing through it. "I told you it wouldn't be the end of the world, and it's not. So you can relax. Okay?"

What was happening? It didn't feel like what he wanted to be happening. Not even close.

"G'night, Ethan."

Do something! Don't let her walk away.

"'Night, Lily," he said.

At least he didn't need another cold shower. Her words had been like a bucket of ice.

Eventually, Ethan got into bed, stacked the pillows under him, and reached for Lily's tablet. The note on the front said, "password 999999."

She was acting like making love on the riverbank hadn't shattered her the way it had him. But he kind of thought it had. She was way too good for meaningless sex. And she was way too good for him, too.

He keyed in the passcode on the old iPad and tapped the Presentation icon. When he hit play, a spinning image cartwheeled onto the page, then filled the screen. The presentation was computer-generated, he realized, but it looked for all the world like the fully renovated Cantina from the outside, front, with the big sliding glass doors wide open, and the taco station and fire-and-water feature in place on the huge flagstone patio that used to be the parking lot. On one side of the station, there were tables and people eating. On the other side, people were dancing.

The view panned into the new addition, over a gleaming dance floor, across the stage, and then behind it, where there were a pair of dressing rooms for guest bands. Back inside, the presentation took him through the kitchen with its devoted veggie station and new cook surface in place, and then back through the dining room with the bar gleaming, the tables in place, new light fixtures. He noticed each light fixture was different. And the tables and chairs were in several different designs too, so he could see what each choice would look like in place.

Upstairs, she'd added a partition dividing the space into two offices, rather than one. He wondered if that was an effort to distance herself from him. Had making love driven them further apart instead of bringing them closer, as he'd feared?

The camera took him out the rear of the building to the new parking lot, then around the right side, where the new main entrance was a big set of double doors almost where the little shed used to be.

The presentation returned to the view from out front, and he saw that he could now manually click through each room. Every item she'd changed popped up with notes when he touched it. The whole thing was brilliant. On the final screen, he touched a summary tab.

She had the whole place laid out right there, as if it were already finished, everything they'd already agreed on and then some, with spaces for him to enter the amounts of the estimates from the contractors for each portion.

He tapped to open the app and figured out how to add his own notes to hers. The stage needed more outlets for amps. The dressing room needed extra guitar strings and drumsticks and fiddle bows for emergencies. And the mic...he wanted it to look old-fashioned, one of those fat rectangular ones with radio call letters on it, only it would say...

What would it say?

What was he going to *name* the place?

Breakfast was long over by the time Lily came downstairs. She'd overslept by hours and only realized during her shower that she hadn't slept that well in weeks. One would think she'd released a little tension.

She'd meant it when she'd told Ethan that making love didn't have to change anything. It had been...beautiful. Wonderful. Everything. And she hoped it would happen again. But she knew it might not.

As soon as Lily took her place at the fully set breakfast table, Garrett came and sat across from her.

She looked at him, then at the table, set for four. "Oh gosh, tell me you haven't been waiting for me before having your breakfast," she said.

Garrett leaned forward, holding a hand to one side of his mouth to stage-whisper, "If I'd eaten earlier, she'd have given me oatmeal, like most days."

"Oatmeal's good for you, especially considering what you have the rest of the day," Chelsea said, heading in from the kitchen with platters of steaming food.

Lily didn't know how the woman did it. She must've heard her moving around upstairs and started cooking immediately.

Her dad came from somewhere, rubbing his hands together.

"Garrett waited for sausage. I, on the other hand, waited for you," he said. "What took you so long?"

"I haven't been sleeping, to be honest. I think it finally caught up with me. And by the way, oatmeal would be better for you, too, Dad." But he was already scooping hash browns onto his plate.

Ethan's chair remained empty. He'd had an early appointment with the bank.

"Bubba was out of here hours ago," Garrett said. Lily didn't know whether he'd read her thoughts or her eyes. "Chelsea, is it all right to call him Bubba when he's not here?"

"I don't think there are rules," she said.

Garrett shrugged. "He was all worked up about the bank and the cantina." He put three sausage patties onto his plate. Chelsea reached out her fork and took two of them back. He never missed a beat in his conversation. "He said to tell you that you're brilliant, and he'll return your tablet when he sees you."

Chelsea said, "Brilliant, huh? What's that about?"

"All I did was put everything we've talked about for the cantina into a presentation for him to show the bank." Then, smiling, she said. "It *was* kind of cool. Animated and all."

She took a cinnamon roll and looked at her coffee.

Reading her face, Chelsea said, "You want a travel mug for that?"

"She sure does," Hyram said. "Here we waited breakfast, and she's gonna take it to go."

"I choose to believe she did it for me," Garrett said, reaching for one of the sausages his wife had stolen. She slapped his hand, then rolled her eyes and let him have it.

Hyram said, "Take two of those cinnamon buns, honey. They were still in the oven when Ethan left so he didn't get one." He put extra emphasis on the name with a make-believe-scowl at Garrett.

Garrett shrugged. "Oh, sure, easy for you to say. He's *always* been Ethan to you."

"He'll always be Bubba in our hearts," Chelsea said. She handed Lily two freshly filled travel mugs and put two over-sized, glaze-dripping cinnamon buns into the big plasticware bowl she'd brought in from the kitchen. "Make sure I get that dish back," she said. Then she shot Garrett a horrified look and said, "Ohmygosh, I'm *old*!"

"No, you're not," Lily said. "I'm the same way with my plasticware."

"Me, too," her father called out. "But I'm also old."

"And I'm...the only one at the table without an opinion on plasticware," Garrett said.

Lily blew them all a kiss, headed out to her car, drove toward Quinn proper, and straight on through to Mad Bull's Bend. She didn't bother with the highway. It was too nice a day. She drove the back roads with her windows down and flipped on the radio.

A familiar voice filled the car. Ethan's voice, crooning his heart out in that lonely, longing song that had made her fall in love with Quinn before she'd ever seen it. "Home." She smiled and let the notes and his deep, rich tone wrap around her, and she sang along, but softly so she could still hear him. She even added a little harmony, and wondered why tears sprang to her eyes when he sang the final lines,

> Land of my biography
> Too good for the likes of me
> In my dreams, I'll always be
> Home

Her chest swelled with emotion. And more, a niggling in her mind that he really meant it. Ethan Brand thought Quinn, Texas was too good for him. He thought his family was too good for him. He thought she was too good for him, too.

The final note died and the DJ said, "That was Ethan Brand, roaring back onto the scene with a just dropped runaway hit that's already burning up the charts, 'Home.'"

An ad came on, so she lowered the volume. Runaway hit? Climbing the charts? Ethan hadn't mentioned it. Though, obviously, they'd been focused been on other topics. Still, this was huge. Did he even *know*?

CHAPTER THIRTEEN

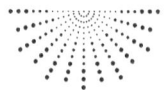

*L*ily drove into Mad Bull's Bend the back way, so she had to cross the bridge. She looked down over, wondering if she could pick out the spot downstream where she and Ethan had been all tangled up in each other and in bliss. A knot of longing formed in the pit of her stomach, and a delicious shiver danced up her spine.

Minutes later, she was pulling into the cantina's parking lot, surprised to see multiple vehicles already there. "Samwell Beckett General Contracting" was painted on the sides of three of them. She got out and made her way among the workers, who noticed her—some more than others—some with big, friendly smiles and hardhats coming off. She smiled back and looked around until she spotted Ethan.

He saw her at the same time and came her way, grabbing her arms when he reached her. "I took that presentation with me to the bank. They approved the financing in like ten minutes."

"They would have anyway, Ethan. You're a Brand."

He barely paused in his enthusiasm. "Then I called Burdick and told him he had the job. I also hired the electrician, and the plumber-slash-water-feature guy and told them they could start today.

"You seem so excited!" She was surprised. He hadn't been this into the honky-tonk until now.

"Seeing it all done in that presentation…" He shook his head. "Lit a fire under me, Lily."

When he said "fire" it sounded like "fahr" and made her want to kiss the accent right off his lips. His phone signaled. He reached into his pocket and silenced it without even looking. "Dang thing's been goin' off all mornin'," he said. "Listen, I have an idea for the name." A power tool started growling, then. Lily took Ethan's arm and pulled him into the kitchen, where it was quieter.

"You should probably check your phone," she said.

"In a minute," he said. "I want to call the place Two Lilies."

She blinked and repeated the words back to him. "Two Lilies?"

"Yep. I been thinkin' and thinkin' on this, hear me out, okay?"

"Okaaaay." She really had hoped he'd want to talk about something else, but…he was wound up, wasn't he?

"First, because I can see your heart is really in this place. And I don't have the kind of vision you do, and it's…it's you. Second, to bring a little bit more of your mom down here to Texas. And third, it's a nod to the fact that there are two unique Lilies, not two versions of one. And even if we're the only two people who read it that way, I figured…" He trailed off with a shrug, watching her face.

She lowered her head because tears sprang into her eyes and she didn't want him to see them. "I love it," she said. "But it seems like your name oughtta be in there somewhere too."

"Two Lilies can be Two Lilies forever. I mean, if you're okay with it. On the other hand, Ethan Brand's would have to be changed, you know, if I decide to sell the place."

The sentence was a gut punch. Wow. Okay, so she was right when she'd said that nothing had changed. Not for him, anyway. Good to know.

He met her eyes quickly, reminding her he was pretty good at reading her. "Is somethin' wrong?"

She pasted on a smile and wondered why it hurt so much. She'd been very clear with herself, hadn't she? She'd decided that having sex with him wouldn't change anything, that she wouldn't let it change anything. But it had. At least for her, and she hadn't meant it to, but it had.

"Lily Ellen?"

Spine straightening, chin rising, she said, "You should really check your phone."

"Why? You know somethin' I don't?"

She raised her eyebrows and nodded hard. He pulled out his phone and its screen was a solid column of notifications. He started with the text messages, she noted, leaning up to look. His manager, all caps, lots of exclamation points.

Ethan looked up, his eyes round.

"Don't look so surprised," she said, burying hurt under her happiness for him. "It's a great song. You're a great artist."

"I've just been stuck for so long…"

"Maybe now you'll be unstuck."

"Maybe I already am," he said. "I've had to stop to jot down lyrics three times this mornin'."

She smiled and it was genuine. If his block was gone…then being with her must've helped, right? Or maybe just the excitement of the work on his honky-tonk finally getting underway.

"My mom used to say that sometimes getting away from a job for a little while is important. You'll either realize you miss it and go back with more passion, or you'll realize you're happier without it and find a new path."

"Which of those has happened to you, Lil? With your job at the hospital?"

She looked around. She loved working with Ethan, but she was in love with him. She loved being with him, regardless of what they were doing. But she also loved working on this project and she was good at it. It was hard to tell which was influencing her feelings about it more.

"You're taking too long to answer," he said. "Do you miss your job as a nurse?"

"I don't miss my old job, no. I still feel bad that I failed at it, you know?"

"You didn't fail, you chose to leave."

"No, I couldn't hack it. I'd like to think if the chips were down, I could, but I'm not gonna risk a patient's life to find out for sure. As for this job…I love it, so far, but I think it's too soon to tell if this is what I'm supposed to be doing. Depends on how it goes, I guess. But never mind me, this is about you. What else does your manager say?"

He frowned at her for a moment, but she nodded at his phone, so he resumed scrolling messages. Then his smile returned and darn near blinded her. "We're debuting on Billboard at number nine next week!" He grabbed her and hugged her right up off her feet, turning her around in a circle. When he stopped, they went silent, as she gazed down into his eyes and tried to remind herself she was done chasing him, and that making love with her had not made him want to stay.

She needed to toughen up her heart.

"Downloads, sales, and plays are all up," he said, as he set her down again, returning his attention to the phone. "Ang is getting a lot of interview requests. Holy…three of them are network shows."

She raised her brows. "That's fantastic, Ethan."

For some reason he touched her again, sliding his hands down her arms to clasp hers and bring them to his lips. He kissed them and said, "You did this. All of it."

"You did it," she said.

She wanted his arms around her, and the only way she could stop gazing into his eyes with her heart pouring out was to look somewhere else. At the floor, at the workers she could see through the porthole windows in the kitchen doors. They were out there milling around the place like the world wasn't reversing polarity every couple of minutes.

Fortunately, the sound of a vehicle skidding into the parking lot and a door slamming provided the perfect distraction. Frowning, Ethan headed through the double doors into the main room of the cantina. Lily followed.

Willow was heading for the entrance. She was in uniform.

"Well, this can't be good," Ethan said. "She looks serious as a toothache."

Lily said, "Let's talk to her outside, okay? You've got all these people busy. They don't need distractions. Much less, gossip."

Ethan grabbed his hat and they stepped out just as Willow reached the door, so she backed off a few steps. She wore her hair pulled back. It hung in a long braid down her back that was probably against regulations.

She didn't bother with preamble. She said, "We found Gringo Sombrero," she said, "Out past the onramp in an old brown Buick with front end damage. He was in the pull-off by the river there, where folks park to go fishin'...unconscious behind the wheel."

"Oh no," Lily whispered. "I knew he was hurt. I feel awful."

"*You* feel awful?" Willow asked. "I'm the one who hit him. I hope he didn't wait too long to get help, you know?"

"How bad's he hurt?" Ethan's only reaction to the news had been a quick lowering of his head. It was still lowered, but he didn't have his hat on to cover his eyes.

"Busted ribs. Concussion. Been unconscious since we found him. No ID on him, and the car's registered to an Olive Dennison, New Mexico, deceased. Natural causes. I'm running his DNA."

"I want to see him," Ethan said. "I need to talk to him." His gaze shifted to Lily's. And she knew why he wanted to see the stranger—to ask whether he'd had anything to do with Angus Silver's *accident*.

"Once he wakes up, you can head over," Willow said. "Doc says other than the accident, Gringo's the healthiest un-homed person he's ever seen."

"I never pegged him as un-homed," Lily said. "Why would he sleep in the shed, when he had a car?"

Lily had always figured Manny knew who he was, but Manny said he had no idea. The guy had just started showing up one day. Never said much. Helped break up a couple of fights, stepped in when help was needed, and then just went back to his perch. Always paid in cash. Tipped well.

He wasn't in the cantina every day. But he'd been there a lot of days, right up until they'd closed for the re-boot.

"I want to see him now," Ethan said.

"Give me a half hour and the DNA will be—" Her phone pinged. It was already in her hand. She looked at it and said, "It's in now," before tapping a button, and walking away, out into the parking lot. Her brown boots tapped and she spoke low to someone on the phone, then suddenly louder. "Are you serious right now? Holy..." And then she turned slowly, staring at Ethan, and Lily knew something was up.

"Okay," she said. "Okay." She was walking back as she said it, sliding the phone into a hip pocket, biting her lip. She met her cousin's eyes then, and said, "Gringo Sombrero's name is Jeremiah Thorne. He was serving time, but got released early in exchange for his testimony against a kingpin who was already in for another crime, and who's since died in prison."

Ethan looked at Willow, his face slowly changing. Curiosity was replaced by something that might've been dread. "Who was the kingpin?"

"His father," Willow said. "Vincent de Lorean."

The words landed, but they sat on the surface of Ethan's brain for a moment. And then they sank in just enough to make him say, "But that would make him my brother."

"Half-brother," Willow said. "Different mother. He's two years older than you."

He was shaking his head slowly. He sought out Lily's eyes. "I have a brother. All this time, I've had a brother. And he's been right here...for how long?"

"He got paroled a year ago," Willow said. "And that's around the time he first started showing up at Manny's, as far as I can tell. Maria agrees."

"Well, what the hell was he doin' here? Watchin' the place? Or watchin' me? Was he still workin' for de Lorean, or whatever's left of his crew? And if not, then why didn't he say anything?" He wasn't asking anyone those questions, really, just letting them spin from his brain into his words. "Why didn't he tell me who he was?"

"Why don't we head to the hospital and see if he can tell us anything himself?" Lily asked. She reached up to close her hand on the back of his neck.

Her hand was cool. He liked it there. "Yeah, let's do that. Talk to him. I don't even..." He trailed off, distracted because she'd moved her hand away.

"You okay to drive, cuz?" Willow asked. "You look a little shell-shocked."

"I'll drive him," Lily said. "I've been dying to drive that big truck of his anyway."

Willow, hearing the same double entendre Ethan had, snort-laughed and tried to pretend she hadn't by coughing and clearing her throat.

Lily shot her a quelling look and Willow gave what she probably thought was an innocent shrug. Ethan saw every bit of it but pretended he hadn't.

To change the subject, he thought, Lily opened the cantina door, put her fingers to her lips and gave a whistle. Everyone turned, power tools went silent, safety glasses slid up onto heads.

"We're going to be out for a bit. Anyone need anything before we go?"

As one, the team returned to work, lowering their safety goggles and letting their tools answer for them. Only Burdick gave a real reply, and it was merely a thumbs-up, before he returned to work.

"Guess they're okay without us. Come on, Big Guy." Lily put a hand on Ethan's upper arm, right around his bicep. He really didn't *mean* to flex, it was automatic. Her fingers moved over his arm in what felt like appreciation.

"Let's go meet your brother. Remind me to call him Jeremiah and not Gringo Sombrero like I've been calling him for a year."

"He came up that often, did he?" he asked.

"Oh he's a hot topic among the She-Brands." She gave him an eyebrow wiggle and walked around his truck to the driver's side. So he got in the passenger side and looked over at her in his seat. She looked like a doll sitting in a human's chair. "You can adjust the, uh—"

"I know, I got it." She'd already been running her hands along the bottom and sides of the seat in search of controls. She moved his seat upward and forward, and still looked small, but at least she could see over the steering wheel and reach the pedals.

He buckled up. She adjusted the mirror and shifted. "Find us something on the radio, will ya?"

He turned on the radio. His song was ending, as a Willie Nelson standard started up, "That was your idea, right there."

"It was Baxter's idea, wasn't it? Around the bonfire?"

"The song was your idea."

"You should probably always listen to my ideas, then."

"I should probably at least consider it."

"I'll hold you to that."

He looked over at her. She was entirely focused on driving, leaning forward in her nervousness, going slower than necessary. He said, "Hey, don't be nervous about the truck. You can't hurt this thing, it's a beast."

"Now, I know that to be false. I saw what happened to its predecessor. It got hurt plenty."

"I guess that's what insurance is for."

She didn't relax. He didn't blame her; it was an expensive ride and everyone knew how fond of it he was. But he liked Lily a hell of a lot more.

Whoa, that notion had come right out of the blue.

"You think it's okay, leaving the work crews alone?" she asked.

"They're gonna have to work when I'm not around watchin' 'em, and they'll either do great or drop the ball. Better to see how it goes now than later."

She nodded. "Yeah, but…most of the time one or the other of us would be here," she said.

That wasn't going to be true for much longer, Ethan thought. Still, there was no point bringing it up now. She got all funny every time he mentioned leaving town. But that had always been the plan.

It only took fifteen minutes to get to the hospital in El Paso.

They signed in, got passes to stick onto their shirts, and headed to the hospital room. Lily knew the staff, and she knew her way around, having worked there. She squeezed his hand and said, "I can wait in the waitin' room. We just passed it."

He nodded, but didn't release her hand. He was staring at the door, completely unsure what the hell he was doing there, what he was about to learn. This was his brother, the son of the man who'd murdered his mother. Then again, Ethan was also that man's son. Biologically, at least.

What sort of man was Jeremiah Thorne? Was his soul as black and bloody as their father's, or as torn and tormented as Ethan's own, or somewhere in between?

He tapped the door twice, then opened it and stepped inside.

But the hospital bed was empty.

Lily squeezed his hand, then tugged him with her as she spoke to a passing nurse. "Hey, Sally. We're looking for the patient who was in this room."

He let her pull him around to face the nurse she'd stopped in the hallway. She had red hair, and redder eyeglasses. "Hey, Lily. Great to see you!" She hugged Lily, and he had to let go of her hand then.

After the hug and a speculative but quick look his way, Nurse Sally said, "You mean Mr. Thorne?"

"Yeah, bushy beard, dirty blond hair," Lily said.

"Yeah, that's him. He signed himself out, 'bout a half hour ago."

It felt to Ethan like a blow to the mid-section.

"Was he okay to leave?" Lily asked.

"We'd have kept him overnight," she said, "But he'll prob'ly be okay. Sore, but okay."

Gone, just like that.

"Wait, wait, who took him downstairs?" Lily asked, and when Ethan shot her a questioning look, she said, "Rules are rules. Somebody has to walk discharged patients out, make sure they're safe till they're off the property—"

"So they don't trip over a pebble and sue us," Sally put in. And they shared a look. "I took him down myself," she said. "You know, the guy's not bad-looking under all that hair."

He saw that Lily agreed with that opinion, and a dark cloud tried to move in.

"Did you see who picked him up?" Lily asked.

"Taxi," she said. "I watched him get in, then headed back to the floor."

"Thanks, Sally."

"Any time. You're a little bit famous around here, you know." She was speaking to Lily but her gaze shifted to Ethan, as he was the reason.

"Infamous, maybe," Lily corrected.

Then Sally leaned in and whispered loud enough for him to hear, "He's even better looking in person, isn't he?"

Lily tucked her arm through Ethan's and said, "Way better." Then she walked him down the hall toward the elevators. She didn't take her arm out of his until the doors closed. Then she did, though, and he realized it had been for the other woman's benefit.

Marking her territory, maybe?

For some reason the notion made him stand a little straighter.

"We can call the cab company," Lily said. "We can find out where they took him."

He lowered his head, shook it slowly. "He knew he'd been ID'd," he said. "So he knew I'd be comin'. That's probably why he left." The elevator doors opened, and he stepped out, hands in his jeans pockets, heart somewhere in the vicinity of his boots.

Lily couldn't get a minute alone with Ethan for the next several hours. They'd returned to the cantina and worked all the rest of the day. He'd driven back, readjusting his seat and mirrors to their previous positions with the push of a button.

It had been a long day, but the crews had finally cleared out. The cantina was missing a wall, and industrial plastic had been draped in the opening, inside and out. The parking lot had been jack-hammered to pieces and hauled away in dump trucks. The bare ground underneath looked rough, and so did the building.

You had to break a few eggs, she figured.

Finally alone in the place, she leaned her elbows on the plastic-covered bar top. "How are you holding up, Ethan?"

He looked her way. He'd been standing in the doorway, looking outside, but he turned then. She could tell he was trying for all the world to act normal—as if his life hadn't been turned upside down today. Again. "I'm all right."

"That's not a real answer," she said.

He shrugged and changed the subject. "Sam left us a copy of his purchase order. Likes to get approval as he goes, so there's not an issue later, he says. Mainly it's lumber, nails, insulation, wiring, about forty other things like that. I went over it item by item, but there are a few choices we need to make before he can send it in. Seating, fixtures, flooring."

"The fun stuff," she said. "We can do it now, if you want. Everyone's gone. It's quiet."

He looked at his phone and she thought he was checking the time. "Why don't we do all that after dinner? Chelsea will have it ready and waitin', and I feel like a jerk when I drag my carcass in late after she's worked so hard."

She lowered her eyes.

"I'm sorry. I don't mean to brush you off."

"No, it's fine. It's just everyone's always there. It's hard to get a minute."

He reached out and broke their rule, as if they hadn't shattered it already, by stroking his thumb across her cheek. She braced her spine to keep from shivering.

"Why don't we meet on the front porch after everyone's gone to bed?" he asked.

She let her eyes latch onto his, because there was no point fighting it. She said, "How are you, really, Ethan?"

His brows bent a little, as if he were asking himself the same question. "I don't think I know."

"I can't even imagine," she said. "You find out de Lorean's dead and left you everything including the cantina, your reputation is flayed in the press only to rebound higher than ever, you have another hit song on your hands, then you learn you have a brother, only to have him vanish. And all within the space of a week."

She'd left out the part where they'd made love, because she didn't think it had been as life-altering to him as it had been to her. Especially not in comparison to all the rest.

"I've been thinkin' how he's been here this whole time, watchin' the place. And then that brown paint on the Caddy."

She nodded slowly. "You think he's the one who caused the accident," she said. It wasn't a question.

He lowered his eyes. "Part of me wonders—"

"Whether he's a chip off the old block?" she asked.

Ethan nodded. "Maybe he's a piece of shit like his father. On the other hand, how wrong can it be if he did ram the Caddy? The dead man had just threatened the woman I-I-I..."

"Ay-i-i," she muttered when he trailed off, but she kept it low and her head down.

"...obviously care about."

It was the lamest finish ever. He kept going, though, and she tried to follow along, but the only thing she could hear was the voice inside her mind wondering if he'd been about to say, "the woman I love." It seemed like what predictive text would have filled in.

"Jeremiah...he seemed like a good guy, didn't he?" Ethan asked, taking the focus off them and putting it back onto his newfound sibling. "I don't really trust my judgment here."

She wanted his brother to be a good guy, for Ethan's sake, so she pulled her head out of her heart and tried to focus on helping Ethan find his footing in the storm. "I already told you I thought he was a decent guy. Maria's ex beat the tar outta my brother over tacos, right there." She pointed at the spot.

The tale had been recounted to her in vivid detail...by Maria, not Harrison, who would rather forget it. "He helped."

"Pulled a gun, as I heard it," he said.

"So did half the other customers. And that's not the only time he's jumped in to help. He's busted up bar fights, and shown unruly drunks the door a dozen times, according to Manny."

He nodded slow.

"Do you think he might've come here to watch out for you? Big brother style?"

"I don't know."

"I mean, maybe he wanted to get to know you," she said. "From a distance, for whatever reason. Maybe he has the same twisted-up notions about the sins of the father that you do. Maybe he thinks he's unworthy somehow, by virtue of his DNA."

He acknowledged her words with a shrug, and didn't even try to argue with her or deny what she'd said. They walked side by side to his pickup. The late afternoon sun was blazing its reflection in the chrome bumper, and she had to cover her eyes.

He opened the passenger side for her, and she climbed in.

"I think you should look for him," she said, when he got behind the wheel and started the engine. "I think you should track him down and get answers to these questions. I think it's gonna eat away at you until you do."

He looked at her for an extended moment, given that he was also driving, but he kept the truck between the ditches all the same. "It's not," he said. "I'm disappointed but not devastated."

"Why do you think that is?"

His brows went up. He pushed his hat back farther on his head. "Frankly, Lily, I think it's bein' around you all the time."

She was so surprised she had to clench her jaw to keep it from dropping.

"You have that effect on folks," he said, easing the truck around a bend in the road.

Her surprise shifted ever so slightly toward irritation. "What effect?" If he started acting like she was her mom two-point-oh —him of all people—she was going to jump right out of this truck.

"Soothin', I guess." He sent her a smile that turned instantly to a frown. "Why do you look offended?"

"That's who my mother was. I thought you said you could see me for who I am, and not as her sainted reflection."

"I thought I made that clear when I explained the name of the honky-tonk." He pulled the truck to a stop on the roadside, then he turned, watching her face, and he said, "I want you to consider one thing regardin' your argument—which, if it were true, would piss me off, too. I can't imagine how I'd hold my head up if everyone I knew expected me to live up to Garrett Brand."

"You expect it of yourself," she said.

"I don't—"

"Oh come on. Isn't that the reason you think you can't live in the same town with your own family?"

"That's different."

"How, exactly, is it different?"

"I—" He looked away from her, then looked back, then shook his head. "We're talkin' about *you*. And how wrong you are about the way I see you. Can we just stick to that for now?"

"Fine. Tell me you don't see me as some kind of glowing being, beaming light and love wherever she goes."

He turned fully in his seat, facing her. His eyes moved over her face. He opened his mouth to speak and then he closed it again. And then he folded her into his arms and kissed her.

She was surprised, and then she melted. All her anger just

pooled at her feet, and her body went soft against his. She held on tight, and the idea of how upset Chelsea tended to get when folks were late for dinner faded away so fast she couldn't find it. A few minutes in, he lifted his head.

"I *do* see you beamin' light everywhere you go, Lily Ellen."

Why'd he have to ruin it? She turned face-front and crossed her arms over her chest with a huff, but he was still talking.

"I don't think you could turn it off, even if you tried. It's who you are, and you need to keep one thing in mind if you're fixin' to deny it again."

She turned to face him so he could see her roll her eyes. "What's that?"

"I never met your mamma."

He could've sprouted antlers and surprised her less. This had not occurred to her.

It was impossible for Ethan to judge her based on her mom's sheer perfection. He'd never had the chance to know the first and best Lily.

Otherwise, he'd see how much she paled by comparison.

"You're an amazin' woman, all on your own." His voice was soft and low, a deep whisper that stroked her nerve endings in paths of fire.

And I'm in love with you, she thought. *Say it. Say it!*

He didn't, though. He faced front, put the truck into gear and resumed driving.

They didn't talk again. Lily didn't want to talk, so she turned on the radio to fill the silence and tried turning over and over in her mind what Ethan had said.

Linda Ronstadt's cover of "Desperado" came on.

The radio had a sense of irony, didn't it?

CHAPTER FOURTEEN

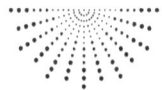

That evening, Chelsea served a thick stew in heavy pottery bowls, with homemade bread for dipping. It was just the five of them; Lily, Hyram, Ethan, and the couple who'd adopted and raised him, whom he still called Uncle and Aunt rather than Mom and Dad.

"This is delicious, Chelsea," Hyram said. "This better than mine. What's your secret?"

"My secret is that Garrett makes the stew," she said.

"And my secret," Garrett said, "is soy sauce, two tablespoons."

"I make him use the reduced sodium kind." Chelsea glanced her husband's way with a smile and their eyes met. The love between them kind of lit up the room.

Lily sighed and glanced at Ethan. He seemed quiet and deep in thought. He caught her looking, so she shifted her focus lower, and it fell on the crockery bowl in front of her. "I agree the stew is phenomenal, but it's these bowls I can't get over," she said. "I've never seen any like them."

"Right?" Chelsea asked. "A local artist makes them. I'll take you to her shop sometime."

"I'd love that."

There came the sound of a vehicle, and then the screen door creaked, and seconds later Willow was joining them in the dining room.

"I'll get another bowl," Chelsea said, starting to get up.

Will held up a hand, "No, it's fine, you don't need to—wait, is that Uncle Garrett's stew?"

Chelsea grinned and went to the kitchen, returning with another heavy ceramic bowl, gray on the bottom half, blue on the top, little handles on either side, brimming with stew, still steaming hot.

Willow accepted it and chose the seat next to Ethan, which was across from Lily. She said, "So I was trying to track down Jeremiah Thorne," she began.

"Why?" Ethan asked. "He didn't do anything illegal. Trespassin', I guess, but I think gettin' hit by a truck was prob'ly punishment enough, don't you?"

She shrugged. "His car is a 1982 Buick Electra. Color's listed as brown. Dark Brown Firemist, to be exact. I looked it up. It was a premium color, cost extra."

Lily and Ethan exchanged a quick look, and Lily was sure Willow noticed it before she went on. "I'm checking it against the brown paint sample we scraped off that wrecked Caddy."

Ethan stopped with his spoon halfway to his mouth and looked across at his cousin. "Why would you do that, Will? Why would you go lookin' to cause trouble for my brother?"

She took a small, soft breath through parted lips.

Garrett said, "She's doin' her job, Bubba."

"Ethan," he said. "And no, she's not." He faced Willow again. "Jeremiah wasn't implicated in any crime, was he? He wasn't a suspect. You're digging into him just because he's my brother. Is that even legal?"

"You...I..." She shoved her bowl of stew away and stood up. "I thought you'd want to know who he is. Whether he's a decent guy or a piece of shit like your father."

Ethan shot to his feet too. "Don't fuckin' call him my father!"

Garrett stood up slower and sent his quelling look at them both until they sat back down. Then he did, too.

"Willow was trying to help," Chelsea said. And then to Willow, "You should've talked to him first."

"Right, even if he killed a guy?"

Garrett got up and left the room. When he came back, he had a folder, which he set beside Ethan on the dining room table. "If he killed the guy, he killed a killer who'd just threatened one of our own."

Ethan reached for the folder, but Garrett put a hand over his. "Not at the table, Son. I can nutshell it for you. Angus Silver was the muscle for his older brother's fentanyl trade in Texas and New Mexico. Got paid to rough up the dealers who got greedy. But he was sloppy, messed up so many times, big brother Nathan sent him to El Paso to run his own small time protection racket. He likes hurting people."

"What people?" Ethan asked.

"People who cross him. Most often it's the loved ones of people who cross him, usually women. There've been murders, disappearances. There's photos in that there folder, and they aren't pretty." He lowered his head, then returned to his own seat. "Seven arrests, but he's only gone to trial twice and never convicted."

"Why not?" Ethan asked.

"Witnesses change their stories. Evidence disappears. Somebody forgets to cross a T or dot an I or check their brake lines before a road trip. He's slippery. Or he was."

"So when he threatened me..." Lily whispered.

"He wasn't kidding," Willow said. She blinked and lowered her head.

Garrett said, "Now you're getting it. I've been worried about repercussions from the older brother, Nathan Silver, so I been lookin' into things off the books. I went out to pay Nathan a visit. *Condolences on your brother dying in my county, we've ruled it an accident, call me if you have any questions,* you know the drill. Silver said his brother's driver, Terrence Clay, had told him the same story he told us. Said he was so shaken up he'd asked for time off and was currently visiting family in Florida. I asked if he'd heard from Clay since he left, and he said no and asked if I had. I got the feelin' he actually had no idea where the kid was."

Ethan sighed. "I spoke with him for a few seconds, before Angus sped off. Advised him to get away from that crew or he'd end up dead or in prison."

"Maybe he listened after that wreck," Willow said. "So are we lookin' for him?"

"Doesn't seem necessary," Garrett replied. "Nathan didn't seem suspicious about the accident. My plan was to close the case and put his mind at ease."

Willow shook her head hard and smacked the table. "Well, you might want to clue somebody into your master plan, Uncle Garrett. I already sent the sample out for comparison."

Garrett nodded. "It's good police work, I'll give you that. When, uh, did you send it?"

"This morning. Dropped it into the mailbox in front of the station before I came here."

"Huh," Garrett said.

Willow sighed and reached for her stew bowl, and the meal resumed under a cloud.

When Willow left, looking miserable, Ethan noticed Lily follow. The two were on the front porch for another fifteen minutes, and he imagined Lily was doing that thing she did. She had a way of making a person feel better just by being around them. She didn't like hearing it, but it was the truth.

He helped with the cleanup while his cousin and Lily talked, and then he headed up to his room so he could argue with himself in private. He'd reached the end of his ability to deny Lily whatever she asked of him, even if it was kids and a dog and a white picket fence. But she'd decided to stop trying.

His honest and immediately reaction had been crushing disappointment and anger with himself for waiting too long and missing his chance. And now, with Jeremiah maybe tangled up in a murder, maybe on the run...

Killing was wrong. But this killing might've saved Lily's life. How could he judge Jeremiah for that, if he'd even done it? Hell, Ethan might've done it himself if he'd had all the information.

He stopped pacing for a moment when that thought crossed his mind, because it seemed like one he hadn't had before—the notion that he could do violence in Lily's defense. That was the way he felt about his family. She'd become every bit as important to him as they were.

And yet he'd just been reminded how toxic his true bloodline was. Willow wouldn't have sent that sample if Jeremiah had been anyone else—anyone besides a son of de Lorean. That hurt, but it was logical. You can't dip good water from a poisoned well.

Dammit, Lily deserved better. He was going to let her fall in love with him and then leave her behind in the end, and he knew it. But he was out of goodness, out of nobility, out of ideals, and he didn't think he could turn away from that look in her eyes one more time. Not now that they'd been together once. Not now that he knew what he was missing.

He glanced at the clock on his nightstand. Another hour, and he'd head down to meet her on the front porch. To choose freaking light fixtures. And he was going to be with her again, if she was still willing. He wouldn't make promises, he wouldn't talk about the future, he'd make sure she understood that he had nothing to offer her beyond the moment.

He paced. The time dragged. He brushed his teeth. His beard was coming in, but he thought she liked the extra shadow on his face in the afternoon. A couple of times, she'd run her hands over his bristly cheeks in a way that made him think so.

He took out the guitar, sat on the bed and tried to work on a song he'd started, but he wasn't feeling it. His emotions were tangled and knotted and he had no idea how to sort them out.

His phone rang and he checked. Angelo Barrone, his manager. It occurred to him how good it was not to feel dread when he saw the caller ID. Every time Ang called lately, it had been with good news. Maybe he'd have something else to celebrate with Lily tonight.

Lily donned a long sweater with deep pockets in deference to the nighttime chill, over jeans and her favorite bedroom slippers. Grabbing her iPad, she left her bedroom, pulled the door closed without making a sound, and tiptoed to the stairway. She didn't want the Elder-Brands getting ideas.

Although, they already knew there was *something* going on between her and Ethan. The whole clan knew.

She sighed, crossing the living room floor to the front door. It was open, with just the screen door closed. The soft strum of Ethan's guitar wafted through, and she smiled at the sound till he hit a bad chord and swore under his breath.

She lowered her head and pushed the screen door open. It creaked its special creak that had etched itself into her brain with all the time she'd spent at the ranch. That sound said, "Welcome home. You're among family here." She hoped Garrett never got around to oiling the hinge and taking the ranch house's voice away.

She stepped out and closed both doors behind her, so she and Ethan wouldn't wake anyone with their voices.

The strumming stopped and Ethan got up off the porch swing and leaned his guitar against the railing.

"I didn't know if we were still on for this," she said, "with everything else." She only looked at him for a second, then crossed the porch to lean on the railing, arms straight, eyes on the layers of color in the sky. Night had fallen. The sky was turning from purple to blue to indigo, meeting the rolling meadows and trees. A full moon was just beginning to crest the distant horizon. The night air smelled of horses, dry Texas ground, and the yellow roses blooming nearby. "Figured I'd enjoy coming out, either way."

He came to stand beside her, but he didn't say anything, and when she turned to search his face, he didn't return her gaze. He looked out at the view, like she'd been doing. But she didn't think he was really seeing it.

"Is everything…okay?" she asked.

He shook his head, still not looking at her.

She pressed a palm to his cheek to turn him her way, then she searched his eyes, and thought they might have been moist. Over a brother he'd never known he had?

"I'm so sorry, Ethan. It's no wonder if you're messed up."

He took a deep breath, then he said, "I sent you the options we have to go over." He nodded toward the iPad, lying atop the porch rail.

Lily frowned. "Don't you think we should talk first?"

He shook his head slightly. "About what? My half-brother is apparently a killer. Runs in the family. If I wasn't expectin' that, I should've been. Blood will tell, isn't that what they say?"

"It didn't in you." His attitude surprised her and ticked her off a little bit. He was acting almost flippant. Like he was working really hard not to give a single damn about his brother, what he was or wasn't, what he'd done or hadn't, why he'd run away when Ethan had come to meet him.

"I'm not a lawbreaker, it's true. Raised by a lawman, so that stands to reason. But I'm still an asshole." He finally met her eyes, gazed into them, and then shook his head sadly.

"I don't know what you're talking about, Ethan. You're a good man."

He sighed. Then, "Why don't you open the file I sent, and let's make some choices?" He pushed off the railing, meeting her eyes only briefly, flashing a fake-as-hell smile, then returning to his spot on the porch swing, more distant than he'd been since they'd made love on the riverbank.

He had a glass of something on the little table next to the swing. Whiskey, maybe. She rarely saw him drink anything other than beer, and she'd never seen him drunk or even tipsy.

His voice was a little gravelly, but if he didn't want to share his feelings, she supposed she couldn't make him. She reached for her iPad, went to sit beside him on the swing. A few taps and there were four different table options on her screen. Each type had multiple color options.

Okay fine, business it was. "We haven't talked about color scheme," she said. "But since our tacos will be world famous, and in honor of Manny, and us being so close to the border, I was thinking we should keep the green, white, and red."

He nodded. "I was thinkin' the same."

"The tables and chairs we took out of there and stored are so old you can't match them anymore. Besides, they're kind of..." She made a face.

He said, "Yeah," and slid closer, leaning over her to start tapping options. "Round or square?"

"Square," she said. "Round is cozier, but square is neater, and we need to keep it organized for maximum seating."

He ticked the X on all the round tables.

"Wood or metal?"

"Wood holds smells. What do you think of that shiny silver one with the ceramic tiles?"

Ethan tapped a set to make it larger. The table had a stainless-steel frame and a white ceramic-tiled surface. The matching chair had a white vinyl cushion. "I don't know if tacos go with white," he said.

"For sure." She leaned even closer to tap the color options tab, and a whole rainbow dropped down. "Has to be red or green," she said. She tapped each color to see how it looked.

He said, "Why not both? We can put red inside and green outside or even mix 'em up."

"Oh, or group them in color blocks to mark the sections for wait staff!" she said, snapping her fingers. "I'm a little worried about breakage though, with ceramic."

He reached across and tapped her screen, opening the detailed notes on the table. "Says here's they're installed with cushioning under the tiles," he said, "It reduces breakage risk, and they come with a lifetime warranty. A tile breaks, they'll replace it." He glanced at her face. "This is your favorite, set, isn't it?"

She nodded, scrolling to the next section of the document, which displayed a dozen light fixtures. "Especially if we go with these." She pulled the iPad her way and tapped and tapped.

After the light fixtures, they looked at the second cooler options for the kitchen and a smaller secondary cooking surface for special orders.

"I think we should let Hyram pick those," Ethan said.

"Oh my gosh, he'll *love* that!" She looked at him smiling. He'd become lighter the minute they'd focused on plans for the cantina. "Good then, I think that's it."

His eyes were on her face, and they turned serious. A hole bigger than the Gulf of Mexico opened up in her heart. Hell, he was going to end it between them once and for all, wasn't he?

She set the iPad aside, took a breath, closed her eyes. "Whatever it is, just say it."

She felt his palm on her cheek and opened her eyes again.

He held her gaze firmly and said, "I have to leave."

The heartbreak in her eyes was plain as day, even though her expression didn't change on the surface. It was subtle, and yet as clear as a shout. "Leave? *Now?*"

He nodded. "Ang wants me out gigging to support the single. Big venues. And he's flogging me for the next album."

"Is he aware you can't do both of those things at the same time?"

"I made him aware of it. But I had to admit I'm not writing a damn thing. Or haven't been, till recently. So he's found some promising freelance songwriters with pieces he wants me to try out."

"But you wrote all the songs on your first album. People will expect—"

"I know. But I had to weigh that against the power of strikin' while the iron's hot." Ethan knew he was full of shit, of course. He didn't want to leave; he *had* to leave. That call had come in the nick of time to prevent him from driving a wedge into his family, if it wasn't already too late. "The new single will stay on the charts for a couple of months, but after that, I need to have something ready to go. At least another single. A new one."

"Oh."

The word was as heavy as if it had been coated in lead before she'd spoken it. And then, her head still lowered so he couldn't see her eyes, she asked, "What about the honky-tonk?"

"I'm gonna have to ask you to manage the renovations without me."

"But—"

"I know you can do it, Lily."

She raised her head slowly. "I have no doubt I can do it. But you…I mean, we…" She got up onto her feet and walked a few steps away from him. Without turning to face him she said, "What about us? You drop this news on me like nothing has happened between us, but it has, and you can't just pretend…"

Her voice had grown tighter, and he thought she didn't leave the sentence unfinished on purpose. He moved to stand behind her and slid his hands over her shoulders. "I'm not pretendin'. I just need…" What did he need? Say something, he thought. He needed to get away from her before he broke her heart and violated the bonds of his family. It had been easier before, when he only saw her on holidays, and only for a couple of days at a time. He could keep his hands off her for a couple of days at a time.

But now that they'd…this was unbearable. And just when he'd decided to give up, be with her and damn the consequences, his manager had given him a way out.

He thought all those things in the space of a heartbeat. Aloud he only said, "I need to do this. That's all."

"Why are you so sure being with me would end so bad it would tear up your family, Ethan? What is it about me that makes you—"

"Nothin'! Nothin' about you." He spun her around and immediately knew what a huge mistake it was, because now he was face-to-face with her, falling into her huge blue eyes, right through the tears shimmering on their surface. "But I know it couldn't work with us, not for long. I'm not…"

"Not what? Don't stop, Ethan, please. That's the longest sentence you've said to me since…ever. You're not what?"

He lowered his head. "I'm not good enough for you. And believe me, Lily Ellen, I wish the hell I was." He kissed her then, because he couldn't help himself, and the fact that he couldn't help himself solidified his decision.

She softened in his arms, melting against him, kissing him back, and that was his signal to let go. He gazed into her eyes only briefly when they flicked open. "I'm real sorry I'm hurtin' you like this, Lily Ellen. But just think how much worse it would'a been later." Then he turned and walked into the house, straight up the stairs into his bedroom, and closed the door.

He hadn't even taken his guitar.

Lily had dropped Ethan's abandoned guitar on the sofa on her way inside. Then she'd stopped by Chelsea's liquor cabinet and taken a bottle of wine and a glass to her room. She drank most of it before crying herself to sleep.

So when she opened her eyes to the irritating and persistent birdsong right outside her open bedroom window, the room was blurry and her mouth felt like swamp muck. Her head ached. Her eyes were all sticky.

Smacking her lips repeatedly and grimacing at the bad taste in her mouth, she flung back the covers and slid to her feet, but as soon as her head was upright, the room began spinning. She grabbed onto the bedpost to keep from falling over. Catching sight of the near-empty wine bottle, she groaned.

Dragging herself to her feet, she shuffled to the bathroom and stood beneath a cool shower to try to rinse the alcohol from her brain. Eventually, she got out and brushed her teeth, gagged on the toothbrush, dragged a comb through her hair, pulled it into a ponytail, and finally, put on her most comfortable pair of sweats and a baggy tee with a sports bra, though she'd have preferred no bra at all. Everything that touched her skin hurt.

Stupid man, making her feel so miserable. Well, now that

she'd had time to think, she had an earful for him. Just wait until she saw him this morning. She pulled on her thickest, softest socks. As she scuffed out of the room and down the hall, she passed Ethan's bedroom.

The door was open. The bed was made.

She kept going down the stairs. He'd taken his guitar off the sofa, so he must've been up before her. The smell of coffee beckoned so strongly that it overcame the nerves rioting in her stomach at the thought of seeing him at the breakfast table.

Only, she didn't. Nobody was at the table, and it had been cleared, except for some flowers in the middle—bluebonnets and black-eyed Susans—and a fat brown accordion file. How late had she slept?

Chelsea came in from the kitchen, two big mugs in her hands. "Heard you coming down the stairs," she said, then saw Lily's face and blinked. "My goodness."

"I owe you a bottle of wine," she said by way of explanation.

"Then you need this more than I realized." She put a mug in front of Lily, then took a seat.

Lily sank into the chair, not entirely on purpose. "Ethan's leaving."

Chelsea reached across the table to cover her hand with one of her own. "He's already left, hon."

"What?" Lily looked up fast, blurting the word in a knee-jerk reaction, despite that she'd heard Chelsea perfectly well.

"He said he had to get an early start. He left that for you." She nodded at the thick folder. "Said to tell you he'd be in touch."

"Huh." She couldn't meet Chelsea's eyes. This was too much, and she was going to burst into tears in front of her at any moment.

"Listen to me, Lily. I'm gonna talk to you like I would if you were my own daughter." Chelsea clasped her hand tighter. "This is not over. He's scared. I can see that. I think this has more to do with his own issues about who he is and who his father was, and my sister's death, and now this brother coming out of the woodwork."

"He doesn't see me," she said.

"How could anybody not see you, Lily? You beam."

She didn't, though. Why did everyone keep saying that?

She took a deep, nasal breath. "He says he's not good enough for me. Thinks I'm some kind of angel."

"More that he thinks of himself as some kind of monster," Chelsea said. "But that's not fatal. Neither of those things is. You just have to show him the difference."

She shook her head slowly. "Honestly, Chelsea, I think you were right to begin with. I don't want a man I have to work this hard for." She sipped her coffee, sipped it again. Her spine straightened a little. Then she said, "Can I get a to-go cup?"

"Sure. Where you going?"

"The cantina. Apparently I'm the one running things while he's singing to horny honky-tonk honeys."

"He only has eyes for you, Lily. You want some breakfast first?" Chelsea asked.

"I'm good."

"I made blueberry muffins."

"I could take one to go."

Chelsea went to get a muffin. Lily opened the folder and looked inside. On the very front was a letter from Ethan. She glanced at the kitchen, where Chelsea was warming her bun in the microwave. Ther was time, so pulled out the single sheet of paper, written in Ethan's messy scrawl.

> *Hey, Lil,*
>
> *You're probably mad as hell at me right now, and I don't blame you. But I want you to set all that aside and consider this offer. For all you'll be doing now that I have to go, I ought to double your salary. But I didn't take out a big enough loan to do that. So I'm*

offering something else instead. Half-ownership. You're doin' all the work anyway. Think about it.

I'll be home for the grand opening. We can do up the paper-work then, if you agree. Everything you need to run things in the meantime is in this folder.

Do whatever you want with the remodel. I've loved every idea you've had, so cut loose. I can't wait to see it.

Ethan

Nothing personal. Nothing about his feelings, or that he'd miss her. Nothing to give her any modicum of hope whatsoever. God, why did she even care?

The dam broke, and her tears spilled.

Chelsea came in from the kitchen with the bun in a plastic container in one hand, and a bottle of ibuprofen in the other, but she set them aside and wrapped Lily in her arms. "Oh hon!"

Lily sniffled and wiped her wet cheeks. "Sorry," she said, then she nodded. "He left me that."

Chelsea looked at the note and when Lily nodded, she picked it up and read it quickly. And then, very slowly, a smile spread over her face. "Don't you see what this is, Lily?"

"I don't know." She sniffled harder. "Guilt, maybe?"

"No." She slid the letter back into the folder. "He can't let go of you. He tells you he's leaving, that you can't be together, and then he immediately finds another way to tie himself to you."

Lily blinked, lifting her head to meet Chelsea's eyes, which immediately went soft and sympathetic.

Chelsea handed her a paper napkin. "He probably realized how angry you'd be at him walking away like this and got scared you'd tell him to take this job and…you know. So this is his solution. He can't let go of you. He probably doesn't even see it himself. Yet."

Lily took the napkins and wiped her tears. "You think that's what it is? He's trying to hold onto me?"

"I'm a psychologist," she said. "And I think it's blindingly obvious."

Lily considered that, and that he was naming the place after her. Well, her and her mom, but her really. That didn't seem like the act of a guy who didn't want to be with her.

She couldn't help the sigh that escaped her, or the way her eyes fell closed. "I really, *really* don't want to get my hopes up again," she said.

"Focus on the cantina, then," Chelsea said. "I kind of think you've found your calling, there. Your father does, too."

"You guys talk about me, do you?"

"Of course we do. We chat about our kids while cooking together whenever he's here." Chelsea dropped the ibuprofen and the plastic container into the gaping top of Lily's shoulder bag and leaned in to kiss her cheek. "Have a great day, Lily." And then Chelsea's phone buzzed from where she'd left it lying on the table.

"You, too," Lily said, and started to turn, but then Chelsea grabbed her forearm.

"Hold on, hold on." She was staring in alarm at her phone, which she then showed to Lily.

> Garrett: Minor fender bender outside the station —all good. I'm fine.

Lily's brows shot up. "He had an accident?"

Chelsea tapped his face on her screen and put the phone on speaker as it rang on the other end.

Garrett picked up with the words, "Hello, hon. I told you I was fine."

"I'll be the judge of that."

"Well, hold up a second then."

Ellipse dots did their teasing dance and were then followed by a seconds-long video of Garrett with his arms out at his sides, turning in a full circle, to show himself unscathed while someone else apparently held his phone.

Lily laughed softly.

Chelsea rolled her eyes. "What happened?"

"Ah, I had a brain fart. Backed right into the mailbox outside the station."

"The mailbox?" Chelsea looked at Lily, frowning.

"Yeah. Before the morning pick-up, too. Mail everywhere. I gathered it up, though. Hope nothin' got lost. Gotta go. Love you, babe."

"You hope nothing got lost," Chelsea repeated.

"Nothin' to worry about," Garrett went on. "Back bumper's scraped up, is all. I'll be home for lunch, and I'm buyin', okay?"

"Okay. Love you." She hung up. Then she smiled and met Lily's eyes. "Sorry to hold you up, like that. Scared the crap outta me for a minute."

"I'm glad he's okay. Are you sure you are? Accidents are scary."

"Oh, I'm not sure that was an accident," Chelsea said. "And I'm pretty sure something *did* get lost in all the spilled mail."

And the light dawned. "Willow's paint sample?"

Chelsea shrugged, eyebrows high, but yeah, that was clearly what she thought.

"Go on, now get busy. You have a lot on your plate."

CHAPTER FIFTEEN

"This ain't no honky-tonk," Ethan said when Ang finally came in through the dressing room door with his name on it. Sure, it was just printed on a piece of paper in a frame where you slid in a fresh sheet with every new performer, but he'd never had his name on a dressing room door before in *any* form. So far this trip, it had been on dang near all of 'em, and every venue a little bigger than the one before. But none had been what this one was. "This a full-blown concert hall, Ang."

"Not a very big one, though," Angelo said. Then he waggled a finger. "Not *yet*." He closed the dressing room door behind him and took a look around inside, nodding in approval.

"Looks big to me," Ethan said.

"Meh, three-thousand, give or take. You ready? They sent me to tell you two minutes, and it's already been one."

"Three *thousand*?"

Someone knocked, then a voice called, "Ready for you on stage, Mr. Brand. Sold-out crowd."

Ang pulled out his phone tapped a button, and said, "Note to self. Three-k sold out. Upsize the venues."

"I need a minute," Ethan said.

Ang frowned at him, then shrugged and opened the door, revealing an eager-looking young man standing on the other side.

"He needs a minute," Ang said, and closed the door while the kid was going, "What? What?" and trying to look around him at Ethan.

Ethan sat on a chair that was too small in front of a mirror that was too big and reached for his phone.

It played a guitar riff just as he put his hand on it and Lily's pretty face lit up the screen. His smile was so wide, he thought she could probably hear it. "I was just gonna call you," he said by way of greeting.

"Aren't you about to go on?" she asked. "Don't let me make you late. I just wanted to say 'break a leg.'"

"Thanks. I have a minute." He slid a look at Ang, and Ang read it perfectly, held up two palms, and exited the room. Ethan returned to his call. "Lil, this is...it's not a bar. It's a concert hall."

"I know."

"How?"

"You sent me your itinerary. I looked it up. It has three-thousand forty-five seats."

"They said it's sold out."

"Oh, Ethan that's wonderful!"

"My knees are knockin'."

She laughed softly and the sound of it made him laugh too. Then she said, "Nobody's gonna see that, though. They're gonna see a big, strong, broad-shouldered, handsome-as-hell cowboy with more confidence than he could hold in a ten-gallon hat."

"I wish you were here," he said, and then he couldn't believe he'd said it. It had just come out. They hadn't talked. He'd left her. And they hadn't *really* talked.

He was an idiot. What if he lost her? What if she decided he wasn't worth all the trouble?

"I'd be there if I could," she said.

"How's Two Lilies goin'?"

"Great. I even have a surprise for you in progress. But you're late to the stage," she said. "Get out there and do your job. We can talk more later, okay?"

He nodded. "Yeah. Okay."

"You've got this, Ethan. You're amazing, you know."

She disconnected before he could say anything back.

Ethan heaved a heavy sigh, set his phone down, and picked up his guitar. When he opened the door, Angelo was standing in front of it, fists on his hips in a "none shall pass" stance. The young man on the other side of Ang had peach-fuzz whiskers in uneven patches his mom probably nagged him to shave.

The kid said, "Phew." Didn't make the sound, actually said the word, "Phew. Let's go." Then he turned and led the way to the stage, and a disembodied voice said, "Ladies and gentlemen, Ethan Brand."

He walked out there to the loudest applause he'd ever received. He couldn't even hear his bootsteps cross the stage to the mic. He looked out into the spotlight's glare, gave a wave, and said, "Thanks, friends. I 'preciate that." And then he didn't know what else to do, so he just started playing.

As soon as his pick crossed the strings, he fell into the music and left his nerves behind.

Everybody in the Brand clan had gone out to one or more of Ethan's shows. He left their names with the crew at every venue. Hers, too, and she hoped he understood why she couldn't get away. If he didn't already, he sure would when he got home, because the Two Lilies Honky-Tonk was going to be amazing.

Lily walked through the place after nearly everyone else had gone home. It was her favorite part of the day, walking through alone, admiring the progress. Even if she wasn't quite alone tonight.

The walls were freshly painted in color blocks of green, white, and red. Their wall sockets naked, wires sprouting from some. The wide doorway into the addition was untrimmed, but the color was in place. She could hardly wait to apply the border she had planned. She would stencil it herself, a line from one of Ethan's song's, she just hadn't decided which one.

Everyone had gone except Willow, who'd been sticking to her like glue ever since Ethan had left. Everyone got nervous when they'd learned the dead man's driver had returned from wherever he'd been, and was once again working for the Silvers —big brother Nathan this time. But they hadn't heard a word from the fentanyl king. His younger brother's death had been ruled an accident, and apparently the young driver hadn't told him any different.

Willow was sitting at the bar with a long-neck bottle of beer, not in uniform, so not on duty. Her hair was loose and long, and every contractor and employee in and out of there was halfway in love with her. She seemed genuinely oblivious to it, though.

As Lily recalled it, even Gringo used to lift his head a little when Willow walked past his table, his sombrero tilting up enough to expose his usually hidden eyes.

She walked into the addition, which had slabside walls she and Ethan had picked out over a phone call one night. She called him as often as she could think of a reason. And since they were in business together, reasons abounded. She even called him when a text would've done. She felt his absence as profoundly as a black hole where her heart should be. Not just emptiness, but a vacuum.

They never talked about anything, though. Well, they talked about everything, but nothing real. Nothing deep. Nothing about what the heck they were to each other.

"One more week," she whispered. It echoed in the vast emptiness of the new space. The stage was up but covered in tarps to protect it. She'd seen it, though. Gleaming wood surface, plugs and outlets, lights hidden within the flooring. The wiring was still a mad tangle at the back of the stage, "One more week."

"Think it'll be ready?" Willow had come in, too. She was standing in the archway, still holding that beer.

"There's not that much left, really. I...I did something, Will, and I'm dying to show somebody, but I need a vow of secrecy."

"Secrecy from my cousin?"

"I know, family first, but—"

"I'm in. Tell!"

Lily took Willow by the hand and quick-stepped back through the dining room, past the stairs, then around the bar and into the kitchen.

"I already saw the new cooler," Willow said.

"Not that." Lily opened the basement door, flipped on the light switch and led the way down. "Leave your beer."

She heard the tap of the bottle meeting a nearby countertop, then Willow came behind her. At the bottom of the stairs there was the same basement as before, but it had a section walled off, with another door in its center.

"This wasn't here before, was it?" Willow said. "How the hell have you had a crew down here without me knowin' it?"

"Why would you notice a crew moving in and out of the kitchen?" Lily shrugged. "Besides, your focus has been on watching me."

Willow shrugged. "Ethan asked me to. He'd be here doin' it himself if you'd have let me tell him that driver was back in the picture."

"The driver hasn't talked. Maybe he's afraid he'll be blamed."

"If he wasn't fixin' to talk, he wouldn't've come back," Willow said.

"If he'd talked, the brother would be here lookin' for that brown Buick. But he hasn't so much as shown his face in this town."

"That we know of."

"You worry too much, Will. But I sure do appreciate you lookin' out for me. And keepin' the driver's return to yourself. Ethan's on a roll. He doesn't need anything tripping him up in the middle of it." She took a deep breath. "You ready?"

"Ready, but I might've already guessed."

Lily opened the door. A light came on when she did, and they stepped into a recording studio. The walls were lined in gray soundproof padding. There were microphone stands suspended from the ceiling, and one wall had a wide pane of glass with the control booth behind it, just no controls yet.

"Holy...this is a recording studio."

Lily nodded fast.

"And Ethan doesn't know about it?"

"Only the crew knows about it. And Samwell Burdick, the general contractor. He hooked me up with this company that does them exclusively and came with great references from some big names. Isn't it great?"

"Wow."

"I was looking into what studios with comparable setups charge for time, and it's a lot," Lily said. She'd been dying to share this plan with someone. "So not only can Ethan use it when he's in town, but it can be an extra revenue stream when he's not. And a perk for our guest performers!"

Willow's brows furrowed. "You *are* good at this."

"I kind of am, aren't I?"

"Not 'kind of." She looked around the room, nodding. "This is amazing. This is gonna floor him."

"I hope so. I did financial cartwheels to make room for it in the budget."

"You did great. Not that I'd know if you didn't, but it sure looks good to me."

"I hope so." They went back out and headed upstairs. "I've been second-guessing it ever since they started work," Lily said.

"Why? What could possibly be the downside?"

They emerged into the kitchen. Lily snapped off the stairway light and closed the basement door. "It might come off like...like I'm trying to keep him here. Like, 'what's your excuse now?' you know?"

Willow listened, nodded, and picked up her beer from where she'd left it on the counter. After a long pull, she said, "I don't think he'll see it that way. I think he'll see it for what it is. A gift from someone who cares. I kinda want you to have your upstairs bathroom, too, though. That's what you gave up for it, isn't it?"

Lily didn't confirm or deny. But that was exactly what she'd done.

They went outside and Lily locked up behind them just as a box truck pulled onto the strip of pavement they'd left alongside the building. By the end of tomorrow, it would extend around back to the bigger parking lot. The flagstone patio was taking shape in the front.

"What's this now?" Lily asked.

The guy did not get out of his truck. Just backed in and sat there, so she went over and tapped his door. It opened, and the driver held up one finger as he tapped his phone. "One second, ma'am, I have to notify the sender before I deliver the package. It's in my notes."

"Ooookay." She frowned at Willow, but then her phone rang. "Ethan?"

"Is it there? Delivery guy just texted he was in the driveway."

"Well, yes, I guess it's here then. What is it?"

"The sign. I got the sign."

"You got the—"

"I'd've consulted you but I wanted it to be a surprise. And then I thought you might hate it, and I've been second-guessing myself ever since I put in the order."

"Oh, for cryin' out loud," Willow said, rolling her eyes.

The driver opened the back, lowered a ramp, and rolled out a dolly holding a well-wrapped rectangle as tall he was. "Where you want it?"

"Inside, for now," Lily said.

He rolled it right up to the big double doors. Lily handed her phone to Willow so she could unlock it. The driver rolled the package inside. She signed for it, then turned. "Will?"

Willow had walked a few steps away with her phone, but she came back and helped her tear off the brown paper.

The sign was a large, old fashioned-looking metal one, with two perfect lilies painted on it. They stood back-to-back, one white with a thin red stripe, and the other red, with a thin white stripe.

"Lily Ellen?" Ethan said from the phone.

Willow handed it to her and she brought it to her ear, as it was no longer on speaker. Willow must've been speaking to him when she'd walked away. "I'm here."

"Look close," he said.

She did, noticing in the contrasting-colored swirls of the petals, there were initials. LM in red, on the white rose. Her mother's initials. Her own initials, LE were in white on the red lily.

"Two *different* lilies," Ethan said. "But they both have some of the other inside 'em."

She had tears in her eyes, so she turned away from Willow, who took the hint, and went back outside to wait for her. "It's beautiful, Ethan. Thank you."

"You're not mad? Soon as I ordered it, I knew I should've consulted you on the design."

"I'm not mad. I love it."

"Good. How are things?"

"Busy and stressful and sometimes frustrating."

He waited a moment, then added, "But good?"

"Ask me on opening night."

"I'm sorry I'm not there helpin' you."

"And I'm sorry I haven't been in the crowd supporting you," she said. "Everyone's been to a show but me."

"Like you've had a free minute, much less a whole night."

"We watched your interview on Nashville Today. You were perfect."

"I felt like my voice was shakin' the whole time."

"It must've been shaking on the inside, because you came across steady and clear."

"I hope so."

"When are you…" *Coming home* danced on the tip of her tongue, but she bit it back as it would've sounded needy. "…heading back?"

"The final interview is Friday afternoon."

"That's opening night!" She said it too fast and knew it.

"I know. I know, I'm sorry. But I'll be there on time, promise. I'm performing. How can I *not* be there?"

She nodded, then said, "Okay."

"I gotta run, I'm on in a minute."

"Stay on pitch," she said. "See you soon." Not soon enough, though. She missed him like she'd miss a limb. And she was tired as hell of waiting for a real conversation with him.

"It's perfect," Lily whispered.

Tomorrow was opening night. Tomorrow Ethan would be home. "I hope Ethan thinks so, too."

"How could he not?" Drew asked. "It's amazin'. And that

letterin' over the doorway!" She pointed at it, singin' the line from "Home." "My treasure's at the rainbow's bend, where I began and where I'll end."

"She stenciled it herself, you know," Willow said. "I helped."

Maria widened her eyes. "I didn't know you were so artistic, Lil."

"I'm not. Willow's help was mostly going behind me, touching up my goofs."

They all laughed. They were in the original section and had come in from the new main entrance around the right side, so they'd already walked through the addition, seen the stage and dance floor, and the lighting. The front was lined with glass, portions of which could slide open wide. They'd also added retracting wooden walls to the outside. They could be locked in place from inside or outside in case of bad weather. They were closed as girls moved past them and into the original part of the cantina.

Lily was keenly aware that her sister-in-law had still not said whether she liked the changes. Of them all, Maria had loved Manny's Cantina most—the place *and* its tacos. She was looking around, nodding, noticing every little thing, and her opinion meant more than she probably knew.

"Well?" Lily asked. And she realized Drew and Willow were also watching Maria, awaiting her verdict.

Maria nodded slow and said, "It still feels like the cantina—if it had spent a weekend at a makeover spa, and maybe had a little work done." She moved closer to the bar, same bar-top as always, same stools, newly covered. Maria slid her palm over the surface. "You had it refinished."

"It was getting a little sticky," Lily replied and the others nodded.

"The tables are different." They were square, red and green. She pulled out one of the chairs—diner style, round padded seats on a shiny chrome frame—and sat down, then lifted her butt, then lowered it again, testing. "Mmm. Definite improvement."

Lily went behind the bar, pushed a button underneath, then nodded toward the front as the outer walls retracted, revealing the glass they'd covered and what used to be the parking lot beyond. Now it was a flagstone patio as wide as the entire building, with a long counter down its center. She pushed the button again, and part of the glass retracted, as well.

"That is so cool!" Drew said, clapping her hands and running outside onto the patio to check things out.

Maria smiled and Lily's heart lifted. She hurried outside to where Drew had discovered the fire-and-water feature, right in the middle of the long strip that was half outdoor taco bar and half the regular kind of bar. The near half was lined with lidded stainless-steel containers, some heated, some cooled. The farther half included an under-counter cooler for drinks and mixers, a set of taps, and rows of glasses. The counter had its own mini-awning, peaked in the middle, that ran the length of it.

"Lily," Maria said. "You freakin' killed it."

"Really?" Lily knew she had. But she was thrilled that Maria thought so, too.

Drew said, "Reverend Wheeler's gonna be so teed off when nobody wants to have their weddin's in the church anymore."

Lily hadn't thought of that and felt immediately worried. "Maybe we should stick to just doing receptions."

"I was kiddin'." Drew put a hand on her arm. "You're a nervous wreck, aren't you?"

"I am."

"I don't think you need to be. It sure looks ready to me."

"It better be ready," Maria said. "Grand opening is tomorrow night."

"We'll know for sure after Friends and Family tonight," Lily said. "If anything's gonna go wrong, we'll find out then. You're all coming, right?"

"Of course we're all comin'," Maria said. "Your dad's makin' tacos without Rosa's supervision. That's his final exam."

Lily laughed with the others, but inside she wished Ethan could be there tonight, too. Friends and Family Night was a dress rehearsal. Her dad and his two young helpers—could you call them sous chefs in a taco place?—would get a real-world trial run. So would the kitchen equipment, the wait staff, and the stage. She'd hired Dirt River, the local band she and Ethan had danced to that night at The Waterin' Hole, right before they'd had sex on the riverbank and she'd fallen even harder.

Manny was coming, family and all. Lord, she hoped he didn't hate it.

Willow, who stood on her right, put a hand on her shoulder and she realized she'd fallen quiet and probably looked on the verge of panic. "You need a spa day, woman."

"After the grand opening, I might need a spa *week*. But not today. Too much to do to get ready."

Maria put an arm around her from her left, and Drew hugged her from behind and said, "We got you, girl. What can we do to help?"

"I hate not bein' there tonight," Ethan said. He was sitting in the too-small easy chair in his otherwise nice trailer, waiting to go on stage for the final show of this run, but his heart wasn't in it. It was a county fair in New Mexico, and the crowd was the biggest yet.

He was closer to home than he'd been in weeks. Maybe that was why he was feeling Quinn's pull on his heart so powerfully. But it was odd. He never felt homesick.

Ang was in the hard chair with his back to a mirrored dressing table. He held up the newspaper he'd brought in a minute ago. It was folded open to a page showing the familiar Billboard chart. "Again, 'cause you don't look like you heard me, you're sitting at number five this week."

"I know. It's...great."

Angelo gave a long, low whistle. "You get a call from home, did'ja? Your dog die or something?"

He shook his head. "I should be there tonight. At Two Lilies."

The manager rubbed his salt-and-pepper-stubble chin. "Grand opening's *tomorrow* night, isn't it?"

"Tonight's Friends and Family," Ethan said. "Like a test run."

"Ah, right. I forgot places do that before they open."

"I don't think I ever knew. But Hyram—our cook—said it'd be courtin' trouble to open without it."

He was tired. He'd done three interviews on country music podcasts, two on local network affiliates, and one had been on the nationally syndicated show *Nashville Today*. And that was huge. In between he'd done two dozen shows in venues ranging farther from home than he had yet, and bigger than he'd ever filled, pulling in capacity crowds at every one of them.

He'd slept in more hotel rooms than he could count with every piece of his flesh, blood, and bones aching to be home. It was an entirely foreign emotion.

He'd even done some songwriting. Heartbreak songs. They seemed to be his vibe these days.

There was a tap on the door. "Two minutes," came through in a muffled voice, then footsteps retreated.

"You look like you lost your best friend, son," Ang said. "You can't go out there like that. You need something to pick you up."

Ethan rose from his chair. "You ever suggest that again and I'll be lookin' for a new manager."

Ang held up a hand, "Whoa, come on, I didn't mean drugs. I meant—" He rubbed his chin again, then nodded. "This is an early show, right?" He'd pulled out his phone, was tapping and scrolling, and talking more to it than to Ethan. "And whaddya got, like a podcast tonight, that interview tomorrow, and then— that's not so bad."

"Yeah, I'll get through it."

"Not what I meant." He got up and paced back and forth while tapping. There were whoosh sounds every twenty taps or so. "Done. You're free."

Ethan blinked at him. "What do you mean, I'm free?"

"I mean, you do this show and you're done. Go home. I just postponed everything else. They want their interviews, we can set 'em up remotely. Maybe do one from the honky-tonk later in the week. They'll eat it up."

Ethan blinked at his manager, who'd always been a decent guy, but had never treated him like this before. "Normally, you'd tell me to buck up and do the work," he said.

"Yeah, and you bucked up and *did* the work. Now my job's changed. I'm not beatin' the bushes to get you decent gigs. We're just sorting through for the best offers now. My *new* job is seeing to it that you, Ethan Brand, stay happy and healthy and well-adjusted. You want to go home, then home you go."

The smile that split Ethan's face then was so big it almost hurt. His throat even tightened up. He was going home. Tonight!

"I'm not even fixin' to text her," he said. "It'll be a surprise."

"Her?"

"Them," he corrected. But it had been Lily's face in his mind, her shining blue eyes full of delight. She was always so happy to see him. She made him ten feet tall.

Ang was scanning his face and nodding in a self-satisfied way. "*There's* the guy this crowd's waiting to see. C'mon, Ethan, I'll walk you out to the stage."

CHAPTER SIXTEEN

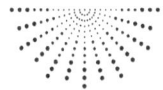

*T*here were still two hours until everyone would arrive, and Lily didn't know how she was going to contain her nervous energy for that long.

"Everything is perfect, Lil," Harrison said, sliding his arm around her shoulders. "Look at what you pulled off, and mostly on your own." He'd been looking around the place, same as she was, but he looked down to meet her eyes then. "I'm impressed by you, little sister. Blown away, as a matter of fact."

She lowered her head, smiling hard and fighting an actual giggle that bubbled up into her throat. "Thanks, big brother. That means a lot, coming from you."

"Ooh, smell that?" he asked.

Their father had started cooking, if the aromas were anything to go by. Her brother's bride was in the kitchen, too, and Cat Shaw was taking her first shift behind the bar. Turned out she was an experienced drink-slinger with some time to kill, plus she loved working with Hyram. Seeing them together... well, she was pretty sure her mom was smiling down and egging them on.

Just then the kitchen doors opened, and Maria thrust her

head out. "That's what was missing! The smells!" She waved a hand toward her own face as if to inhale them all the better and vanished back inside.

"She's probably driving Dad crazy," Harrison said.

"Are you kidding me? He adores her. But don't be surprised if he puts baby notions into her head."

"Baby notions?" Harrison's eyebrows shot up almost to his hairline, which made Lily burst out laughing.

"You should see your face!"

"Well, it's just…we have a five-year plan."

"You have all the time you want," Lily said, "I'm just saying, the old man's been making noises about it. You don't have to grant his every wish, you know." But then she rolled her eyes. "Five years, though?"

"Well, yeah. Maria's taking over the vet clinic from her mom, and that's gonna be an adjustment."

"Huh."

"What, you disapprove?"

"Oh, gosh, no! I just—hope I don't have to wait five years for one of my own."

Her brother looked at her in surprise. "I didn't know you had baby wishes, Lily."

"I didn't either, but all Dad's yammering about you and Maria making him a grandpa got me to thinking about it, and I realized, I really want to be a mom. I want to be the kind of mom our mom was."

"You'll be even better," he said, and he leaned down to kiss her cheek.

A white van pulled into the new driveway that curved around the building, past the main entrance, to the big parking lot in the back. It looked like a re-purposed delivery truck. "That's Dirt River." She bounced on the balls of her feet in excitement.

"Dirt who, now?"

"The local band I booked! I want them onstage before everyone arrives. I can't wait to hear what they think of our setup. They're going to use our built-in amps, our microphones, the whole shebang." She'd had a crash course in operating all of the above from the installers. Ethan would be better at it, though. He worked with those things all the time.

The thought of Ethan sent a wave of something both delicious and terrifying through Lily from her toes on up, as she hurried through the addition past the stage, through the backstage area to the brand-new stage door. She opened it and waved at the four young men who were already out of their van, unloading instruments, and carrying them across the pristine black parking lot that was twice size of the old one.

Tomorrow, Ethan would be home, she thought. And her heart clenched. Tomorrow, in time for the grand opening.

Harrison went outside to lend the guys a hand, and then they trooped in with guitars, keyboard, and several parts of a drum set, all of them greeting her as they passed. They were excited to perform in Ethan Brand's new honky-tonk during its opening week. And the higher Ethan rose on the charts, the more excited they got.

She hoped the exposure would help them out.

When the last of their stuff was in, she closed the door and returned to find the guys on the stage, setting up, plugging in. They didn't need her to tell them what was what.

"What do you guys, think?" she asked, pushing a button to extend the solid retractable wall over the glass, then stopping halfway. "Open or closed?"

"It'll still be light out at seven," said Lupé, a drummer with a neck as thick as his bulging biceps. "I think closed."

His three bandmates nodded, so she pushed the button again and close the barrier all the way.

Harrison said, "Way better. Much more intimate, and we still have the view from the side windows. It'll give everyone time to take the place in, before you dazzle 'em with even more."

"After dark, I can flip on the party lights and turn on the fire-and-water feature from in here." She pulled a remote out of her apron pocket and wiggled her eyebrows. "Then I'll open the slider for the big reveal."

Another vehicle pulled in, a gray mini-van with a florist's logo on the side.

"I didn't order flowers," she said. But she unlocked the side doors, their new main entrance. The vehicle hadn't pulled all the way around to the parking lot but had stopped right in front of them.

A smiling woman with gray hair in a pixie cut got out from the driver's side and a younger woman from the passenger side as the rear hatch rose. Lily stepped out, and the older one came her way with a clipboard.

"You're the owner?"

"Co-owner, sort of." No paperwork had yet been done. Everything really depended on Ethan's return, how things were between them, and whether she felt like she could keep working with him without being in a constant state of heartache. Wanting him and not having him might be easier from a distance.

But lately, it kind of seemed like he might feel the same way she did. And yet, he wasn't here. And he hadn't said a word about having changed his stance on things, or altered his belief that he couldn't live in Quinn, in the shadow of his noble family.

"We can set them up for you, no extra charge," said the older of the two.

"I don't even know what—I didn't order flowers."

Frowning, the woman brought the clipboard back around. "Ethan Brand ordered them. Two lilies for each table, one red, one white. Special emphasis on each one having some of the other's color in it. There's a crystal vase for each set. We managed to get enough for fifty tables, as requested. That sufficient?"

"Oh...my gosh. Ethan did that?" Lily opened the sliding door wider, and the two women began carrying in long slender boxes with lilies lying inside beneath a layer of clear plastic just tucked around the edges all the way through to the original cantina. The dining room, she reminded herself.

Lily helped, impressed by how tenderly the women handled each stem, and hurried to the kitchen for a pitcher of water. After she'd filled all the pretty crystal vases, she checked her watch thinking she'd killed an hour, but only twenty-four minutes had passed.

Willow's SUV pulled in next. There wasn't room for it to pass the parked van, so she pulled out around onto the grass. Lily tapped the voice memo app on her phone and said, "Widen the entrance strip so it's never blocked by a stopped vehicle."

"That's a very tiny problem," Harrison said.

"May that be the only flaw we find the entire night," Lily replied, and then she heard a crash and some shouting from the kitchen.

The roar of the crowd was deafening when Ethan wrapped the show, held up his guitar and took his final bow. And while they kept on cheering as he crossed the stage, he didn't have any intention of coming back out for an encore. The lights shifted all at once, from him to the crowd, and it was a relief to have them out of his eyes. He looked out, just before he reached the curtain, just to take it in once again. He'd been doing that after every show, gazing out at the crowd once the lights went out and he could see. Trying to really appreciate the folks out there. It was hard to believe that many people had paid money just to watch him stand on a stage and sing his songs.

He was writing every night. He'd already told Ang there'd be no need to buy songs elsewhere.

He gazed out from the darkened stage, feeling great, and then suddenly...not so great. A large sombrero was moving through the mostly empty space in front of the front row.

Ethan stopped walking, narrowing his eyes, trying to see the face beneath the hat. Instead, a hand tapped the front brim, like a greeting.

It was him!

He moved fast, tapping down the concealed stairs, through the partitioned runway to his trailer, dropped his guitar there, and kept going, veering forward. He pulled his hat low over his eyes, hoping not to be recognized when he moved back through the dispersing crowd toward where he'd seen the hat.

But he needn't have hurried.

It was on the head of the fellow who stood in the secure parking lot to the right of the audience. He was leaning against Ethan's big red pickup truck.

Ethan had been moving fast, and came to a clumsy stop when he saw the stranger there. Then he moved more slowly until he stopped right in front of him. The other man's head was still down-tilted, his face still hidden beneath the sombrero's brim.

So Ethan said his name. "You Jeremiah Thorne?"

He lifted his head, revealing a bushy, untrimmed beard and blue eyes that were vivid and dark. "Yeah. And your brother," he replied. He watched Ethan's face, his eyes unflinching.

"So I been told. Same father, different mother."

"Different mother, same ending."

Ethan's breath hitched in his chest. He had to swallow before he could speak and when he did, his voice sounded strangled. "De Lorean killed her?"

"She killed herself. But he caused it, yeah." He broke eye contact, looked around them instead.

The crowd was still dispersing. Ethan saw a group of teenage girls watching them intently. Probably deciding whether he was himself or not. He had a hundred questions for Jeremiah. But they clearly couldn't have a conversation out here. "You uh, want to talk in the trailer?"

"In the truck," he said. "We need go get a move on."

"Where we goin'?"

"Like the song says, home. And there's reason to hurry, so go get your shit. I'll explain on the way."

Ethan met his brother's eyes. They were dead serious. "I'll go get my shit." He unlocked the pickup's doors, using the keypad, as the keys were back in his trailer. "Be right back."

Jeremiah nodded and got into the passenger side to wait.

Ethan didn't know his brother, so he sure as hell didn't trust him. He was calling his uncle Garrett before he got five steps away.

"Son," Garrett said when he picked up. "How was the show? You done already?"

"Just finished up." He walked into the trailer, pulled his big bag out from under the bunk, and laid it unzipped on top. "Listen, my um…my brother's here. Waitin' for me out in the truck. He says we need to hightail it home."

"Why's that?" Garrett asked, his voice suddenly serious.

"Hasn't said yet. Thought I'd best check in with you while packin' up to head back." He gathered his bathroom gear and dumped it in. Most of his stuff was still in the truck. He had some kind of mental block about unpacking, this trip.

"You're comin' home tonight? That'll thrill everybody. 'Specially Lily."

"Yeah, but keep that to yourself." He looked around the room, gathered up some clothes, a notebook, and pencil and threw those in. That was everything but the guitar.

"Ah. I gotcha," Garrett said. "It'll make for a great surprise. What're you, about two hours away?"

"Closer to three," he said. "Everything's all right, then?"

"Everything's fine. We're s'posed to arrive in two hours for the meal, but we'll still be there in three. Drive safe. Your brother comin' with you?"

"Looks like."

"Good. Use the time to get to know him."

"I will. Keep an eye on things, okay?"

"She's surrounded by family, Bubba. She's safe. I'll head over early, soon's we hang up, if it'll make you feel better."

"It would," Ethan said. And for some reason his old man calling him Bubba hadn't even chafed that time.

He pocketed the phone, put his guitar into its hard-shell case, and headed back out with the duffle over one shoulder and the guitar case in his hand. He slung the bags into the back of the truck and got behind the wheel.

For a while, he had to focus on the bumper-to-bumper crush of vehicles trying to get out of the fairgrounds all at once, but eventually they pulled out of the crush and onto the highway.

That was when he finally said, "I don't know what question to ask you first. Why have I never known about you?"

"I didn't know about you either, till a coupla years ago. Our father didn't want us to know about each other."

Ethan kept taking short looks at him as he spoke. "Why not?"

Jeremiah shrugged. "He was training me to help him run the biz, he said. But he was really getting me just entangled enough to take the fall for somebody's fuckup. Somebody more important. I was sure he'd get me out. But he didn't. After a year, I got my own lawyer, had him set up a meeting with the prosecutor. Told 'em everything I knew and they turned me loose early."

Ethan nodded slowly. He listened with care. His brother's voice was deep, with a rasp at the lower registers. He seemed the epitome of calm.

"And then you started hanging out at my family's favorite little cantina."

"I was still working for Dad, you know. He was running his organization from behind bars. He didn't know I'd talked— wouldn't have known until I testified, but he died before it got that far. Meantime I had to play along. If he'd found out—I'd be as dead as our mothers."

Ethan winced when he said that.

"He sent me to Manny's Cantina to look things over, he said. I knew by then I had a brother. I knew his last name was Brand and he lived in Quinn, Texas, and how close that was to Mad Bull's Bend. And while I was there, I saw one of your cousins, heard her talkin' about you."

"Which cousin?"

"The drop-dead gorgeous one," he said.

Ethan crooked a brow. "They're all gorgeous."

"Willow." Jeremiah looked out his window at the passing scenery. "She was sayin' something about Bubba being as big as his dad even though he was adopted, and I knew it was you. Took another six months of my hangin' around that cantina to learn that Bubba Brand was Ethan Brand, the country singer." He shook his head a little self-deprecatingly. "I should've known first time I saw you, though. You have our father's eyes."

Ethan managed not to grimace.

"When Dad died, the lawyer told me he'd left you everything and you were plannin' to refuse it all, so I'd be next in line to inherit it. I can't afford to turn it down." He shook his head. "Not the business, though. That's done. I'm cashin' out. Let other crooks fight over his territory."

"That's probably smart."

"Yeah." He sighed. "But he told me, Dad's estate guy, that he'd signed the cantina over to you in some kind of side deal with Manny, and that you were keeping it. And that worried me."

"Why's that?"

"Dad was tied up with seven other little places like Manny's, was washing money through all of 'em. Since he died, his biggest rival, Nathan Silver, has been moving in, taking over where Dad left off. Had his kid brother Angus running that end of things for him.

"That clears up a lot," Ethan said. "Angus made me an offer. I told him to shove it where the sun don't shine."

"I'm aware."

Ethan looked at Jeremiah. He was working his way up to the accident that might not've been an accident, so he probably ought to quit interrupting him.

"Two other business owners told him to shove it, too," Jeremiah said. "The nail salon and one of the bars. The owner of the nail salon's adult daughter was found floating in her backyard swimming pool a few days later. It was ruled an accidental drowning. I even bought it at first."

Ethan looked at him sharply. "At first?"

"Yeah. The strip club was owned by a smart-ass entrepreneur who thought the days of shakedowns were over once our father kicked it. His young bride turned up dead in an ally. She'd been beaten and raped."

Ethan swore in an entirely un-Brand-like manner.

"He's fond of taking out his rage on young women. You see what I mean? And I saw him come talk to you. And I knew you'd tell him to take a flyin' leap. And I knew he'd go after one of the women in your life. Willow, or Maria, or Lily, or young Drew." His words had come faster as he'd gone along.

"I believe you," Ethan said.

Jeremiah nodded, as if that was important to him.

"But he wasn't trying to shake me down, exactly. He wanted to buy the place."

"Either way, if he doesn't get what he wants, people die."

Ethan took a breath and asked the question. There was brown paint on the Caddy," he said. "Was that you?"

Jeremiah nodded. "It was only supposed to be a warnin'. Run him off the road, then get up in his face and tell him who my father was, talk a big game, put a little fear into him. That's how Dad always did it."

Ethan nodded.

"The passenger bailed. But the passenger wasn't Silver. It was his driver. Silver was behind the wheel. I didn't see that coming." His eyes had gone distant, and Ethan knew he was remembering. "I was stalled there in the road. He tried to ram me, broadside. I got her started, slammed her into gear, and shot out of the way." He let his chin drop low. "I couldn't believe it when he went over the side," he said. Then he took a deep breath. "I killed a man."

"You didn't kill him, you just ducked. And you saved a life in the process. A life I'd have hated like hell to see end."

Jeremiah glanced sideways, his lips curving up at one corner. But the slight smile died before it was fully born. "But there's still the brother. Nathan."

"So Willow told me."

"Nathan's bad news, Ethan. Makes Angus look like a Boy Scout. I left the hospital, because if they'd arrested me for trespassing in your shed, I wouldn't've been able to keep an eye out, and if Nathan got wind of what had really happened, he would have come back for vengeance. He'd assume it was you, since you're the last person his dumbass brother messed with. I had to get close to him. Find out what he knew."

Ethan frowned hard. "That's where you've been." Jeremiah nodded. Then Ethan asked, "Close to him, how?"

"Doesn't matter. What matters is that Angus's driver came back, and he talked. Nathan knows that accident was no accident, and he's not gonna let it go. I got this information earlier today, and I been tracking you down ever since. He'll try to get revenge."

"I'm not even there," Ethan said.

"But everybody you love is."

Their eyes met. Ethan sensed his brother was telling him the truth, and he pressed down harder on the accelerator.

Lily couldn't keep the smile off her face. Everyone was enjoying the food, the drinks, the band, the dance floor. If only Ethan were there to see it all. There'd been a minor disaster in the kitchen, a collision and some spilled taco beans, possibly due to too much help out there (Maria). But since then, everything had been smooth, fun, and joyful.

"You're beaming, you know that?" Her brother came up to stand beside her near the front of the room.

"If I am, it's with relief. This is…" She looked around at the smiling, dancing, taco-devouring people she loved. "It's almost perfect."

"Would be if Ethan was here, huh?"

She shot him a quick look. "Well, yeah, I guess. He's the only Brand missing."

"The only Brand *you're* missing, you mean?" Harrison winked, then slid an arm around her shoulders. "Maria has high hopes for the two of you, you know."

Surrounded by noise, laughter, and music, she arched an eyebrow. "What kind of hopes?"

"I'll leave you to ask her that for yourself. Meanwhile," he tapped his knuckles on the front-facing glass, "I'm dying for the big reveal, and you said as soon as it got dark. And if you look out the main entry doors, you can see it's fully dark now. So?"

Grinning, she grabbed his forearm and pulled the remote from her apron, thumbed buttons, she said, "Lights, water, fire…"

"Fire?"

She nodded, then waved a hand to get the band's attention. They got her signal and wrapped up the song. Then the band leader said, "I believe our lovely hostess wants us all to turn our attention toward the front. This party's about to spill outside. Hit it, Larry."

A drum roll ensued. Lily pushed the button to open the wooden panels so they'd slide open on that gorgeous fire-and-water feature, party lights, outdoor tables, and perfect flagstone patio.

Only, the doors didn't move.

She could hear their motor humming, but the doors were not budging. "Heck, I knew something would go wrong." She aimed the remote and thumbed the button again. "I wonder if somebody fastened the storm locks."

Harrison frowned at her.

"On the corner, there are slide-bolts on the outside to hold the barricade in case of a storm."

"I'll go check," Harrison said, then he told the others, "Patience, everyone. Two seconds." He walked over to the right side, where the main entrance was, but when he went to go through, the doors were locked.

He turned to send Lily a puzzled frown.

That was when the power went out, plunging them into darkness.

Lily couldn't believe it. "What in the world—"

Glass shattered in the dining room as a ball of flames smashed through a window and hit the floor, spreading a pool of liquid fire. Lily ran for the fire extinguisher and was reaching for it just as another fireball came through another window, smashing into the wall of bottles behind the bar. Cat Shaw screamed and covered her head with her arms as glass shattered and alcohol fed the flames. Her sleeve was burning and a wall of fire rose between her and the extinguisher.

Lily ran to her. She smothered Cat's burning blouse with a

towel and saw flames rising up, blocking the kitchen doors, illuminating her father's terrified face in the portholes. "Go out the back!" she shouted. Then she pulled Cat with her into the addition, shouting, "Smash the entry doors!"

But before Garrett Brand even picked up a chair to do so, another firebomb smashed through those glass doors, and fire again spread like spilled destruction. Harrison grabbed her arm, pulling her away from the flames. "All the exits are blocked. What do we do?"

"Stage door," she shouted. But she needn't. The others were already running in that direction, following the band, who'd entered that way.

Harrison had his arm around Maria, Lily realized. It was so dark she didn't know where they'd picked her up, and the others were only shapes and shadows picked out by the spreading flames, but increasingly blocked by smoke.

She bent low, so did Harrison, and they brought up the rear, she hoped. It was dark and chaotic and noisy and she couldn't be sure everyone was together. Someone might've been in the restroom or checking out the second floor.

When they neared the exit, she saw the uncles up front, smashing at the stage door, which had somehow been blocked from outside. Drew screamed and her father Ben folded her into his arms.

"This was no accident," Willow said, from somewhere close. "This was that freakin' Silver."

"God, I hope Dad got out," Harrison said. "What if they blocked the kitchen exit too?"

Lily took a breath and choked on smoke. "We have to go upstairs!" she shouted.

"The smoke will be worse up there, won't it?" Willow asked.

"Yes," she said. "But we can go out a window and onto the roof."

"A few at a time," Garrett said. "Too much smoke to wait

around up there long. Get up top, out the window onto the roof and keep goin'. Don't come back inside, no matter what. Do you hear? You come back in, you slow us down. Women first, git up on up there."

"Not without our men," Chelsea said, latching onto his hand.

Something exploded, and everyone screamed and crouched down. The roar seemed louder after that, the smoke denser, the very air hotter.

Lily yelled, "Top of the stairs, to the right, that's the closest window. We have to hurry! Smoke's getting worse." She grabbed Drew's hand, she didn't know why. "Hold your breath up there and get out fast. Ready?"

Ethan texted Lily ten times, but there was no response, and that made the panic inside him grow.

"Still nothin'?" Jeremiah asked from the passenger seat.

Ethan shook his head left and right. "Nothin' better have happened to her."

"Nothin' better have."

Jeremiah had tossed the sombrero and poncho into the back and Ethan wondered if he'd only worn them to make sure he'd be easy to spot in the crowd, the opposite of the reason he'd worn them before.

He looked back at the clothing briefly. Jeremiah saw the look. "I wanted to be anonymous in town. Didn't know if anyone in Mad Bull's Bend would know me by sight, so I kept my face covered." He ran a hand over his full beard. It seemed reddish in the dashboard lights. "Kinda eager for a shave now that you know. Didn't want to take the time, though."

"I appreciate it."

"You love her, huh?" Jeremiah asked.

Ethan actually gasped. It was an odd reaction. He didn't remember ever gasping before.

"I picked up on it the first time you two came into Manny's together. Maria and Harry were with you—sorry, Harrison—and Willow."

"What, exactly, would you say you *picked up on*?"

He shrugged and said, "I don't know. You just seemed like a couple, you know? I was surprised when I found out you weren't."

He grunted and kept driving.

"She's a rare beauty, if you don't mind my saying so."

"I don't mind you sayin' so. I agree with you."

Jeremiah nodded. "It's more than a pretty face, though, it's… a light. Comes from inside her, you know what I mean?"

"I do. She gets mad when I say it, though."

"Got a temper on her," he agreed, grinning from behind his beard. Then, his smile dying, "I sure hope she's okay." He looked down at Ethan's phone, face-up in the console.

Ethan was painfully aware of its uninterrupted black screen. "We're almost there. Ten more miles."

CHAPTER SEVENTEEN

*L*ily held her breath as she raced up the stairs. She was holding Drew's hand and had a death grip on Orrin's wrist to pull him behind her. Without lights it was dark as pitch, and smoke was a thin fog hanging in the air. She needed to take a breath. The window was to the right, and she realized they'd have never found it on their own. Lily took Drew's hand and guided it to Orrin's. When they latched onto each other, she found the window, opened it easily, reached behind her and pulled them to it. Orrin put one leg over the sill and helped Drew climb out, then he reached back for Lily, but she saw him turning, put her hands on his ass, and shoved him the rest of the way out onto the roof.

Her eyes were burning. She stuck her head out the window, as far to one side as she could, to take a breath. Then she ducked back in, and ran to the top of the stairs, and shouted, "Send more up!"

The open window was creating a draft, drawing the smoke right up the stairs and out the opening, but there was no help for it. If she closed it, the rooms below would fill.

Rosa and her daughters waited below. Lily thought of

Manny and his recent heart attack, and knew she should've grabbed him first, but she guided Rosa and the girls to the window and got another breath as they climbed out. Orrin & Drew remained on the roof to help, so Lily went back to the stairs and down them into the deafening roar and impossible heat. There were vaguely human shapes in the smoke, all crouching low on the dance floor. Flames were roaring in the original part of the cantina, and heading this way fast, and the main entrance was a curtain of fire. No way out but up.

The biggest shape came her way, those broad shoulders so like Ethan's that for a second she thought...

Garrett Brand pressed a blessedly soaked towel to her face, then his hand to her shoulders to push her down low. She didn't know where he'd got the wet towels. Right, she'd put a big water cooler backstage for the band. Garrett took Manny and Chelsea up the stairs.

Lily lowered the towel and shouted over the roar, "Top of the stairs, to the right!"

As Garrett's form faded into the smoky staircase, Willow grabbed her mother, who grabbed Penny, who grabbed Kirsten, who grabbed Esmeralda. It was too many at once. Lily got in front of them, broke up the group, motioning them low again, pumping her palm to convey some should wait while others went up. Then she sent the rest.

She'd given away her towel and she needed it again. Somebody handed her one. She lost track of how many passed, of who was left behind. Garrett was up and down the stairs many times no longer letting her guide people up. It was so hot! Her skin felt sunburned. She couldn't hear anything but the fire's roar and furious crackling, like bones being crushed in the teeth of a giant.

"Lily, come on."

It was Garrett again. He was pressing another wet towel to her face. "The others?" She asked. "Is anyone—"

"Everyone's up."

"My dad? The kitchen crew?"

"I don't know, Lil." He put an arm around her and they turned toward the staircase. Then there was a *whoosh* as flames blasted up the stairway like a blowtorch, following the draft.

Lily screamed as she and the man who'd become like a second father to her over the past year, backed up into the darkest darkness they could find. They sank to the floor in a corner near the stage.

"He never even got to see it," Lily said. Her chest kept spasming and she didn't know if it was from the smoke or the grief. Garrett's chest must be doing the same, because he was clutching it...Oh no. Oh no. "Garrett!"

But the big guy dropped like a sack of feed, flat onto his back on the floor.

"Garrett!" she shrieked.

But he didn't move. Hell! She knelt and pressed her fingertips to his neck, then laid her head on his chest to be sure. No pulse.

The defibrillator was behind the bar, beyond a pool of fire. She couldn't get to it. So she placed her hands over his chest, and started pumping, and counting. She gave him two breaths in between, because something told her to do it that way, rather than the newer method of all compressions, no breaths. But she felt it, he needed the air. So she gave him her own.

She started to cough. Her wet towel was beside Garrett's head, but she had to keep pumping. Then all at once, he dragged in a loud long breath, only to start coughing. She rolled him onto his side and pressed the wet towel to his face and said, "Just slide yourself this way, Garrett. Can you do it?"

He nodded from behind the towel, and she got behind him, grabbed him under his arms, and he pushed along with his feet. They made it to the very front of the stage, the furthest spot from the fire.

Garrett lifted the wet towel to her face. He said, "You should've left me, girl. We ain't gettin' outta this."

"Sure we are. You gotta have a little faith."

He coughed lightly then rubbed his chest. "Tell me somethin', Lily. Did I have a heart attack just now?"

"I mean, it stopped beating. It was probably the smoke."

"Or maybe the sausage." He offered the end of his wet towel to her. She lay down on the floor beside him so it would reach and held it over her face. "So my heart stopped altogether, did it? I was...dead?"

"What's the movie line? You were..." She coughed hard and her eyes stung and watering and her chest burned. "You were only *mostly* dead."

"Then it was real."

"What was?"

He met her eyes, shook his head slow. She could hear his breaths because they whistled in and out of his lungs. His voice a rasp, he said, "You're a helluva nurse, Lil. Should you ever want to go back to it, remember that."

As they neared the exit to Mad Bull's Bend, an ominous orange glow hung low in the sky. Ethan didn't slow down when he got off the highway. His heart was already frozen with dread before he saw Two Lilies engulfed in fire, and barreled over the grass, across the patio.

"The roof!" Jeremiah shouted, pointing. "Back up, turn on the fog lights."

Ethan did both, then dove out of the truck and ran toward the building before he even realized what he was seeing. People were on the roof, family, filing toward the farthest end, then inching lower along the peak, dangling from their hands, and dropping to the ground. He ran to them, Jeremiah right on his heels.

Manny's family, all five of them, were huddled off to the right, and he spotted Hyram still in his white apron. Cat was with him, but not Lily.

Nearly everyone was off the roof by then, and many were talking and shouting at once. He ran back a few paces to see if Lily was up there, but he didn't see her.

A small hand grabbed the front of his shirt. Chelsea.

"Garrett and Lily are still in there!" she screamed. "They didn't make it out!"

"Get everyone out of the way," he said, and ran back to the truck. He got behind the wheel and slammed the door. The other door slammed too, and he realized Jeremiah had returned to his spot in the passenger seat.

They locked eyes. Something connected. His brother nodded, pulled his seatbelt on and said, "Hit it."

So Ethan hit it.

Lily was having trouble keeping her eyes open. Even down flat on the floor, there was no good air. But she was conscious enough to hear the thunderous crash and see the blazing lights that suddenly pierced the darkness. She held her hand before her eyes and looked into the light.

Ethan's truck, like a fiery red steed with blazing eyes. It backed up slightly, leaving a gaping hole behind. And then Ethan was coming toward her, a tall, broad, Stetson-wearing shadow framed in light. He crouched low and scooped her up into his arms. "I got you, Lil. I got you."

"Your father," she croaked, and managed to point limply.

He turned, dropped back to one knee, still holding Lily.

"Dad."

Garrett pushed himself up. "I'm alive."

"I got him, Brother." A bearded man pulled Garrett's arm around his shoulder, gripped him around the waist, and helped him get up onto his feet. The flames roared closer, drawn by the fresh oxygen coming in through the gaping hole.

"Gringo Sombrero?" Lily asked.

"Ma'am."

She let her head fall against Ethan's chest, and rocked with his steps as he carried her out through the hole his truck had made in their beautiful honky-tonk. "Did my father get out?" she croaked, surprised her voice sounded so deep and hoarse.

"I saw him. He looked okay. Cat too."

There were flashing lights and firefighters on the outside. There were hoses attacking the flames, and there were Brands everywhere. A medic came running and pressed an oxygen mask over her face. "Over here, bring her over here."

A few more steps and Ethan was lowering Lily onto some EMT's gurney and taking his arms away. She sat up and pushed off the mask, reaching for him. "Ethan!"

And then his arms were around her again. "It's okay, I'm right here."

"Ethan." It was a whisper this time. Her cheek was pressed to his, and she felt a teardrop that was not her own. Startled, she drew back to look at his face. Flashing red-and-white lights painted it in the darkness, and made the tears on his cheeks flash like diamonds. "Ethan?"

He put the oxygen mask back over her nose and mouth and then smoothed her hair out from under the elastic band. He looked around, and she followed his gaze as best she could. The fog in her mind was fading, though, as the oxygen did its job. She saw Garrett in Chelsea's arms, ignoring the medics who tried to get at him. She saw Elliot Brand, Trevor's dad, sitting on the tailgate of a firetruck, breathing oxygen through a mask like she was. He'd been among the final group to escape out the window.

She pulled her mask off and said to the medic beside her, "His heart stopped in there," she said, nodding Garrett's way, and she heard Ethan gasp.

He looked his father's way, as the medic spoke into a mic clipped to his shirt, apparently to the EMTs who were pestering Garrett, because they got very serious very fast and Chelsea looked suddenly thunderstruck.

"We need to transport her, Mr. Brand," the medic said to Ethan.

"I'm ridin' in with her if you think you can work around me."

The guy nodded, and Ethan eased Lily's arms from his neck. She lay down so they could collapse the gurney and rolled her into the back. Ethan climbed in after her, and the EMT said, "I'll ride up front, but if anything changes—"

"Got it.

Before he could close the rear doors, her father and brother were there, leaning in.

"Baby!" Hyram cried.

She lifted the mask again. "I'm okay. But make sure Garrett is."

"We have to go," The EMT said. "You can meet us at the hospital."

Lily gave Harrison and her dad a thumbs-up even though the EMT's urgency had her concerned. Beyond them, she saw Garrett climbing into the second ambulance under his own steam, Chelsea right beside him. Then the rear doors cut off her view, and in another few seconds, the ambulance lurched into motion. She was pleased to see the second one's flashing lights right behind them.

Ethan took Lily's hand in both of his, and pressed kisses to it. Everything had taken on a dreamy quality, and consciousness was a fraying thread.

He bent closer, and spoke softly, his deep voice caressing her ear. "I'm never leavin' you again, Lily Ellen. I'd appreciate it if you'd return the favor, and not leave me, either."

She blinked up at him. "Imma pass out soon," she said. "Or did I already? Is this a dream?"

"It's a nightmare. I almost lost the only woman I've ever loved, and the only one I ever will. I got a lot more to say to you, girl, but before you go passin' out, I had to get that much said. I love you. Don't deserve you, but I love you."

She pressed a hand to his bristly cheek and smiled. "I love you, too." She tried to say it, at least, as the thread of consciousness broke and she drifted away.

3 DAYS LATER

Ethan stood at the ruins of Two Lilies Honky-Tonk.

The original structure had burned to the ground, and only charred beams and ash remained. The new addition had sustained such heavy damage to the inside that it would need to be gutted, but the external structure was mainly intact. There was a dozer working to clear the debris.

A car door slammed. He turned. And there was Lily walking toward him. She had a bandage around her head, wore jeans, boots, and a lightweight red flannel shirt unbuttoned over a tee.

She walked right up to him.

He said, "I thought they were keepin' you one more night?"

"Yeah. So did they. But once they told you to leave and let me get some rest, I saw no more point in hanging around." She looked over at the ruins of their place, shaking her head slowly.

"I'm glad everyone's okay. I know what a blessing that is, but I'm pretty devastated you never even got to see it."

"I saw some. Willow took a pile of pictures before things went bad. They were saved in her cloud. It was beautiful, Lily. Perfect. The lettering over the archway—shoot, I loved it so much my heart hurt."

She stared at him, right into his eyes, and he stared back. There were two feet of space between them and he didn't know whether to close it up or not. He'd made a pretty powerful declaration in the ambulance. And she hadn't responded, so he didn't really know where he stood.

But he was planning to find out.

"You seen the headlines?" she asked.

He nodded. "They got Nathan Silver dead to rights on arson and attempted murder. He's going away for a long time."

She came closer, put a palm on his cheek. "That's nice, but not what I meant. *You* are all over the news. Quinn wants to throw you a parade, you and your brother."

He shook his head slowly. "You saved everyone in there, Lily. You and Garrett, and then you saved him too. He showed me the bruise on his chest, you know. The shape of your little hand. Said he's gonna get it tattooed there so it never fades."

She lowered her head. "And then you saved us both. You saved me, the one everybody thinks is a light-beaming angel, and you saved your father, the most loved man in Quinn County. I don't know how your delusions of unworthiness will ever survive it."

They were walking side by side toward where the cellar stairway opened into the earth. A lot of ash and rubble had fallen in there. Lily looked around, spotted some tools, and went to pick up a pair of shovels.

"Let's dig this out," she said, handing him one. "See if your surprise survived."

They started digging, clearing debris from the basement stairway.

"I didn't know you'd done anything in the basement," he said.

"You said you trusted my judgment. I made an executive decision."

She went into the basement and tried the door, and then he helped, and they got it open. "We need a flashlight."

"Here, we'll use my phone." He turned on the flashlight feature, then he went through it and aimed the light around the room they had entered.

"It's okay!" she breathed. "It's not even damaged. Oh, gosh—"

"Is this…Lily, did you put in a recording studio?"

"Just a small one. And the fire didn't touch it!" She put her hand over his on the phone to guide it to the padded walls, and then to the glass. "The booth is over there. The glass isn't even broken. There's not much equipment yet. The boom mics came with the package, but I figured you'd want to pick the rest yourself, and—"

He pulled her around and right into his arms, and then he kissed her long and slow. He loved the taste of her lips, the feel of them, soft beneath his. He didn't know how he'd ever thought himself capable of not being with this woman.

"It's perfect, Lily Ellen. I love it. I'll use it while we rebuild. The place was fully insured, the bank insisted on that. We'll just start again."

Ethan took her hand, pulled her out of the studio and back up the stairs. They stepped out into bright Texas sunlight. The dozer was running again, several yards away. It was time. He'd thought maybe a nice dinner or something, but no. No, he'd waited as long as he cared to.

He looked her right in those big blue eyes of hers, and he said, "Lily, do you remember the ride in the ambulance?"

"Of course I do. Why?" She lifted her eyebrows. "You're not gonna try and take it back, are you?"

"Take what back?"

"Did I dream it, then?" She turned away, pressing a hand to her forehead. "Was it just from the smoke? I thought…you said you'd never leave me again. You said you loved me."

He pulled the ring from his pocket while her back was to him. He'd bought it right after they'd made him leave the hospital last night at the end of visiting hours. They'd let him stay the two nights prior. Well, *let him* wasn't exactly accurate. They hadn't physically removed him, though, so same result.

He'd called the jeweler at home last night, woke him up, made him come open the shop.

Lily was still turned away. He dropped down on one knee, and said, "You didn't dream it. But you didn't reply, either."

"I tried to." She turned around then, and saw him on his knee, holding the ring up like an offering, and she froze. Her eyes went so wide he thought they might pop, and she clapped a hand over her brilliant smile.

"I don't know why I fought it so hard, Lily. I mean, I do. You're too good for me, were then, are now, always will be, but danged if I've been able to convince you of it."

"You'll never convince me of that."

"Then I guess you better marry me."

"I guess I'd better."

"Is that a yes?"

She nodded. "Yes."

He got up, wrapped her in his arms, and scooped her right off her feet. He held her up so high he had to tip his head back to kiss her.

Ethan Bubba Brand knew right then that he'd finally found his country kind of love. She'd been waiting right here at home.

EPILOGUE

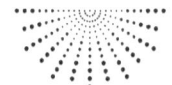

THREE MONTHS LATER

*L*ily sat beside Ethan on the swing, on the front porch of the ranch house. They were building one of their own, out past the family plot on North Brand Lane, but it would be a few more months before it was ready.

The grand re-opening of Two Lilies had been a smashing success last night. Ethan had performed the first single from his new album, *Down Home they Call Me Bubba.* Lily thought most of the town had turned out. Dirt River had opened for him.

As for Jeremiah, he'd come in for the opening after being away on business, he said, but he still had shadows in his eyes, and a haunted look. He came and went, doing who knew what, but he'd been there for their wedding.

After the grand opening, Ethan called for an after-party at the ranch, and everyone had spent the night. Which made the timing perfect, Lily thought, for their little surprise.

The sun was about to rise.

Garrett and Chelsea came out on the front porch every

morning with their first mugs of coffee to watch it come up together, and they watched it set together every night. It was a tradition Lily intended to adopt and continue, and had, so far, every day since their small, private wedding and backyard reception.

Chelsea's footsteps padded on the stairs. She was always the first one up. She would put the coffee on. Lily and Ethan had left the big front door open, so they would hear the others coming. Only the screen door was still closed.

A few minutes later, Garrett came down. Lily heard their morning kiss, and knew Chelsea was handing Garrett a mug and then hugging her own mug between her hands. And then, side by side, leaning into each other, they'd mosey to the front door, and open it to come out onto the porch with their first cups of coffee to watch the sun rise together while the whole world was quiet.

The screen door creaked its old familiar whine. And then Garrett said, "What in the all-fired get-out is this?"

Lily giggled. She couldn't help it, and Garrett looked from the little basket at the front door, to her and Ethan on the porch swing.

Chelsea knelt and pulled at the small blanket they'd tucked inside the basket. Beneath it there was a pair of booties, a rattle, and an ultrasound printout. She picked it up, rising slowly and facing Ethan and Lily. And then she grinned, and said, "Baby?"

"Mm-hm," Lily said, nodding.

And then Chelsea was hugging her and they were both bawling, and Garrett was clasping Ethan's hand and slamming his shoulder. "Dang, son, I was beginning to give up hope for grandkids! Congratulations!"

"Is there a due date yet?" Chelsea asked. "How are you feeling?"

More footsteps came from the stairs as Hyram descended.

Chelsea quickly put the photo back in the basket and pulled Garrett out of the way.

Hyram opened the screen door, looked down at the basket, and didn't even need to pull the blanket aside before he was grinning and slapping his thigh and yelling "hot damn!" like a true Texan.

His shout woke the household, and soon the whole crowd was on the front porch, celebrating and high-fiving and hugging each other. Maria leaned close and whispered, "Thanks for takin' the pressure off me, Sis."

In the middle of all that love, Ethan kissed Lily. She laughed against his mouth to the cheers and happy tears of their huge and ever-growing family.

ALSO BY MAGGIE SHAYNE

SMALL-TOWN CONTEMPORARY SERIES

The Texas Brand

The Oklahoma Brands

The McIntyre Men

The Texas Brand: Generations

THRILLERS & ROMANTIC SUSPENSE SERIES

Brown and de Luca Return

The Fatal series

Shattered Sisters

Danger After Dawn

PARANORMAL ROMANCE

The Portal

Wings in the Night

The Immortals

By Magic

ABOUT THE AUTHOR

New York Times and *USA Today* bestselling novelist Maggie Shayne has published 112 novels and novellas for numerous major publishers. She also spent a year writing for American daytime TV dramas *The Guiding Light* and *As the World Turns*. But her heart was in her books, and she'd found it impossible to do both.

Now, she is excited to be publishing with dream-publisher, Oliver Heber Books and she's having more fun than ever.

Maggie lives in a century-and-a-half old farmhouse with two waterfalls outside, in the rural hills of Cortland County NY with her husband Lance, who builds waterfalls for a living, and their dogs. There are always, always dogs.

Sign up for Maggie's NEWSLETTER!
Early looks at covers, new and upcoming releases, behind the
scenes trivia, dog pictures, and sometimes a recipe!

MaggieShayne.com
Sign up at the top of the page.

- facebook.com/MaggieShayneAuthor
- instagram.com/MaggieShayne
- bsky.app/profile/maggieshayne.bsky.social
- bookbub.com/authors/maggie-shayne
- amazon.com/author/maggieshayne
- goodreads.com/maggieshayne